THE
END OF
OLYMPUS

Also by Kate O'Hearn

Pegasus

THE END OF OLYMPUS

KATE O'HEARN

Aladdin

NEW YORK LONDON TORONTO SYDNEY NEW DELHI

ALADDIN

An imprint of Simon & Schuster Children's Publishing Division
1230 Avenue of the Americas, New York, NY 10020
First Aladdin paperback edition November 2017
Text copyright © 2016 by Kate O'Hearn
Cover illustration copyright © 2016 by Jason Chan
Also available in an Aladdin hardcover edition.
All rights reserved, including the right of reproduction in whole or in part in any form.
ALADDIN and related logo are registered trademarks of Simon & Schuster, Inc.
For information about special discounts for bulk purchases, please contact
Simon & Schuster Special Sales at 1-866-506-1949 or business@simonandschuster.com.
The Simon & Schuster Speakers Bureau can bring authors to your live event.
For more information or to book an event contact the Simon & Schuster Speakers Bureau
at 1-866-248-3049 or visit our website at www.simonspeakers.com.
Cover designed by Karin Paprocki
Interior designed by Mike Rosamilia
The text of this book was set in Adobe Garamond.
Manufactured in the United States of America 1017 OFF
2 4 6 8 10 9 7 5 3 1
The Library of Congress has cataloged the hardcover edition as follows:
Names: O'Hearn, Kate, author.
Title: The end of Olympus / by Kate O'Hearn.
Description: First Aladdin hardcover edition. | New York : Aladdin, 2016. | Series: Pegasus ; 6 | Summary:
Emily is contending with great changes, including diminished powers, but goes to London to rescue
Agent B and others from the CRU, where she makes horrible discoveries about the agency's history.
Identifiers: LCCN 2016025402 | ISBN 9781481447171 (hc) |
ISBN 9781481447195 (eBook)
Subjects: | CYAC: Pegasus (Greek mythology)—Fiction. |
Mythology, Greek—Fiction. | Conspiracies—Fiction. | Fantasy. |
BISAC: JUVENILE FICTION / Legends, Myths, Fables / Greek & Roman. |
JUVENILE FICTION / Action & Adventure / General. | JUVENILE FICTION / Girls & Women.
Classification: LCC PZ7.O4137 End 2016 |
DDC [Fic]—dc23
LC record available at https://lccn.loc.gov/2016025402
ISBN 9781481447188 (pbk)

For my family,

those still with me

and those who have gone ahead.

Always with much love.

And for Pegasus—

It's been an amazing ride, my sweetest friend.

"KEEP YOUR RIGHT ARM UP!"

Emily raised her staff higher and stood before Diana, panting, sore, and exhausted, awaiting her next attack. When Diana lunged, Emily countered with a tumble and spin maneuver that saw her back on her feet and striking Diana's staff from the side.

In response, Diana dove down low and came back up under Emily's defenses, knocking the staff from her hands. It flew several feet away and crashed to the ground.

They had been training for most of the day, and the fatigue was starting to make Emily sloppy. Her long black hair swept into her eyes, and her hands were slippery from sweat. She was trembling with exertion as she retrieved her staff.

They were in the remains of the amphitheater, on what was left of the stage. It would be some time before another performance could be hosted here, as most of the repairs to Olympus were focusing on the homes. The invasion by the Titans who had escaped the prison Tartarus had caused almost complete destruction, which the Olympians were only now recovering from.

But while the amphitheater awaited repair, it made a very good training ground, with little chance of them being disturbed.

"Higher!" Diana repeated as she attacked again. She cut down with her staff and slipped easily through Emily's defenses, striking her in the side. Emily grunted and went down to her knees, gasping for breath.

"You see, if you do not keep your arm up, you leave yourself vulnerable."

Behind her, Pegasus neighed loudly and came forward. He put himself between Diana and Emily and pawed the ground.

 2

"Yes, I know she is tired," Diana said to the winged stallion. "But Emily has a body now. She must learn to use it properly and to protect it. She is an Olympian, and most of her powers are gone. If we ever go against the Titans again, she must be prepared to fight in hand-to-hand combat."

Emily looked up at Pegasus, grateful for the brief respite he'd given her. "I'm okay, Pegs. Diana's right. I must learn this." Still panting, she raised her staff, preparing to engage the powerful huntress once again.

But Diana didn't move. "No. Pegasus is correct. I am pushing you too hard. You may take the rest of the day off."

Emily glanced up at the sky and saw the clouds going pink as the sun started to set. There wasn't much of a day left to take off. "Thank you," she said. "Same time tomorrow?"

Diana nodded. "We will start first thing with bow training and then move on to swords." As she started to leave, Diana called back, "Pegasus, make sure she eats plenty of ambrosia. She needs to keep up her strength."

Emily pulled a towel down from Pegasus's neck and watched Diana leave. "Does that woman ever get tired? Look at her. She didn't even break a sweat or mess her hair. I'm soaked and hurt all over!"

There was a twinkle in the stallion's eyes, and Emily knew he was laughing at her. "Yes, I know, I've got a real body and I'm not used to doing these physical things. But I'm getting stronger. I can feel it."

Pegasus nickered and nodded.

After she wiped her face, Emily looked around. Scars from the recent battle were everywhere. A whole section of the white marble amphitheater's upper seats was gone completely. The statues along the avenues had all been broken and were only now being slowly replaced. Jupiter's palace, containing the apartment she shared with her father, Pegasus, Joel, and Paelen was being rebuilt after the Titans had razed it to the ground.

When the Titans had poured into Olympus, they'd destroyed everything in sight. Earth hadn't fared much better. She and her friends had gone to Hawaii to look for a power shard that lay deep in the Diamond Head volcano and the Titans had followed them. The

Hawaiian island of Oahu had suffered greatly as the Titans and Olympians had brought the war there—it had soon involved Pele and the powerful Hawaiian gods. Were it not for the intervention of the ancient Xan, Emily wondered what would have happened.

Everything had changed on that one trip. *She* had changed more than she'd ever imagined possible and doubted if things could ever be the same again.

Emily pressed her forehead to the stallion's warm neck. "It's all so different now, Pegs," she said sadly. "Look, Joel and Chrysaor aren't here—they're probably holed up in Vulcan's forge, doing their best to avoid me. Paelen is off somewhere with Lorin. Before, they'd have been here making fun of me and cheering me on."

Pegasus leaned his head back to her and nickered.

"I know what you're going to say. That I'm feeling sorry for myself. Maybe I am. But it just feels like everything is ending. I know things can't stay the same, but why do they have to change so much?"

She inhaled deeply and stroked his strong, muscled neck. "At least you're still here. That's all that matters. You and me—'Team Pegasus' forever."

Pegasus snorted again and lowered one of his wings to invite her up onto her back. Without hesitation, Emily climbed up. She didn't care where they went, as long as they were together.

The stallion's hooves clicked on the marble stage as he started to trot and then entered a cantor. He opened his powerful wings and took off. Emily didn't need to ask where they were going; she already knew.

Her favorite place in all Olympus—the lake with its smooth, soft silver sand that went up to the warm waters. It was calm and still and always eased her troubled mind.

As Pegasus winged his way over the damaged city, Emily was reminded of the phoenix legend. Olympus was rising once again from the ashes of destruction. Ahead she saw the Temple of the Flame, with the fire burning brightly in the plinth. It was one of the few places left undamaged. The Titans had recognized its value as much as the Olympians did. Their plan was to capture it along with Emily, to control her as much as they did Lorin. But they had failed. Now the Flame burned brightly, even if most of Emily's powers were gone.

Sometimes late at night when she was alone in her bedroom, Emily would test herself to see what powers she had left. She could still shoot flames from her hands and hone them down into laser flame. If she concentrated very hard, she could move objects with her mind and could levitate. But it wasn't as easy as it had been before, and she would never risk trying to fly again. All the powers had seemed so scary in the beginning. Now she missed them.

Each day Emily discovered something else she'd lost. There were so many little things she'd grown accustomed to that were gone. She was grateful that she still had the power to heal with a touch, but now, when she used her healing powers, she was left feeling tired and drained.

Riza said it would take time for her to adjust to her new life—"Emily Version II"—as she teasingly called her. And Riza was right. One of the hardest things for Emily to adjust to was not having the gentle Xan's guiding voice in her head.

In order to save them both, Riza's father had separated them. He'd given Emily her Olympian body and had restored Riza. Riza was now a full, immensely powerful and super-tall Xan living on Xanadu. One of the oldest worlds in the universe, Xanadu had become a sanctuary for the people and animals of dying worlds. They were brought there and protected by the ancient Xan. Now that Riza was fully back to herself, she remained guardian of the unique sanctuary. Occasionally she would "pop" over to Olympus for a visit, but most of her time was spent taking care of the inhabitants of Xanadu.

Emily missed her more than she'd expected. Riza had been a part of her for so long; it was like losing a twin sister, and their separation was painful.

Pegasus nickered and drew Emily from her thoughts. They were approaching the silver lake. As the stallion came lower in the sky, Emily saw that their beach was not empty. Unfortunately, one of the visitors to the lake was someone Pegasus absolutely hated.

"It's all right, Pegs," Emily said reassuringly. "We don't have to go down. We can just fly around for a while."

Pegasus snorted again and continued his descent. He whinnied angrily.

This call was answered by another loud, shrill whinny.

"Pegs, no, please, you can't fight him!" Emily clutched his mane tightly. "Just leave them alone. We can go someplace else."

Pegasus was trembling beneath her as he touched down on the sand and trotted closer to his clone, Tornado Warning.

The clone was just as angry to see the original on the beach. His wings fluttered, his eyes went wide and wild, and his nostrils flared in threat.

"Tornado, stop," Lorin called. "Calm down. He's not here to harm you." The tall, beautiful blond Titan was standing at Tornado Warning's head and stroking the angry stallion's muzzle.

Emily wasn't sure what bothered her most. Pegasus's anger, or seeing Lorin and Paelen walking together with Tornado Warning on her secret beach—the one place in Olympus where she and Pegasus could go to be completely alone. Emily felt more than a trace of betrayal that Paelen had brought Lorin here.

She knew Pegasus felt the same seeing Tornado Warning.

Lorin had fallen instantly in love with Pegasus the moment she'd first seen him. But knowing she could never possess the free-spirited winged stallion, Jupiter had given her the next best thing—Pegasus's clone, created in the Area 51 laboratory by the evil government agency the Central Research Unit. The CRU had created many clones of Olympians, and although Jupiter promised to take care of them all, there were some that still caused a lot of trouble. Tornado Warning was one of them.

While he was identical to Pegasus in every way, it was only a physical match. Where Pegasus was an intelligent and respected citizen of Olympus, Tornado Warning was just a flying horse. His behavior was pure equine with none of the grace or elegance of the original.

The one thing they did share was a burning hatred for each other. "It's all right, Pegs," Emily said. "Let's just go!"

"No, wait!" Lorin called as she stroked Tornado's neck to calm him. "These two should become friends."

"I do not think that is a good idea," Paelen warned. "They have a history that is not good."

"I am sure if they spent time together . . ."

"Lorin, no," Emily said forcefully. "You cannot force friendship on anyone. Pegasus is free to choose who he wants to be friends with. Tornado Warning isn't one of them."

Paelen wouldn't meet Emily's eyes. She could feel his discomfort at being caught in what was understood to be Emily and Pegasus's private place. "Come," he said to Lorin. "We should go."

"Why? We were here first." Lorin pouted. "This is our special place. If they do not like us here, they can go. But I am not leaving."

Emily felt her own temper flare. Since Lorin had come to live in Olympus, the tension between her and Emily had not eased. In fact, it had grown. Like Pegasus with Tornado Warning, there was no way Emily and Lorin could ever be friends.

Looking back at Paelen's discomfort, it was obvious this wasn't the first time they'd been here. She watched him closely and could see the conflict in his face. Paelen was loyal to Emily, but he had developed feelings for Lorin and didn't want to disappoint her.

Paelen was a warm, loving person who had been

alone for a long time. He deserved all the happiness in the world, and Emily was glad he'd found someone. She just wished it had been anyone but Lorin. Though she couldn't blame him. Lorin was stunningly beautiful, vulnerable, and capable of great kindness—when she wasn't being a spoiled brat. Most of all, Lorin adored him.

"No, Paelen, it's all right," Emily said. "We'll go." She gave Pegasus a quick nudge. "Come on, Pegs, let's just get out of here."

Pegasus was pawing the sand and snorting at Tornado Warning. But with Emily's gentle prodding, he finally turned away from his clone. But with each step he took, Emily could feel his hesitation. Despite everything, Pegasus still wanted to fight.

When Tornado whinnied again, Pegasus looked back. "Pegs, please, I really need to get out of here *now*."

Pegasus was quivering as he started to trot and then opened his wings and took off. Emily understood how he felt because she felt exactly the same. That beach was their escape. Now that was gone, and it only made her feel worse.

"Let's just go home," she said sadly.

With Jupiter's palace destroyed, Emily and her family were scattered around Olympus, staying with other families. Emily and Pegasus were now living with Alexis and Tom—the two Sphinxes—on the far side of the city. Her father was sharing quarters with Hercules, while Diana had moved in with her twin brother, Apollo. Joel was now living at Vulcan's forge, and Paelen—well, Paelen moved around a lot and didn't call any one place home.

When the palace was rebuilt, Emily was certain everything would return to normal. But until then they would have to wait.

Pegasus landed outside the tall cave Tom and Alexis called home. Despite its wild, rough exterior, when they passed through the entrance, the inside was as opulent as Jupiter's palace. Because they were Sphinxes, Tom and Alexis didn't use chairs. Instead, large, fluffy throw cushions were scattered around the carpeted floor. Tables were much shorter, and dishes, well, they were optional—though Tom was doing his best to try to get Alexis to use cutlery, despite their large lion's paws.

The walls of the cave were draped in tapestries with

woven images showing Olympus in its glory. Near the back of the cave were several statues that had been saved from destruction. When the restorations were complete, these would be returned to Jupiter's palace.

Off the main cave were several secondary caves. These served as bedrooms, and one was used as a small kitchen area.

Emily slid down from Pegasus's back and patted the stallion. "We'll find somewhere else to go walking."

"Walking where?" Tom padded out from the kitchen area.

He was still a sight to see, and in all honesty, Emily was surprised by how much being a Sphinx suited him. His upper torso was muscular and bare and his head and face were the same, though he was letting his hair grow long like a lion's mane. After that, everything about him was different. He had a massive set of eagle's wings folded neatly along his lion's body. His arms and legs were those of a lion, with paws instead of hands or feet, and he had a long tail that swished with every movement.

Looking at him, Emily could hardly remember what he'd looked like as a man—let alone a CRU agent. There was one thing that was obvious: He was happy. When Alexis appeared beside him, his face lit with joy.

Emily felt like an intruder in their home. They had only recently been joined in an Olympian union ceremony, and she hated to disturb what was essentially their honeymoon. But both Tom and Alexis had insisted that she and Pegasus stay with them while the palace was being rebuilt.

"How did the training with Diana go?" Tom asked.

"Fine, I guess," Emily answered softly. "If you don't mind being tortured by a female Attila the Hun."

"I'm sure she's not that bad," Alexis said.

Emily held up her arm where a new bruise was coming to the surface. "Oh no? Even my bruises have bruises."

"Well, I've drawn you a nice hot bath," Alexis said. "We still have some time before supper. Why don't you take a break?"

Emily lounged in the bath, trying to ease her stiff muscles. It had been so long since she'd had a body, she'd forgotten all the little things that could hurt.

Laughter filtered in from the other part of the cave, and she could hear Pegasus nickering lightly. She was glad they were happy. She just wished she could share it. But as she lay back, her long black hair billowed around her.

Black hair, instead of the auburn she'd always had. Her legs were much longer too. And her fingers— they seemed impossibly long and fine. Everything had changed.

When she finished bathing, Emily climbed from the tub, jumping when she caught her reflection in the mirror. She still wasn't used to seeing the stranger that was now *her*.

Emily walked closer to the glass and studied her new face. Her eyes were now a deep sapphire blue with white specks. Riza had given her those specks by slipping some of herself into the mix when her father created a new body for Emily. The skin was smooth without a mark or blemish on it. She was so much taller than before and perfectly proportioned. Everything about her new body was beautiful and perfect. So perfect, in fact, that Emily hated it.

It was hard to admit, but Emily hated everything

about her new life. Her new body, her limited powers, and especially the way everyone looked at her. Inside she was still the same, but the outside had changed, and she missed the person she used to be.

But if she couldn't accept herself, how could she expect others to accept her? It made no sense. "Emily Version II" was stunning. Tall and beautiful, she was a younger version of Diana, with all of her grace and elegance. But still, Emily would have traded anything to have her old body back, with all its faults.

"Emily, are you finished? It's time to eat," Tom's voice called.

"Be right there." It was unbearable to hear her voice coming from that perfect person reflected in the mirror. "Break all the mirrors," she said softly to herself. "That's what I'll do. Problem solved."

She dressed and walked into her bedroom. Tom was there with a sympathetic smile on his face. "Emily, sit down for a moment. I'd like to talk to you."

When she sat, he sat down on the floor beside her. "You know, in all of Olympus, I think I'm the one who understands most what you're going through."

Emily had been trying to hide her feelings from everyone. But the way Tom was looking at her, she knew she'd failed. "What do you mean?"

"You're asking the man who spent ages as a tree what I mean. I was a tree, Emily. Leaves, bark, and roots. Then, from that, you turned me into a Sphinx. So you know full well what I'm talking about. We've both gone through some pretty extreme changes."

"But you wanted to be a Sphinx."

"Oh yes, I did, and I'll be eternally grateful to you and Riza for doing it for me. But that doesn't mean I didn't go through some major adjustments. I still am. You know, of all the stupid things I miss, it's having thumbs. Can you imagine how difficult it is to pick things up with paws?"

Emily dropped her head and chuckled. "I hadn't thought about it."

Tom laughed too. "Trust me. Spoons are no fun. It's a good thing I don't wear shoes anymore, because there's no way I could tie laces with these babies!" He held up his two large lion paws. "I won't even tell you what it's like to shave in the morning." He became serious. "So I kind of know what you're going through. I've seen it on your face and on the faces of everyone else around here."

"It's because I look like Diana."

"No, it's not that you look like Diana. It's because you don't look like Emily anymore. It's taking time for everyone to adjust and for you to get used to yourself."

"But . . ." Emily felt herself starting to break. "But Joel . . ."

"I know," Tom said. "I've seen it too. Joel is hiding himself away in Vulcan's forge as he tries to process the changes in you. That doesn't mean he cares any less for you. It's just going to take him time."

"What if he can't accept me?"

Tom sighed. "Emily, until I met Alexis, I believed I was immune to emotions. I was a CRU agent and nothing more. But the moment I laid eyes on her, everything changed. So I may not be the best one to give advice on relationships. But what I will say is that if Joel can't get used to you, if he can't see that you are the same amazing girl you've always been, then he isn't worthy of you. The loss will be his, not yours."

"It will be both of ours," Emily said softly.

Tom leaned forward, kissed her forehead, and lifted her chin with his large golden paw. "You'll find your way, Emily. I know you will. This face, beautiful in all that it is, isn't yours yet. You haven't worn it long enough to let your character shine through."

"And if it never does?"

"It will, Emily. I can promise you that." Tom shook his head sadly. "Back on Earth, magazines and television were always pushing the idea that external beauty is all that matters. It isn't. Faces and bodies change; we all get older—it's a fact of life. It's what's inside that really counts. Not this temporary exterior."

He chuckled again. "Okay, so it's not quite so temporary here on Olympus, with this immortality thing going on, but you know what I mean. You have been the new Emily for only a short while. Give yourself time to get used to yourself. I'm sure you'll soon see that you haven't changed all that much. Soon as you accept yourself, you'll find everyone else treating you the way they always did."

Emily threw her arms around Tom and held him tightly. "Thank you."

"You're very welcome," he said. "Now, let's go in there and celebrate the return of Emily!"

After dinner Pegasus disappeared into the evening sky without telling anyone where he was going. He returned a short while later with Emily's father. When he touched down, Pegasus wouldn't meet Emily's eyes, and she realized he must have been listening in on her conversation with Tom. He thought she needed her father. Pegasus was right. Of all the wonderful people on Olympus, it was Pegasus who knew her best.

When her father slid off the stallion's back, he embraced Emily. "I still can't get over you being taller than me."

"Not taller," Emily said. "We're the same height."

He grinned. "Maybe, but I seem to be getting shorter all the time. Joel is taller than me now, Paelen, Diana and you."

Emily grinned back, feeling all the better for seeing him. "This means I can do this to you." She ruffled his hair.

As they walked together in the setting sun, Emily

told her father about the encounter with Paelen and Lorin at the beach, and how Joel had been avoiding her. With her father at her side and Pegasus walking behind them, Emily felt her worries start to fade.

Finally they stopped and her father turned to her. "Em, I know this has been hard on you and that you're still feeling very out of sorts because of Hawaii. . . ."

Emily dropped her head but nodded.

"I can't imagine what it's like for you, especially all these changes. But you can't let it get you down. You're alive. That's all that matters—to me and to everyone else. You're alive and we're in this beautiful place. Yes, it's been damaged, but look how fast the Olympians are repairing it. That is what's important. Not that you've changed—or are *much* taller than me."

"But . . ."

"Yes, I get it. Joel is being an idiot. But he's a teenage boy. That's what they're supposed to be! I was the same when I was his age. Heck, I'd be worried if he wasn't an idiot. You've just got to give him plenty of space and time. You'll see. He'll come around soon enough. Besides, worrying won't change things. And that thing with Paelen and Lorin? It's hard, but you have to give them time too. This is all new to Paelen. He's feeling things he's never felt before. I bet you five bucks things get back to normal sooner than you think."

Speaking to her father made all the difference to Emily. She threw her arms around his neck and hugged him tightly. "Thanks, Dad. . . ." They laughed and talked until the sun completely set and stars came out. Eventually, Emily and Pegasus took her father back to Hercules's home. After dropping him off, Emily climbed onto the stallion's back and they took off into the night sky.

"Pegs, I know it's getting late, but I don't feel like going back yet. Can we go flying for a bit? Would you take me somewhere we've never been before?" Pegasus nickered loudly and put on more speed.

Beneath them the night dwellers came out and worked silently in the streets, clearing rubble and helping with the rebuilding of Olympus. With day and night shifts working full out, destroyed buildings were being rebuilt in record time. Emily noticed that a lot of the new buildings were different from the ones that had stood before, and she realized that the Titan invasion had changed more than just her: Olympus itself was different. If it could rise from the rubble, surely she could too.

Pegasus took her higher into the clear night sky. The air was warm and sweet, as always, and the stars and constellations that had seemed so alien to her at first now greeted her like old friends.

"Faster, Pegs," Emily cried excitedly, catching hold of his mane and leaning forward.

Pegasus obliged and flapped his wings harder. He climbed higher in the sky than he normally did and flew over parts of Olympus that Emily hadn't yet fully explored.

They traveled to the neighboring city of Helicon, where the Muses lived, and to Mount Helicon, on the large mountain beside it, where Pegasus had spent a lot of his childhood.

Helicon looked much like the part of Olympus where Jupiter's palace had been, with its cobbled roads and stunning buildings. As always, art and sculpture played a big part in its architecture. Just like the palace area, many of its marble statues now lay in rubble on the street. It was obvious that it too had borne the wrath of the Titan invasion. But also like the main city, it was rising from the ashes.

Farther along toward Mount Helicon, Emily saw a flash of light in the darkness of the mountain. "Did you see that, Pegs?"

Pegasus whinnied and changed directions. Gliding closer, they soon saw a single figure standing on a platform at the very top of Mount Helicon. Emily squinted. Old Emily would never have been able to see any details, especially in the dark. But Emily Version II was able to make out the shape of a woman.

Before Pegasus landed, Emily recognized the woman as one of the Muses, Urania. She was standing before a large telescope and studying the stars. The flash had been from a shooting star reflecting off the glass of the telescope. Urania was best known for her love of astronomy, and she spent most nights up here, cataloging the night sky. Tall and lean, she had long brown hair, which she styled on the top of her head, deep olive skin, and entrancing hazel eyes.

She was dressed in a traditional Olympian gown, but it had dirt smudges all over it. If ever there was a tomboy Muse, it was Urania.

When Pegasus landed, Emily slid off his back. Urania turned and frowned. "Pegasus, what brings you up here so late? And who is that with you?"

"It's me, Urania," Emily said.

"Who?"

"Me, Emily." She held up her hand and summoned a ball of flame. "Flame of Olympus . . ."

The Muse's eyes flashed opened. "Oh, Emily, I am so very, very sorry. I did not recognize you."

"I know," Emily said. "No one does these days."

Urania stepped away from her telescope and came closer. "I heard that you had changed. But my word, child, you are the spitting image of Diana when she was young."

Pegasus nickered and whinnied. Urania looked from Emily to Pegasus and back to Emily again, and her expression changed—became sympathetic. "I am sorry it has been difficult for you. I am certain in time people will see you for you."

"I hope so." Emily walked over to the large

golden telescope. "So are you looking at anything interesting?"

"Actually, I have been watching Titus for Father. He wants to make sure that Saturn does not try to cause more trouble."

Jupiter was the father of the Muses and had a very active part in their lives. "Can you actually see Titus from here?"

Urania nodded. "But this telescope is not my only means of watching. Come, I would like to show you something."

Emily and Pegasus followed the Muse away from her telescope and across the peak of the mountain. They descended some marble steps on the opposite side. When they reached a plateau, Urania walked over to a large stone bowl. It was sitting on the ground, but the top reached their waists.

"Pegasus made this for me a very long time ago. It is filled with water from his spring."

The winged stallion had his own special powers to draw water from the ground. He'd created four springs on Mount Helicon that had healing properties and never dried up. Emily had also witnessed him using his powers at Area 51 to restore Groom Lake and then in the Diamond Head crater in Hawaii.

They walked up to the stone bowl, and Emily peered into the clear spring water. It reflected the stars above but nothing more. "I don't understand."

Urania smiled and waved her hand across the top of the bowl. "Show me Saturn."

The water started to swirl and fill with white fog. Soon images began to move within its depths and the fog cleared.

Emily jumped when she saw the cold, hard face of Saturn staring right at her. The sight of him struck terror in her heart and made her shiver. She could still hear his menacing voice and see the rage in his dark, stormy eyes. He had tried to imprison her in Tartarus, and when that had failed, he'd tried to kill her.

Pegasus nickered and nudged her gently while Urania chuckled softly. "Do not fear, child. He cannot see you. But we can see him." Then she called to the water, "Pull back. Where is he?"

The image changed and seemed to draw away from Saturn's face. He was seated alone on an ornate throne, staring blankly at nothing. The room around him was tall and opulent and adorned with statues— some of them Emily recognized from the prison Tartarus. These were of Saturn, his four brothers, and his top commanders. But apart from the statues, he was alone.

"He actually looks really lonely," Emily said softly.

"I am sure he is," Urania said. "Saturn is a warrior leader to a people who are tired of war. He remains the head of the Titans, but everyone there now focuses on agriculture and the arts. They are rebuilding their lives and society. I have seen nothing to suggest that they are planning another assault on Olympus."

"So we're safe?"

"I believe so." Urania pulled her arm back over the water, and the image of Saturn faded. "Perhaps you would like to try it."

"Really? May I?"

The Muse nodded. "You just wave your arm over the water and say what you wish to see. When you are finished, you bring your arm back to close the image."

Emily looked excitedly to Pegasus. "Finally I can

show you who I've been talking about all this time." She paused and looked at Urania. "Does this show current time, or the past?"

"It will not reveal the past or the future. Only what is happening at this moment."

Emily waved her arm over the water and said, "Show me Agent B—also known as Benedict Richard Williams, from London, England, Earth."

Once again the water swirled and fogged. Emily's heart fluttered with excitement when she first saw the flash of familiar, dark curly hair. This was much better than television. But as the image cleared, she gasped.

Agent B was tied to a chair by leather straps. His hair was longer than she remembered, and he had grown an unkempt beard. One of his eyes was bruised and swollen shut, and he had scratches on his face. He looked as though he'd suffered a severe beating. "Pull back!" Emily commanded. "Show me where he is."

The image obeyed and pulled farther back to reveal Agent B locked in a small dark cell with thick bars on the front. Other men were outside the cell, seated at a desk at the end of the cell block.

"Focus on those men outside the cell."

At Emily's command, the image moved away from Agent B and shifted to the men holding him. Their distinctive black suits and grim expressions left no room for doubt. Finally she said, "Take me farther outside the building. Where are they?"

The image shifted again and seemed to be moving in reverse as it backed out of the cell block, down long, brightly lit corridors, and up through an elevator shaft. Up and up it climbed, until it seemed to float through an old stone wall and into a dark and dusty brick corridor with narrow walls and a low ceiling. Then it came to a set of rough wooden steps, and at the top, went through another old-looking door. It moved along a short corridor with two doors along one wall, marked as men's and women's restrooms. Past the bathrooms to yet another set of steps that opened at the top into a vast concourse filled with people. Large moving information signs hung above a long line of payment barriers. Beyond them were trains loading and unloading travelers. It reminded Emily of a smaller version of Grand Central Terminal in New York.

But none of it made any sense. What was Agent B doing beneath a train station?

From the concourse, the image backed out onto the street. "Stop!" Emily called. She read the sign above the entrance: CHARING CROSS STATION. With the image paused, Emily looked around the driveway entrance to the station and saw black cabs and two bright red double-decker buses.

Emily looked back up at Pegasus. "How is this possible?"

"What is it, child?" Urania said. "I do not understand. Who is this man who suffers so?"

"You won't know him, but that's Agent B. He helped save Olympus when we traveled back in time to the very first war with the Titans. He sacrificed his life for all of us. Then the time line changed and peace was restored with no one remembering what happened. What he did made it all possible. But now, somehow, he is no longer an agent of the CRU. He's their prisoner!"

"Are you certain?" Urania said.

"Yes," Emily cried. "But how?" She was pacing the area, trying to figure out how things could have gone so wrong for her friend. "When I destroyed the weapon, the time line changed and Agent B was restored to his life at the CRU. There is no way he could have told anyone what happened because in the new time line, when the gold box was opened in Greece, the weapon wasn't inside it. So the disaster never happened. No one from Earth could know about that. Only a few of the original Olympians, Titans, and me, remember. But all the Titans are on Titus."

"You are speaking in riddles," Urania said. "What do you mean by time lines, weapon, and disaster?"

Emily shook her head. "It's very complicated and might be hard to understand. But the history you know is very different from what originally happened because we went back in time and changed the past. Trust me. Agent B saved Olympus when Saturn created a weapon that killed Olympians. Without him, none of you would be alive. But until he traveled back in time with us, he was a 'by the book' agent. He was cold, mean, and efficient. When the weapon was destroyed in the past and the time line reset, he would have gone back to being that same coldly efficient agent. I can't imagine what crime he could have committed to end up like that."

She looked imploringly at Urania. "You're sure what we're seeing is happening is right now? Not in the past?"

"I am. The pool only shows present time."

Dread settled in the pit of Emily's stomach. "May I use it again?"

"Of course, child. Feel free."

Emily's hands were trembling as she waved her hand over the water. "Show me Stella Giannakou."

The waters obeyed, and Emily was just as sickened to see Stella, not in her home in Athens, Greece, but instead, locked in a small cell, not unlike Agent B's. There was no wheelchair for her, so the disabled Greek girl was unable to move around her cell. "Show me the guards outside her cell." The image shifted and revealed two men in suits sitting at the desk at the end of the corridor. They were not the same men from Agent B's cell block.

Her voice was little more than a whisper. "Now show me Earl Jenkins and Little Frankie."

The image shifted and showed Earl also sitting in

a darkened cell. Like Agent B, his hair was long and he looked haggard, as though he'd been there some time. Then the image moved to the cell next door. A boy in his teens with a head full of bright red hair sat on the narrow bunk. Frankie wasn't so little anymore. But there was no mistaking that it was him.

Pegasus whinnied, and Emily gasped.

"They've all been captured by the CRU." She looked desperately to Pegasus. "How? How did they know about Stella or Agent B? I can understand about Earl and Frankie, but not them. They were from the other time line."

Pegasus nickered, and Urania nodded. "Pegasus also wants to know why they are being held. That young girl could not know anything useful to the CRU. Why are they holding her?"

Emily focused on the water again. "Take us back out of the building."

The image seemed to repeat the same process as it backed out of the cells, down the corridors, up the elevator shaft, through the public concourse, and out onto the street. "Back up farther, above the city. Where is this?"

The water obeyed, and the image seemed to show them lifting off the ground. They rose above Charing Cross Station and higher into the sky.

"Stop there," Emily called again. The skyline was completely unfamiliar to her. There was a winding river that seemed to split the city in two. Along the edge of the river, not far from Charing Cross, her eyes landed on a familiar building. She had seen it on television and in pictures many times before. "Move slowly toward the river," she said to the water. "I think that's the tower of Big Ben. Take us there." The image shifted and appeared to fly over the buildings. It stopped and hovered above a large, distinctive clock tower rising over a long, ancient building that looked almost gothic with all its pointed spires. "They're in England," Emily mused aloud. "Somehow, Earl, Frankie, and Stella have been taken to London, England."

AFTER LEAVING URANIA AT THE TOP OF Mount Helicon, Emily and Pegasus made their way back to Tom and Alexis's cave. They landed outside, and Emily climbed down from Pegasus.

"I just don't understand how could they know about Stella or Agent B."

Pegasus nickered and pawed the ground. He turned and stared at her. The moment their eyes locked, their connection let Emily see the image of the two of them flying through the Solar Stream.

"You're saying we have to go there to help them?"

When Pegasus nodded, Emily agreed. "I was thinking the same thing. But, Pegs, we both know there's no way Jupiter would let us go. Or Dad either.

Even though Jupiter and a few others here remember them, we both know they'll say I don't have the powers to save them."

"Save who?"

Emily jumped at the voice behind her. She turned and saw Tom and Alexis standing at the entrance to the cave. Alexis's tail with swishing with annoyance and she had bed head. "Yes, Emily, who do you wish to help?"

"Tom, Alexis," Emily said awkwardly. "I'm sorry, did we wake you?"

"You two could wake the dead with your loud voices," Alexis said.

Tom padded closer. "What are you up to? More late-night trips?"

Emily looked at Pegasus, and the stallion nodded. "Can we go back inside? We have something important to tell you."

When Emily explained what they'd discovered in Urania's well, Tom started to pace the confines of the cave. "How could the CRU know about them?"

"That's my point," Emily said. "They couldn't.

The time line changed. Once I destroyed the weapon, a kind of reset button was pushed and everything we went through was erased, just like Agent B said would happen. Olympus wasn't destroyed, and all the Olympians didn't die. It never happened because we stopped it by destroying the weapon in the past."

Alexis was shaking her head. "I have heard this story told and even seen the Pegasus pendant around your neck. I also know your dog, Mike, appeared out of nowhere. But it is still very difficult to understand."

"That's why time travel is so messed up," Tom said. "One little change in the past can have a major impact on the future. It could be altered completely and the people of the future would never know it."

"I still don't understand," Alexis said. "How?"

Tom stopped before her. "Let's say I went back in time and I met your grandfather on the day he was supposed to meet your grandmother. But because I was there, they didn't meet. Because they didn't meet, they didn't get married. Then, because they didn't get married, your mother was never born. Because your mother was never born, she couldn't meet your father. Then you couldn't be born either. So suddenly you, Alexis, would vanish from the future. No one here would ever notice because for them you never existed. But for me, as the time traveler, I knew you did. Everything would be ruined because I went back into the past and distracted your grandfather from meeting your grandmother."

Alexis looked at Emily. "Did that happen?"

Emily nodded. "We did go into the past. But the changes we made were good. They protected this future by destroying a weapon that was destroying it. I remember the other time line, but everyone else doesn't." She looked at Tom. "But I thought it was all over until I saw Agent B and Stella in the cells. Somehow the CRU must know about it."

"But that's impossible!" Tom insisted.

Pegasus whinnied and nickered. He shook his head and snorted.

Emily and Tom both looked at Alexis to translate. "Pegasus is suggesting that perhaps one of the early Titans may have been captured by the CRU and they have extracted information from them."

Emily looked at Pegasus. "How? When?"

Once more the stallion whinnied.

"During the recent conflict on Earth at the Diamond Head volcano," Alexis translated. "Many of the older Titans were at that battle. Perhaps one was wounded and captured. But when the Xan sent everyone home, they missed that Titan, who was left on Earth in the hands of the CRU."

It made a lot of sense. "So it could be a Titan has been tortured into telling the history?" Emily asked.

The stallion nodded.

"This isn't good," Tom said. "Their facility in London is the most secure."

"I remember you saying Area 51 was their most secure," Alexis said.

"It was, for the United States. But the London unit makes Area 51 look small. There are CRU facilities all around the world, and then there are super-facilities. I never went to that London one. The CRU tends to keep their agents in their home country. That way we don't stand out."

"Jupiter must be told," Alexis said.

"No!" Emily and Tom said as one. Tom finished. "We're only just getting over the big blowup in

Hawaii. I think if poor old Jupiter were to hear the name 'CRU' one more time, he might blow a gasket."

"Or get so angry he destroys Earth. Remember, he almost did when he first found out about the clones," Emily suggested. "He was going to turn the Solar Stream on Earth back then."

Pegasus nickered, and Alexis shook her head. "Please, be reasonable. It is too dangerous for you."

Emily stroked the stallion's neck, certain she knew what he'd just said. "We both want to go." Emily paused. "Alexis, you don't know Agent B, but he was very much like Tom. Once we got him away from the CRU, he turned out to be a decent, wonderful man."

"Careful, Emily," Tom said. "It sounds like you have a bit of a crush on him. Those emotions won't help you."

Emily blushed. "No, I don't. It wasn't like that. But I do care for him. He was a really good friend, and he helped me when Pegs died. . . ." Emily looked at Pegasus. "That was the worst, watching you die. But he was there for me. . . ." She stopped. "Wait here. I'll be right back."

Emily ran into her bed cave and opened her personal box. Inside were the journals from their journey into the past, which had been found in the rubble of the palace. Emily picked up Agent B's and ran back into the room. "I haven't let a lot of people see this. It's too personal. But I think you should. This is Agent B's journal. He wrote this message right before the biggest battle with the Titans on Titus." She opened the journal to the last entry and started to read aloud.

> *My dear Emily, if you are reading this and I am alive, shame on you! Close the book right now and put it away. . . .*
>
> *But if you are reading this because I am dead, please, keep going. . . .*
>
> *Emily Jacobs, you are perhaps the most stubborn girl I have ever met. You can be irritating beyond measure, irrational, and infuriating. But you are also one of the most loyal and caring people I have had the pleasure to get to know.*

*We have fought side by side for months
now. We have suffered together, bled
together, and at times we've even
laughed together.*

*As we are facing our toughest challenge
yet, I have the strangest feeling I won't
survive it. If I don't, if it's true that I
am dead, I beg you, please find me in
London. Find me and get me away from
the CRU.*

*Let me know you again. Let me call
you and Pegasus, Joel, the Olympians,
and that mangy mutt Mike my friends.
Please, Emily, find me and save me
from myself.*

*Yours,
Benedict Richard Williams*

"See," Emily said to Tom. "He changed, just
like you did. He didn't want to be a CRU agent

anymore. Before we went into one of the final battles, he gave me his journal and made me promise that if we won and time reset, I would find him. He even wanted me to kidnap him and bring him here or to Xanadu to read his journal. He's put all kinds of messages to himself in it. He really wanted to change.

"But now that I've seen he's locked away and they're hurting him, I can't let it go. I have to save him. I have to save them all—Frankie, Earl, and Stella. I owe them that. We all do."

Tom sighed heavily and looked back at Alexis. "Emily and Pegasus are right. They must go back to find Agent B. We must know who told the CRU about the other time line."

"But that is madness," Alexis said. "He is just one man."

"It's more than that," Tom insisted. "And not just because of a promise made." He shook his head, and his tail flicked. "I am sick and tired of the CRU and their obsession with Olympus. But there is no mistaking that something is up. Whether they've captured a Titan or found out some other obscure way, they're not going to stop coming after us."

Pegasus nodded and whinnied.

"You cannot!" Alexis insisted.

"What?" Emily asked.

"He says he wants to take on the CRU and finish them once and for all."

Tom padded up to Pegasus. "It would be a nice dream, my friend. But I'm afraid they are far too big and powerful for that. What we can do is get those people away from them. Once they're safe, we declare Earth a quarantine world. Meaning no one ever goes back there again."

"So what do we do now?" Alexis asked. "And, Tom, my beloved, you get any thought of going back with them out of your head. Looking as you do now, there is no way you can hide what you are. You will do their mission more harm than good."

Tom dropped his head. "I know. I'd be a liability to you. But what I can do is work as your support team. I'll tell you what you need to know about the super-facility in London."

"I assume you will be taking Joel and Paelen with you," Alexis said.

This had been spinning around in Emily's mind from the moment she'd seen Agent B in the cell and knew she'd be going back to Earth. "No," she finally said.

"What?" Tom cried. "But you four are a team! You can't go without them. Together you are unstoppable."

Pegasus whinnied and nodded his head.

Emily sighed sadly. "We were a team, but not now. Joel spends all this time hiding in Vulcan's forge and won't even look at me. Paelen, well, you've seen him. He's in love. He won't go without Lorin, but there's no way I'm taking her on this mission."

"Emily, listen to me," Alexis said. "Be reasonable. You are a determined person, and I have seen you in action. I know what you can achieve. But you have changed. It wounds me to say this, but if you and Pegasus try to go on your own, you will fail. And in doing so, you will hand yourselves over to the CRU."

"We're not going alone," Emily said as the stroked Pegasus's warm, muscled neck. "Riza has been with me from the beginning. She cares about Agent B and the others as much as I do. When she learns what's happened, Pegasus and I won't be going against the CRU alone. We'll have one of the most powerful beings in the universe with us. We'll have a Xan on our team."

3

DURING THE LONG OLYMPIAN NIGHT, TOM coached Emily and Pegasus on some of the things they might encounter on their journey to London. Though he'd never been to the CRU super-facility, he had visited the city several times.

"It's very much like New York," he said. "Just as congested and just as few places to hide. So get in, extract your targets, and get out again."

Emily listened to every word, and as he spoke, she heard disturbing echoes of the CRU agent he used to be. Suddenly this wasn't Tom the Sphinx talking; it was Agent T, speaking about targets and extractions instead of friends and rescue.

"I understand," Emily said.

While they spoke, Alexis packed two large sacks of ambrosia cakes and bottles of nectar for the long journey through the Solar Stream to Xanadu. She brought the bags to Pegasus and draped them across his neck like saddlebags.

Tom looked out the cave. "All right, it won't be long before dawn, so you'd better get moving." His voice became even more serious. "Emily, listen to me. I want you to promise me, on your word, that if Riza doesn't go with you, you won't go alone. Come back here and we'll figure something out. But you can't take on the CRU alone."

"I promise," she said.

"You too, Pegasus," Alexis said. "No reckless adventures, do you understand me? Emily is still the Flame of Olympus, and we need her." Her voice softened. "And we love you both very much, so please, do not do anything foolish."

Pegasus nickered, and Emily agreed. "We won't." She had changed into her jeans and a sweatshirt. She tied her long black hair back in a ponytail and put her personal items, including the Xan food pouch, in the pack she pulled onto her back. She decided to leave Agent B's journal in her box. She would bring the agent to the journal, not the journal to the agent.

"Now, you've still got plenty of powers left," Tom said. "Don't be afraid to use them. You know the agents you're going against won't hesitate to use their weapons against you." He paused. "I'm deadly serious, Emily. You're different now. You have blood and you have a body—it's Olympian, meaning it's much stronger and tougher, but it still can be hurt. Worse, if they catch you, there is nothing stopping them from cloning you and Pegasus again. Just remember what happened at Area 51."

Mention of the cloning sent a shiver down Emily's spine. "I'll be extra careful, I promise. But with Riza with me, hopefully we'll pop in and then out again before the CRU knew what hit them. We'll be back in no time."

Tom nodded. "Now, I'll tell your father that you and Pegasus have gone to spend some time with Riza. I'm sure he'll understand. But listen to me. If you are gone more than two days, I will have to tell him. Then no doubt we'll all be coming after you."

Emily nodded. "We understand. But can you make

it three days? Remember how long it takes to get to Xanadu through the Solar Stream. That's almost a day right there."

When it was agreed, Tom and Alexis escorted them out of the cave. Tom rose on his hind legs and put his large paws around her. "You mean everything to me, Emily. Come back safe."

Emily hugged him back. "We will. I promise."

Next it was Alexis's turn, and when she embraced Emily, she whispered in her ear, "I am going to keep you to that promise, Emily. Who else will babysit for us?"

Emily inhaled sharply. "Babysit? Are you . . . ?"

The beautiful Sphinx nodded. "I am. So you must come back to us."

Pegasus whinnied in excitement and bobbed his head.

Emily was filled with joy for the two Sphinxes and hugged Alexis tightly. "That's wonderful news! Just you wait. We'll be right back. Then I can plan your baby shower."

With her heart lightened, Emily climbed up onto the stallion's back. She waved and called good-bye.

Just before Pegasus took off, she heard Alexis ask Tom, "What is a baby shower?"

Emily held on to Pegasus's mane as they traveled through the portal between worlds, the blazing light of the Solar Stream whooshing around them. This was one time Emily missed her Xan powers. She could have made this journey in seconds. But with the Solar Stream, it was long and loud, and she couldn't speak with Pegasus. Being left to her own thoughts, she recalled Tom's words that she, Joel, and Paelen were a team.

It hurt to realize that was gone. Joel hadn't actually said he didn't care for her anymore, but his actions spoke louder than words. It had been at least three days since she'd seen him or Pegasus's brother, the winged boar, Chrysaor.

She had tried to visit him several times, but he always made excuses why he couldn't see her.

What had gone wrong? Did her appearance really matter so much? Could Joel really be so shallow? The more she thought about it, the more it hurt. The more it hurt, the angrier she became. It wasn't her fault she'd physically changed. Or was it something else entirely? Was Joel finally tired of all the adventures?

Then there was Paelen—her sweet misfit friend who could always make her smile with his crooked grin. Part of her missed him most. He was always up to mischief, always finding ways to make her laugh. Now he was spending all his time with Lorin. She actually felt sorry for him. Teaching the wild Titan was supposed to be her job. But after everything they'd been through, she and Lorin just couldn't get along. It was Paelen who was left to take over Lorin's education. To make it easier for him, Emily had backed off—but she missed him.

Emily forced herself out of her dark thoughts. Instead she opened the bag Alexis had packed for them and pulled out a few ambrosia cakes. She leaned forward and offered one to Pegasus. Emily smiled as the stallion took the cake gently and nodded his gratitude. Eating her own portion, Emily focused on what lay ahead.

When the long journey finally came to an end, Pegasus slipped out of the Solar Stream over the jungle world. Thick clouds hung dense and full just above the trees, and the fragrance of the rich, thriving wildlife below filled their nostrils.

"It's so good to be back, isn't it?" Emily called to Pegasus.

The stallion whinnied and bobbed his head up and down. The sure, confident beating of his large white wings told her he knew exactly where they needed to go.

It had been some time since she'd last visited Xanadu, and in that time a lot had changed. When Pegasus touched down in the clearing before the Temple of Arious, she noticed all the work Riza had done. The area had been neatly groomed, and the immense statues of the ancient Xan, cleaned of the vines and moss, glowed in the bright sunlight.

"Riza's been busy," Emily commented as Pegasus touched down and folded his wings.

The Temple of Arious itself was almost unrecognizable. Gone were all the vines and trees that sought to reclaim and obscure the ancient building. The entrance and external walls now gleamed of polished marble. Sitting on the top of the flat, squat building were the three helicopters Emily had sent here so very long ago. The Olympians had offered to remove them, but Riza had declined the offer, saying they were now part of Xanadu. They too had been polished to a bright shine.

"Riza," Emily called. "Can you hear me? Where are you?"

Emily and Pegasus waited before the entrance to the temple. After a few minutes, Emily called again, and Pegasus joined in with several whinnies. But for all their calling, the only sound around them was from the wildlife.

"I wonder if she's inside." Emily walked forward and entered the temple. Once again, everything around her looked brand-new. "Does she spend all day cleaning?"

Pegasus nickered with laughter and walked farther inside. He moved toward the stairs that led down to the lower levels.

"Do you think she's with Arious?"

In answer, Pegasus started down. They wound their way through the maze of corridors until they reached the level containing the supercomputer, Arious. The entry doors were open and the lights were on. A distinct humming was coming from inside, which let Emily know someone was in there.

When Emily and Pegasus entered, she was surprised to see Cupid standing at the central control consul with both his hands on the receivers. His head was back and his wings fluttered while he was connected to Arious.

"Arious," Emily said softly. "We need to speak with you."

"Hello, Emily and Pegasus. Welcome back," the soft voice of the computer called. "Give me a moment and I will disconnect with Cupid."

The humming increased slightly. A moment later, Cupid shook his head and removed his hands from the receivers.

"Hi, Cupid."

Cupid jumped and his wings flashed open. He turned quickly. "Flame! I did not hear you come in."

"You can't hear anything when you're connected to Arious."

"True," he agreed as he stepped away from the consul. "But what an amazing experience it is to go in there. Thank you, Arious."

"You are most welcome, Cupid. Feel free to return anytime."

Cupid grinned, and that smile was just as beautiful as ever. His smooth skin, perfect teeth, and blazing eyes were almost painful to look at. After everything they'd gone through, his beauty never diminished.

"I will, have no doubt," he said.

"So, Emily," Arious said. "Do you have something to share with me?"

Since Riza had been separated from her, she had been working with Arious to ensure the supercomputer would be compatible with Olympians, so they could come here and share their collective knowledge as well.

"Not this time, thank you," Emily said. "Actually, I'm looking for Riza. I really need to speak with her. It's urgent."

"I am sorry, but Riza isn't here."

"Is she visiting one of the other sanctuary continents?"

"No. She is off-world. We discovered a sun about to go supernova. There was at least one planet in their system that still had life. Riza has gone there to arrange for the transport of the inhabitants. We will soon be enlarging Xanadu again to take in this new civilization. It has been a very long time since we've done that, and it is exciting."

Emily was crushed. She had never expected Riza not to be here. "Do you know how long she will be?"

"Some time, I'm afraid. Though she did leave something here for you in case you came to visit." Arious hummed a bit more. Then a small drawer on the wall consul popped open. Inside was a beautiful gold ring containing a stunning blue stone.

Emily admired the ring and placed it on her finger. "It's perfect. But I wonder what would happen if I wore this and then used the Flame. Would it burn up?" She looked at Cupid. "Paelen gave me a ring, but it melted when I used the Flame. Now all I have left is the jewel."

"Riza knew this," Arious answered. "She said the ring would not burn or melt. It is indestructible. Though I probably should have warned you: Once you put it on, only Riza can remove it."

"Really?" Emily tried to pull the ring off her finger, but it wouldn't budge. "It doesn't matter. I wouldn't want to take it off anyway. She knows I love sapphires."

"That is not a sapphire, though it looks like one. She hopes you might use it to join her."

"Join her?" Emily looked into the sparkling facets of the jewel again. "Is this what I think it is?"

"Yes," Arious said. "It will open the Solar Stream. She said you can use it to visit her. All you need to do is hold it up and call her name and it will take you right to her. She said she would welcome yours and Pegasus's help, since the world she is on has an atmosphere compatible to you."

"May I join you?" Cupid asked hopefully. "Since visiting Arious, I have been seeing all the things the Xan did and all the places they have been."

Emily frowned. "You want to go exploring? But you've always been so . . . so . . ."

"Hesitant?" Cupid said. "Yes, I have. But after all we have been through, I discovered I have a taste for adventure. For all the horrors of the war with the Titans, I did enjoy fighting for Hawaii."

"You were there?"

Cupid nodded. "It was a wondrous place, and I

met some very *interesting* Hawaiian goddesses. It is unlikely that you would have seen me, as I was not fighting at Diamond Head. So I would like to help Riza save the survivors."

"So would I," Emily agreed. "But we can't, at least not right now. There's a big problem on Earth with the CRU. We were hoping Riza would come with us to help free Agent B, Stella, Earl, and Frankie. They've all been captured."

"Earl?" Cupid cried. "How? He and Frankie were in safe hiding in Wisconsin."

"Trust me; they're locked away in CRU cells."

"You must be mistaken," Arious said. "I have seen Agent B and Stella from your memories. They were part of the alternate time line. There is no way the Central Research Unit could know about them."

"There is no mistake," Emily said. "I've seen them with my own eyes within some kind of magical pool that Urania has. Agent B has been beaten. Earl too, I suspect. They've been imprisoned in London, England."

"And you hope to have Riza help you to extricate them," Arious said.

"If you mean by 'extricate' that I want to free them, then yes. I want to extricate them. Pegasus does too."

Pegasus nodded and snorted loudly. He pawed the smooth floor of the computer room.

"I understand how you feel, Pegasus," Arious said. "And it is a conundrum how they knew. But should Riza leave what she is doing now, many species will perish as their sun dies. Her duty as a Xan is to protect all life."

Emily knew Arious was right, but it felt wrong. The needs of the many did outweigh the needs of the few, and Riza shouldn't abandon what she was doing. But if she didn't help with Agent B and the others, there was no telling what the CRU would do to them.

"What about us?" Cupid volunteered. "We can free them."

Emily gazed at him, completely stunned. She could hardly believe this was the same Cupid who just a couple of years ago was frightened of his own shadow. But looking at him, she could see there was more determination in his face. Despite the fact that time moved profoundly slowly on Olympus, it seemed that Cupid had matured.

Emily shook her head. "We can't go. We promised Tom and Alexis we wouldn't go alone."

"You will not be alone," Cupid said. "I will be with you." He reached for her hands. "Emily, I realize that you have gone through some major changes in your life. But so have I. I have seen Olympus invaded twice: once by the Nirads when you first came to us and then by the Titans. I have traveled to Earth and fought beside you against the CRU. During that time, I became friends with Earl. Knowing that he is in danger is intolerable to me. If you do not go to Earth with me, I will go alone and find him."

"That is not logical, Cupid," Arious said. "You do not look human. Your wings will betray you."

"Of course it is not logical," Cupid agreed. "But it is the right thing to do. I do not know Agent B or Stella. But I do know Earl and Frankie. It would be wrong to turn our backs on them now because of a little danger. Wings can be hidden, but the suffering of friends cannot."

"It's not a little danger, Cupid," Emily said. "It's a lot. Tom said the London CRU unit is a super-facility, the biggest and most dangerous we've gone against."

She looked over at Pegasus. "What do you think we should do? If we go back to Olympus and tell Jupiter, there's no telling what he'll do."

"We all know exactly what he will do," Cupid put in. "He will destroy Earth once and for all. Now that your powers are diminished, you could not stop the Big Three if they rose against Earth."

Beside her, Pegasus whinnied and snorted. Emily looked to Cupid to translate.

"Pegasus agrees with me," Cupid said.

"Pegasus," Arious said. "You are letting your emotions rule your head."

Again Pegasus whinnied as he clopped over to the supercomputer. He snorted and shook his head.

"Yes, emotions and loyalty are important, but so is logic. The CRU is formidable. In the weights and measures of the universe, they are too dangerous for you three."

"You cannot stop us, Arious," Cupid said. "But you can help us."

"Help us how?" Emily asked.

Cupid walked up to the computer and put his hand on the consul. "I have studied you well, my strange silver friend. Long enough to know there is another within you who can help. You have done it in the past for the Xan. You can do it now for us."

If a machine could frown, Emily was sure Arious was doing just that. The supercomputer actually sighed. "Perhaps it wasn't such a good idea for Riza to enable us to communicate after all. You have learned too much about me."

Cupid chuckled. "Perhaps, but it is too late to back out now. And you do not fool me, Arious. I know you wish to go as well."

"What are you talking about?" Emily asked.

"Watch," Cupid said. "Release Arious Minor."

They could hear Arious grumbling under its breath as it clicked and its lights flashed. Finally a small dot of light appeared before Emily and floated just in front of her face.

"What is this?" she asked. She held out her hand, and the dot settled on her palm. There was no heat, but she did feel a light tickling sensation.

"I am Arious Minor," the dot answered in a high-pitched voice. "I am a holographic link to Arious Major. Separate from but part of Arious."

"This dot," Cupid said, "would often go on long journeys with the Xan. It worked as their guide and adviser—always connected to Arious here on Xanadu."

"And witness," the soft, light voice said. "But it has been millennia since I have left Xanadu. I may not have the strength to sustain myself."

"Sure you do," Cupid said. "You are just frightened to be leaving this room, which has imprisoned you for all this time. Come with us. The journey will do you good."

"What good can come from watching you hand yourselves over to the CRU?" Arious Major said in its normal voice.

"If we get into trouble, you could let the others know."

"And the result will be the same. Jupiter and his brothers will attempt to destroy the Earth. Riza and I will have to stop it. It will be a disaster for all involved."

Emily felt the first glimmer of hope. "Not necessarily. If you did come with us, we might be able to get in and out before Jupiter finds out."

"What could I do?" Arious Minor said.

"Well, I was thinking . . . Could you . . . ?" Emily paused. "I don't know how to explain it, but could you get into other computers and figure out what they know?"

"The word is 'interface,'" Arious Major said. "Yes, though I fail to see the importance of that."

"You might not see the importance, but I do," Emily said. "The CRU runs on computers. They use them to lock their doors, to record their knowledge, everything."

Pegasus started to whinny excitedly.

"It is possible," Arious Major said to the stallion. "If what Emily suggests is true."

"What's that?" Emily asked.

Arious Major said, "Pegasus has asked, if I interface with the CRU computers, could I learn all their secrets and thus figure out how to destroy them."

"Could you?" Emily asked.

"Yes," Arious Major said. "If I can connect to the CRU mainframe, I am sure I can enter their network and destroy them from within. We can end them, once and for all."

THEY LEFT THE TEMPLE AND WALKED OUT into the bright sunshine of Xanadu. The jungle was wild and alive and the air sweet with the perfume of flowers. But for all the beauty around them, Emily was focused on only one thing.

"Are you sure you want to do this?" she asked Cupid. "It is Earth, and you know what'll happen if they catch us, and there's a pretty good chance they will catch us."

"I do," Cupid said. "But I also know what will happen to Earl and Frankie if we do not go. So we have no choice."

Emily went up to Pegasus's head. "It's got to be your decision too. Are you sure you want to do this?"

Pegasus snorted, pawed the ground, and nodded

his head. Cupid said, "He says absolutely." But Emily already knew that.

"I want it on the record right now that I believe this is a bad idea," said Arious Minor. "No good can come of handing yourselves over to the CRU."

"We're not handing ourselves over," Emily said. "We're going to free friends. Besides, you're with us. It's you who will help the most when you take their computers down. The CRU would never in a million years expect you there."

"I think it's rather unfair of you to put all the pressure on me," Arious Minor said.

Emily chuckled. "And I think you've spent too much time in my head, and Dad's and Joel's. You're sounding like a human."

"If you're just going to insult me, I'll go back inside."

"No, don't go." Emily smiled. "I'm sorry. But it's funny to hear how your language has changed since I first met you."

"It's called adaptation. I speak in a manner that is best suited to your understanding. If you prefer, I could go back into binary code."

"No, no, I prefer you speaking my language."

"All right, then, I still think you are crazy!"

"And I think you are wasting time," Cupid added. "If we are going, now would be the time."

Pegasus snorted in agreement. He lowered his wing and invited Emily up on his back. The moment she climbed up, there was a flash of familiarity that calmed her more than all the talking to anyone had done. They were going on a mission. There was no worrying what she looked like or what she had lost. There was only the need to rescue her friends.

"If everyone is ready," she called. "Let's go!"

Pegasus entered into a trot and then a full gallop. Beating his strong wings, he climbed steadily into the blazing sky. Cupid was keeping up close beside them. The beating of his wings matched the stallion as they gained speed to enter the Solar Stream.

As they plunged once again into the Solar Stream, somehow Emily could still see the dot that was Arious Minor leading the way despite the blinding lights swirling all around them. Emily was mesmerized by the small dot and focused on it, keeping all the negative thoughts and worries out of her mind.

The journey to Earth from Xanadu was a long one. But after an age, they burst free of the blazing lights and into a star-filled night sky. Just like their previous journey to Earth, Pegasus arrived over open water.

Emily gazed all around, trying to get an idea of where they were. But surrounded by water, she hadn't a clue.

"Do you know where we are?" she called to Cupid.

"Not yet," he responded. "I need to see some land to get a better idea."

"You do not need land," Arious Minor said. "Look up. Use the stars to chart our location. We are currently flying over the Atlantic Ocean, four hundred and fifty-one miles from Ireland. After that, we shall approach the United Kingdom. By my estimates and Pegasus's current speed, barring complications, we shall arrive in London in nine point seven hours."

"Wow!" Emily said. "That's really impressive. So, can you tell us what time of year it is, based on the stars?"

"It is midwinter in this part of the world," Arious Minor said. "Are you not feeling the cold?"

"Actually, no," Emily said. Now that she had a body, she'd thought she might. "Cupid, are you cold?"

The winged Olympian shook his head. "Not at all. Though, if memory serves, I am hardly dressed for winter."

Cupid was right. He was wearing the traditional Olympian tunic with gold belt and sandals. He wouldn't exactly fit in. Neither would she without a winter coat. Of course, that was nothing compared to Pegasus and his wings. They couldn't exactly disguise him as a zombie again.

"We'll have to hide again when we arrive, then try to find some clothes."

Pegasus whinnied, and Cupid said, "Pegasus hopes we can find an appropriate blanket for him."

Emily leaned forward and patted his neck. "Don't worry, Pegs. We'll figure something out."

It had been some time since their visit to Hawaii. But as Emily looked down on the moonlit waters of the Atlantic, she discovered that she missed Earth less and less. After this, she doubted she would ever return. What Riza was doing sounded a lot more interesting than constantly coming here and having to hide.

As the long night passed and dawn split the horizon, they saw the outline of land ahead.

"Is that Ireland?"

"It is," the dot answered. "Shall we go down lower and take a look? I have only ever seen it through the memories of the Xan."

"Why not?" Emily said. "Pegs, do you want to go down lower to see Ireland?"

Pegasus nickered and tilted his wings. Soon they were descending.

"That's amazing," Emily said as they passed over the small country. "It really is the Emerald Isle. Even during the winter, it's green."

As Pegasus winged his way over Ireland, Emily saw more water looming ahead. After that they would reach England. Then what? Once again she felt that stirring in her stomach that they were making a terrible mistake. But what choice did she really have?

By the time they reached the English coastline, the sun was climbing high over their heads, well above the solid dark storm clouds that hung sullenly over the country.

"Looks like we're heading into rain, just like last time," Emily warned.

"This is a good thing," Cupid called. "It will give us cover as we head to London."

"Arious," Emily said, "would you lead us there?"

"Yes, but it's still against my better judgment. You do realize the danger you are putting yourselves in."

"Better us than Jupiter losing his temper and bringing his brothers here to end this world once and for all," Cupid said.

"That would never happen," Arious said. "Riza and I would stop them."

"And that would start a fight between you and them," Emily added. "This is the only way, unless you can think of another?"

The tiny dot went silent.

"Neither could I," Emily agreed. "Without Riza, we're on our own."

Conversation stopped as they approached the shore. Pegasus climbed higher to hide them in the dark clouds. With Arious Minor to guide them, they headed south toward London. But with each beat of the stallion's powerful wings, Emily heard a tiny voice nagging at her to forget Agent B and the others and go home. But how could she abandon her friend to the CRU?

After a while Arious Minor announced that they would soon be approaching London.

"Pegasus, I have an idea," Cupid called. "Would you slow down a bit but keep flying toward London. I will be right back."

"Where are you going?" Emily called as Cupid dipped down deeper into the dense clouds. "Cupid, wait!" But the winged Olympian disappeared into the grayness around them.

"He's very headstrong," Arious Minor said.

"He's going to get us into trouble, that's what he's going to do," Emily said.

A few minutes later Cupid returned and flew in front of Pegasus. "Follow me. I have a plan that will help us conceal ourselves. It is this way."

Pegasus nickered and then started to follow Cupid down into the clouds. When they burst free, they were flying over vast swaths of green fields with the occasional home dotting the land. The style was nothing like Emily had seen before, with red tiled roofs and quaint brick houses. A soft, misty rain fell, and by the looks of the sodden land, it hadn't stopped in quite some time.

"This way," Cupid called. "There is a place ahead that has horses."

They followed the winged Olympian down toward a single property with a small house and a large stone barn. Hedgerows marked the property lines, and a few horses wearing coats were standing in a muddy paddock. With the rain falling, there was no one working outside.

At the sight of them, Pegasus nickered.

"Ignore them, Pegs," Emily said as she patted his neck. "You are much better than they are. They're just horses and you're not."

Pegasus snorted and still didn't seem pleased. It made Emily realize that her best friend also had to overcome obstacles of perception. Pegasus was not a horse, but to look at him, he appeared to be a big beautiful white horse with wings. It made her own quest for identity seem petty and insignificant.

"We'll just take what we need and get going again. You won't even have to talk to them."

They touched down on the muddy ground outside the barn. Cupid ran forward and pulled one of the big barn doors open, and Pegasus trotted inside. There were three horses in their stalls, and they started to whinny noisily at the winged stallion's arrival. One chestnut stallion started to rear up and kick at the stall door.

"Easy," Emily called to the horses as she slid off Pegasus's back. "It's all right. We're not going to hurt you."

But no matter what they tried, the horses in the barn were disturbed by the presence of Pegasus among them. Their screaming increased by the minute.

"Do you want me to silence them?" Cupid offered. "I could make it painless."

"You want to kill them?" Emily cried. "No way! Stealing a blanket or two is one thing. But killing beautiful horses is another."

"But they are noisy," Cupid said. "They will draw attention to us."

Cupid was right. The horses were being very loud. But killing or even hurting them was out of the question. "No, Cupid, you won't touch them! We'll think of something else." Emily walked back to the door and peered out. Despite the noise of the horses, no one was coming out of the house.

"I don't think anyone is home. Wait here. I'll be right back." Emily left the barn, to the loud protests of Pegasus and Cupid. She ran across the muddy ground to the front door of the house. Pressing the doorbell, she waited for an answer. When no one came, she knocked forcefully on the door. After a couple of minutes, she was convinced no one was home.

Emily pushed against the door, and the wood frame creaked and then started to crack. A moment later the door burst open as wood fragments scattered along the floor.

"Well, that was one way of getting in," Arious Minor said as the dot hovered in front of her.

"Could you have opened it?"

"No," the dot said. "But you might have considered that open window over there."

Emily looked at one of the windows near the door. It was slightly ajar. Had she seen it, she wouldn't have had to force the door. "You know, you could have told me about that before I destroyed the door."

"I didn't think you would listen to me."

"Of course I would. You're part of the team," Emily said. "Next time, if you see a better solution, please say something."

"You consider me part of your team?" the dot asked incredulously.

"Of course. Don't you?"

"I must admit, I never thought of it. When I traveled with the Xan, I was expected to remain silent and simply observe. I only spoke when told to."

"In case you hadn't noticed, I'm not Xan."

"But you contain parts of the Xan. I know what Riza did when her father was creating your body."

"Maybe so," Emily admitted. "But still, if you need to tell us something or see us heading into danger, please speak out. Don't wait to be asked. Being part of the team means we all work together."

"I will," the dot said.

Emily noticed how Arious Minor glowed a little bit brighter. "Now, would you do me a favor and tell Pegs and Cupid that no one is home and that they can come in."

"Of course."

The dot of light shot out of the house and across the yard. His words disturbed her. For as benevolent as the Xan were, it didn't sound like they treated Arious Major or Minor very well. In fact, they weren't big on emotions at all. That's what set Riza apart and why she and Riza were so close.

While she waited for Pegasus and Cupid, Emily walked farther into the house. Near the door was a coatrack with several long, dark green rain slickers, which would be perfect for hiding Cupid's wings.

Deeper inside, she saw the home was modestly furnished. The smell of coffee lingered in the air, and when she entered the kitchen, she saw the remnants of a pot still simmering. That smell brought back memories of her own home when her mother was still alive and always had coffee simmering. That smell meant home.

From the kitchen, Emily passed into a small den and off of there, to a neat but cramped room that worked as an office. A computer hummed on the desk, and papers were scattered all around. Taking a seat at the computer, Emily reached for the mouse. Just then, Arious Minor returned.

"Would you like me to help you with that?"

"Sure," Emily said. "Can you do that interface thingy you mentioned and find out where we are and how far we are from Charing Cross?"

"No problem," Arious Minor said. "I would like to see what the technology of this world can do." The dot vanished into one of the USB ports.

Suddenly the screen burst to life with images that flashed faster than Emily could follow. Whatever Arious Minor was doing, he was doing it very quickly.

The sound of shattering glass coming from the other room made Emily jump from her chair.

"Pegasus, be careful," Cupid complained. "You are wrecking the place!"

By the time she reached the den, Pegasus was standing in the middle of the tiny room, taking up most of the space, while Cupid was bending over and picking up the pieces of a broken lamp. The floor was covered in muddy prints from all of them.

"Why are human dwellings so small?" Cupid complained as he put the pieces down on a lounge chair. "I cannot even open my wings in here. I have no idea how Pegasus is going to get back out again. Look, he cannot turn around."

"I don't think they were expecting winged Olympians to visit when they built the house. Why don't you look around for some clothes and I'll stay with Pegs. Arious Minor is using the computer in the office. Just be as quick as you can."

While he was gone, Emily looked around in the small den. Cupid was right. They were going to have to move furniture so Pegasus could turn around and get out.

Standing at the stallion's head, Emily stroked his smooth mane. "It won't be long now, Peg. Are you nervous?"

Pegasus bobbed his head.

"Me too. I just wish Riza were here. She could get Agent B and the others out of there in no time. Then we could go home. Or maybe we could join her on some of her journeys. What would you think of that?"

Once again, Pegasus bobbed his head. "I'm glad. So when this is over, I'll talk to Dad about spending more time with Riza."

"Emily," Arious Minor said as the dot of light

returned to the room. "At Pegasus's average speed, we are just over an hour's flight from London. I have downloaded the maps we need to find our way around the city. Did you know there was something called the Internet?"

Emily chuckled. "Yes. What about it?"

"It is amazing. Filled with so much data. There are some wonderful things on there, but some terrible things too. Humanity has evolved into a very complicated and, I'm sad to say, destructive species with as many people doing terrible things to the environment as there are others trying to save it. Earth has lost too many species because of humanity. I believe Riza should be told. Perhaps it is time we removed some of the more endangered species from this world and brought them to Xanadu for protection. After all this time, it appears humans are not learning from their mistakes."

"That wouldn't be a bad idea at all," Emily admitted. "But did you find anything on there about the CRU?"

"For all the information out there, the CRU are strangely silent. I did find a kind of Dark Internet with information not readily available. I have my suspicions that the CRU work within that darkness. Unfortunately, that computer was not strong enough to help me access it. It would mean me leaving here to follow the trail. I thought it best not to."

Cupid returned to the lounge. He was wearing a pair of baggy jeans and was tearing slits in the back of a shirt to fit over his wings. His tunic and belt were tucked under his arm. "Whoever owns this place is bigger than me. His shirts are massive, and I am swimming in these trousers. I had forgotten how much I hate wearing human clothing."

Emily reached for his Olympian garments. "It's better than these for the moment." She stopped and looked at Cupid's belt. It was finely woven Olympian gold with a diamond set in every other link.

"Cupid, would you mind if I left your belt for the people who own the house?"

"My belt? No. Mother gave that to me."

"I know, but look around. We've stolen their clothes, destroyed their lamp, and dirtied their house. And I broke down their door. We should at least leave them something to pay for the damages."

"But why my belt?"

"Because it has diamonds in it, and they are very valuable here. Besides, I don't have anything to give them."

Cupid grumbled for a bit but finally handed over his belt. "I certainly hope they appreciate the sacrifice I have made."

Emily grinned. "I'm sure they'll be blown away."

Cupid pulled on the flannel shirt and maneuvered his wings through the slits. He tucked it in and sighed. "Before we leave, I want you to write a note to let them know the true value of the gift and that it came from me."

"That sounds fair." Emily went back into the office and wrote up a quick message to the homeowners. When she finished, she offered him the pen. "Do you want to sign it?"

"No, I do not wish to sign it," Cupid said irritably. "I want to get moving before these people come home and find us here."

"I agree," Emily said. "I'll just go get a blanket for Pegs and we can leave."

When they were ready to go, Emily pulled two of

the rain slickers down from the coatrack and gave one to Cupid and kept the other for herself. She pulled it on over her clothes.

Cupid wrinkled his nose. "This smells like the barn."

"Yes, it's a farmer's coat," Emily said. "But it's better than being seen."

"Are you sure?" Cupid complained.

They made their way outside and found that the rain was now coming down harder. But Emily didn't mind. Rain meant people rarely looked up—which gave them a better chance of not being seen as they made their way to one of the world's busiest cities.

Emily climbed up on the stallion's back and patted Pegasus's neck. "All right, everyone, next stop—London. Let's go!"

PAELEN WAITED UNTIL LORIN RETIRED TO
her bedchamber in Vesta's home before leaving. He
walked back to where he was staying in the caves of
the night dwellers and felt guilt settle in his chest.

Seeing Emily's disappointment at the silver lake
was still weighing heavily on his mind. He knew that
beach was her special place where she and Pegasus
went whenever she was troubled. So why had he let
Lorin talk him in to taking her there? It had been a
terrible mistake. He had given in to Lorin because it
was easier than saying no to the Titan, even though
he knew what could happen if Emily found out.

But Emily did find out, and seeing the hurt on
her face was worse than anything he could imagine.

Yet for all of Emily's pain, Lorin seemed oblivious. Perhaps it was because she had not yet learned how to read expressions, or—and Paelen really hoped this wasn't it—that she enjoyed making Emily suffer.

Whatever the answer, Lorin still had a lot to learn. One of the biggest things being that Pegasus was a free individual and not Emily's pet. Somehow she couldn't grasp that and was always asking him to tell Emily to give Pegasus to her.

Not even Jupiter giving her Tornado Warning was enough. She may have loved the winged horse, but Lorin still wanted Pegasus.

"Stupid, stupid, stupid," he repeated to himself as he smacked his head. "Why did I do it? Why did I take her there?"

Ever since the events in Hawaii, nothing was the same. Emily had changed completely. Riza was a separate and powerful Xan, and Lorin was in his life. The Titan was beautiful and smart, and for reasons he could never understand, she seemed to care deeply for him. But Paelen wasn't sure what he felt. There was so much he liked about her and some parts he even loved. But there were other parts he didn't like.

Lorin's overwhelming jealousy of Emily was one of her biggest faults. It was almost out of control, and because of it, he had been put in charge of teaching the Titan instead of Emily.

Paelen felt conflicted. Emily was his dearest friend. She was the first person ever to show him that he was more than just a thief. That he had value and belonged. But now he was neglecting her because of Lorin.

In all his life, he'd never understood the complications of relationships. He'd never really wanted to until he'd met Emily. Part of him was happy that she had found something special with Joel. But another part of him was sad because he always wished she had chosen him instead.

Emily hadn't, but Paelen took pleasure knowing that at least she was happy with Joel and that she was his friend. But after Hawaii, that also changed. Emily and Joel weren't spending time together anymore.

As happy as Paelen was about his relationship with Lorin, he also grieved because his friendship with Joel and Emily was different. Why did it have to change? Why couldn't they all be friends?

It was getting late, but Paelen couldn't sleep. He looked down at his winged sandals and sighed. "Take me to Vulcan's forge."

The tiny wings flapped in acknowledgment and lifted him up in the air. They carried him silently above ruined buildings. Like everything else in his life, Olympus itself was a wreck.

The journey was short and, even though it was late, the glow of the forge was shining through the large double doors.

Touching down outside the doors, Paelen peered in. The workspace around the large forge was unbearably hot and cramped. Tools of unimaginable use hung on the walls and down from the tall ceiling. The floor was filthy from the coal that was being shoveled into the fire.

Joel was standing beside the forge. His shirt was off and he was covered in a film of sweat and grime. His artificial arm worked the billows, blowing strong winds into the flames to stoke the fire into surrendering more heat for the steel that was being worked within its glowing embers.

Chrysaor, the winged boar, was lounging on rags

in the corner. Somehow he managed to sleep despite the overwhelming heat and noise.

Directly across from Joel was Vulcan. Hunched over on his artificial legs, he was wielding a massive hammer as he pounded out glowing red steel on an anvil. From first impressions, it looked like they were making weapons. A lot of them.

"Joel!" Paelen called from the doors. He knew better than to enter without announcing himself first. He'd made that mistake once before, and creeping up on Joel had surprised him. Joel had reacted instinctively and struck Paelen with a blow from his silver arm, which had driven him across the forge and into a large barrel of oily water used for cooling forged metal.

Joel looked to the entrance and nodded at Paelen. Then he motioned to Vulcan that he was taking a break.

"Hey, Paelen, what's up?" Joel was his normal, smiling self as he wiped sweat off his brow with a grimy rag.

"I need to speak with you. I did something really stupid and I cannot get it out of my mind. I do not know how to fix it."

Joel grinned and punched him. "So, what else is new? You're always doing something stupid. That's what everyone loves about you. Whoever you did it to must understand that by now."

"It was Emily."

Joel's smile vanished, and he frowned. "Emily? What did you do to her?"

At the mention of Emily's name, Chrysaor rose and joined them outside the forge. He snorted at Paelen.

"Well, I did not mean to," Paelen said to the boar.

"You didn't mean to do what?" Joel demanded.

Paelen looked down at his winged sandals. "I took Lorin and Tornado Warning to the silver beach. Then Emily and Pegasus came. Lorin refused to leave, so they had to, or Pegasus would have started fighting with Tornado."

Chrysaor squealed in anger while Joel shouted, "You did what? What on Earth possessed you to do that?"

Paelen frowned. "We are not on Earth, Joel. We are in Olympus."

"You know what I mean. Why did you do it?"

"Lorin had seen it in Emily's mind when they were connected. She has been nagging me to take her there."

"So why didn't you say no?"

Paelen dropped his head. "Well, she used that 'look' on me, and I just could not say no."

The winged boar continued to squeal at him.

"I am sorry; I know it was a mistake!"

Joel was shaking his head. "So if she asked you to put your hand in Vulcan's forge, would you do it?"

Paelen shrugged. "If she used that 'look,' probably."

"You moron!" Joel said. "You should never let a girl get that kind of control over you. It just leads to disaster."

"Well, you feel the same about Emily. Or at least you used to. You would have done anything she asked of you."

"What's that supposed to mean?" Joel challenged. "What do you mean 'used to'?"

"You know what I mean. You have been avoiding Emily because she does not look the same. Everyone in Olympus knows you do not love her anymore."

"What?" Joel cried. "That's a lie."

"Is it?" Paelen asked. "When was the last time you spoke with her?"

Joel paused, wiping his brow again. "I dunno, yesterday maybe."

Once again, Chrysaor squealed. This time he was looking at Joel.

"What?" Joel said to him.

"It has been more than four days," Paelen explained. "Chrysaor and I were there, remember? She asked us if we would like to join her at Apollo's home to have dinner with Diana and her father. You said no, and the two of you walked away. I could not go because of Lorin. So none of us went. But, Joel, you did not see Emily's face when you and Chrysaor left. You hurt her. We all did."

"But . . . but I've been really busy," Joel said defensively. His face was changing and getting angry. He pointed back into the forge. "Look in there. What do you see? Weapons! Vulcan and I have been working nonstop making weapons to arm every Olympian. The Titans nearly destroyed us, here and in Hawaii. If Riza and her family hadn't been there, we'd all be dead now."

Paelen shook his head. "It was Emily who saved us. She was the one who sacrificed herself by leaping into the lava and retrieving the shard. It was Emily, not Riza."

"Even so, we need to arm ourselves."

"Did you tell her what you were doing so she would understand?"

"No," Joel said. "But I shouldn't have to explain. She knows me."

"Does she?"

Speaking to Joel and hearing his excuses made Paelen realize just how much they'd both neglected their friend. "Joel," he finally said. "How do you feel about Emily now that she looks so much like Diana?"

Chrysaor squealed, but Paelen shook his head. "No. Let him answer, because his feelings have changed."

"I—I don't know what I feel," Joel said. "It's complicated. Emily just doesn't seem like Emily anymore. She's changed so much, it's like she's a different person. She's taller, a lot stronger, and even though her new face is beautiful, it isn't *Emily*."

"But it is," Paelen said. "Only the outside has

changed. Inside she's still the same person. How would you feel if Emily looked at you differently because of your silver arm?"

Joel shook his head. "It's not the same. This is just one arm. All of Emily has changed."

"Do you think she does not know that? That she is not having a difficult time adjusting to everything?"

"Well, maybe," Joel said. "But this is big. Sometimes I feel like the Emily we knew died in that lava and that a new person called Emily is here, trying to take her place."

Paelen heard the excuses; he'd even made some himself. But hearing them from Joel made it worse. He'd thought their feelings for each other could survive anything.

"Joel, we have both hurt her when she needed us most. Does what someone looks like on the outside mean more than what is on the inside? If I changed completely, would you stop talking to me too?"

"Don't be stupid. Of course not."

"Then why is it different for Emily? Is it because she is a girl and you expect her to look a certain way?"

"It's because I loved Emily, the old version with

the brown hair, freckles, and pretty blue eyes," Joel snapped. "Not this . . . What does she call herself now . . . ? 'Emily Version II,' with her jet-black hair, deep blue eyes with white flecks, and not a zit or freckle in sight. Paelen, this new Emily is just too perfect. She's perfectly strong, perfectly tall, and perfectly beautiful."

"So?"

"So I want the old, imperfect Emily back!"

"And because she cannot look the same, you no longer care?"

Joel shook his head and combed his fingers through his dark hair. "I don't know, okay? Is that what you want to hear? I just don't know. Does that make me a bad person? Probably. An idiot? Definitely. But some changes are just too big to accept."

Paelen tilted his head to the side. "You know, I always believed there was nothing on Olympus or any other world that could ever get between you two. But I was wrong." He looked down at his sandals. "Take to me Alexis's home."

Paelen felt a lump in his throat as the sandals carried

him silently toward Alexis and Tom's cave. He knew it was late, but guilt and regret kept him moving. He should have said something sooner and not let this go on so long. Even if it meant waking her, he needed to speak with Emily to apologize for everything.

Landing in front of the Sphinxes' cave, he peered in and was surprised to see the lights on. Tom was pacing the floor while his long tail swished in the air. Alexis was sitting down with a worried expression on her face.

"Hello," Paelen called. "May I enter?"

"Of course," Tom said. "It's good to see you." He peered past Paelen. "Where's Joel?"

"He is working at the forge with Vulcan. They are making weapons in case the Titans attack us again." Paelen dropped his head. "I actually came to speak with Emily. I know it is late, but I must see her."

"I'm afraid she's not here," Tom said.

"Not here? Is she out with Pegasus?"

Tom nodded. "You might say that. Please come in. I think we should talk."

"Tom, no," Alexis said. "We promised Emily. It has not been long enough."

"I know, but I've been thinking that letting her go was a terrible mistake. Even with Riza, they're risking too much."

Paelen felt a thud hit his stomach. "What kind of mistake? What is Emily doing?"

"Tom, we must not," Alexis said. She faced Paelen. "Everything is fine. Emily will be back soon. You may leave us now."

"Back from where?"

Tom approached Alexis. "I'm sorry, my love, but I can't keep quiet. Not about this. Emily means too much to us, and I know they're walking into danger."

The more they held back, the more frightened Paelen became. "If this involves Emily, you must tell me!"

"But she did not wish to involve Paelen or Joel," Alexis insisted.

"Not involve us," Paelen cried. "Why not?"

Tom shook his head. "Because you're not a team anymore. Emily knows it, and so do I. But I fear she has bitten off much more than she can chew this time. I'm still tempted to go to Jupiter."

"No!" Alexis gasped. "You cannot. We promised Emily, and that is one promise I intend to keep. Her fears that Jupiter will destroy the Earth are valid. He will if he finds out."

Paelen's mouth went dry. "Tom, Alexis, listen to me. You must tell me what has happened. Where are Emily and Pegasus?"

Tom sighed. "They've gone to Xanadu to get Riza. Then they plan to go to Earth to attack one of the biggest CRU facilities in existence."

"What?" Paelen cried.

Tom nodded. "Sit down and listen. I don't care that things have changed between you three. Emily is in danger, and you and Joel are going to find her whether you like it or not. You will find her and help her, or I swear you'll both answer to me!"

It was dawn by the time Paelen left the cave. "Faster!" he shouted at his sandals as they winged their way back to Vulcan's forge. Even before he touched down, he was running into the inferno of heat. Joel and Vulcan were standing together, inspecting a new sword, while Chrysaor was once again in the pile of rags.

"Joel!" he cried. "Joel, it's Emily. You must come!"

Vulcan put down the sword. "What has happened to Emily?"

Paelen repeated the story he'd just heard from Tom about Emily and Pegasus going to Xanadu to collect Riza and her plan to go to England to free the CRU prisoners.

Hearing his brother's name, Chrysaor joined them and squealed loudly at the end of the story.

"They have taken my Stella!" Vulcan cried. "How is this possible?"

"You know her?" Paelen asked.

Vulcan nodded. "Of course I know her. It was Stella's design for the flame-sword that saved us in the first Titan War. This is her design we are making right now. Those swords were the only things we Olympians could use against the Shadow Titans." He looked at Joel. "Go into the back of the forge and call out the name 'Maxine.'"

"Who's Maxine?"

"Just do it!" Vulcan commanded.

When Joel returned a moment later, a wheelchair

covered in dust and cobwebs was following close behind him, moving on its own. His eyes were wide. "What is this?"

"This is Maxine, Stella's wheelchair. I made it for her a very, very long time ago. The sweet child's legs did not work, but with Maxine, Stella could get around just as well." Vulcan looked at Paelen. "You will not remember her, but you and Stella were very close. You were such an old man by then, but you and Brue lived with us in our mobile forge. I always thought if your ages were not so different, you and Stella would have been perfect for each other." Vulcan chuckled with the memory. "In your old age, you went back to your thieving ways. We were always finding my tools hidden under your bunk."

"I remember none of this," Paelen said.

"So you should not. It happened in another time line, as Emily and Agent B called it. Once Emily destroyed the Titan weapon that was killing us, time changed. You do not remember it because for you it never happened. But I was there, in the first war, and remember it well. I cared very deeply for Stella. So did you, Paelen."

"Now the CRU have taken Agent B and Stella," Paelen said. "Tom and Emily insist there is no way they should know about them—Earl and Frankie, yes, because they are from this time line, but not Agent B or Stella."

"Unless someone who was there told them," Vulcan suggested.

Paelen nodded. "That's what Tom believes. He thinks in the fight on Hawaii, one of the older Titans may have been captured and told them about the other time line and war."

Joel spoke for the first time. "This doesn't make any sense. Even if the CRU found out about the other time line, so what? What do they expect by taking Agent B and Stella? The weapon was destroyed. It is no good to them."

Vulcan shook his head and started to look around the vast forge. He picked up tools and brought them back to his workbench.

"What is it?" Joel demanded. "What are you doing?"

"I am seeing what we need to take with us."

"What do you mean take with us?"

Vulcan stopped looking around and came back. He slapped Joel across the head. "Use your brain, boy! There is only one reason why the CRU would take Stella and Agent B. Not because of what they know but because of who they are."

"What do you mean?" Paelen said.

Chrysaor squealed, and Vulcan shook his head, sighing. "How you two have managed to survive this long is beyond me, so I will explain it to you slowly." He pulled out a stool and sat down. "In war, deep friendships and loyalties are formed, just as you two care for each other. But the first war with the Titans was different. You will not remember, but you were both there. We all fought together in the most terrible circumstances possible for a very long time. It was grim, violent, and filthy. But Agent B and Stella were with us all the way. The bonds we all forged ran deep. The CRU must know this and are using it against Emily and all of us who were there."

"For what?" Joel said. "I still don't get it."

Paelen slapped Joel across the head. "Vulcan is right. Use your brain, or is the heat in here getting to you? Do you not see? If Agent B and Stella meant so much to Emily, they would be the perfect bait in a trap so deep, not even Emily could escape."

Vulcan went back to work, furiously racing around the forge, gathering weapons and supplies. He piled them in a large sack and stopped long enough to say to Joel and Paelen, "Change your clothes and meet me back here when you are ready. If Emily and Pegasus are off to Xanadu first, we may still be able to catch them."

"We're going to Xanadu?" Joel asked.

"No," Vulcan said in irritation. "That would take too long. The moment you boys are ready, we must try to catch them up on Earth before they reach Charing Cross."

EMILY, PEGASUS, AND CUPID FLEW STEADILY toward London through the driving rain. But the worse the weather became, the better Emily liked it. If she could barely see Cupid winging beside them, what chance did the people on the ground have of spotting them in the sky?

"We are approaching London," Arious Minor announced. "Perhaps we should find somewhere near the station to land while we wait for darkness."

Emily agreed and called forward to Pegasus. "We're almost there. We should find somewhere to hide until tonight."

Pegasus nodded and came down lower in the sky. Bursting free from the low-hanging clouds, they got their first glimpse of the city. Emily's initial impression was that it was very pretty, with winding streets and narrow alleys. It also had some very oddly shaped buildings. But it was different from New York City or Las Vegas. The buildings weren't nearly as tall.

They followed the course of the river that cut through the city until they passed the Tower of Big Ben that she'd seen in Urania's pool. Finally, Arious told Emily they were above Charing Cross Station.

"How about down there?" Emily pointed out to the winged stallion a taller roof on a neighboring building. There were four large gray exhaust ports that almost looked like castle turrets. "Can you land down between those big smokestacks?"

Pegasus whinnied and tilted his wings. He expertly maneuvered between the stacks and landed lightly on the roof. Cupid landed behind him and tucked in his wings.

Emily slid down from the stallion's back and peered over the edge of the roof to the street below to see if anyone had seen them. They were only five stories high at most. But judging by the number of umbrellas she saw, it seemed no one had witnessed their arrival.

"Now we wait," Cupid said as he pulled the green rain slicker over his wings. He stood beside Emily, peering out over the city. There was congestion on the road, with cars, tall red double-decker buses, and black cabs all trying to get to various places.

"Have you ever been here before?" Emily asked.

Cupid nodded. "A very, very long time ago. Back then it was called Londinium and was just a rough settlement. The island was mostly ruled by the Romans. This city looks completely different and infinitely more interesting. It will be a pity to cut off all connection to this world, but seeing all these changes, perhaps it is for the best."

They stood together on the rooftop, watching the day giving way to night. The colorful city lights came up and reflected on the wet sidewalk and roads. Emily walked over to the other side of the roof and peered down on the entrance to the Charing Cross Station. It was the same entrance she'd seen in Urania's pool. Somewhere beneath that old Victorian building, her friends were being tortured.

"I wonder why the CRU chose such a busy location for their super-facility. It seems dangerous when so many people use the station."

"That's a good question," Arious Minor said. The small dot was hidden under Emily's thick black braid.

"I mean, if the CRU are obsessed with capturing anything unusual, why put it here? How do they get them inside if this is a busy train station? What if someone escapes? They could do a lot of damage to the city."

"Perhaps it was built before this was a big city," Arious offered. "I read on the Internet that Charing Cross Station was opened in 1864, so the CRU might have been here before then and the station was built on top. From what we have learned, the CRU are all over the world, but no one seems to know their origins. They are as much a mystery as those they hunt down."

Emily agreed. Tom didn't know, and in all their time together, Agent B hadn't been able to tell her a lot either. "Guess we'll never know. But when you were in the computer, did you find a way in? I don't think we want to take Pegasus in through the front doors. He might draw a bit of attention."

"Though it would be interesting," Arious Minor said. "But from the plans I saw, there is a delivery entrance on a side street. However, the station is open late each night, so we have a wait ahead of us."

Emily nodded and went back to Pegasus. She brushed his wet mane out of his eyes. "The station closes very late. But Arious Minor says there is a private delivery entrance we could use to get in." She pulled down the sack of ambrosia cakes and nectar. "While we wait, we might as well eat." She fed Pegasus first before she and Cupid ate their portions. Then she pulled out the Xan food hat and ordered up a large dish of chocolate ice cream for the stallion.

As the hours ticked by, they stood together on the roof, eating and watching the traffic start to thin. Later in the evening, the traffic picked up again, and Arious Minor explained that Charing Cross was in the theater district and that some of the shows were now letting out.

They watched crowds of well-dressed people with their umbrellas dashing into the station to catch the last of the late-night trains while cabs streamed into the station entrance to drop off their passengers.

It was a few hours later before Emily crossed the roof again and gazed down at the station entrance. This time Pegasus and Cupid joined her.

"It looks like they're finally closing for the night," Emily said. "They are turning off the lights. When it's quiet, I think we should move."

"So, do we have a plan?" Cupid asked.

Emily shrugged. "Not really. Just get in there and try to get the others out while doing as little damage to London as possible."

"That is it? That is our plan?"

"Can you think of anything else with just the four of us taking on a CRU super-facility?"

When Cupid shook his head, Arious Minor came out from under Emily's hair. "Do not forget, Emily, that you have powers. Not as strong as before, but you are still a formidable fighter and part Xan. Do not hesitate to use them to free your friends."

Emily nodded. "Well, this isn't going to get any easier. Let's go."

Pegasus dropped his wing, inviting Emily up.

Once on his back, she patted his neck. "This is it, Pegs."

The stallion opened his large wings and leaped out from between the air vents. He glided down to the ground and landed on a side street. Emily climbed back down and covered the stallion's wings with the blanket.

Cupid landed beside them and pulled on his raincoat.

"All right, Arious," Emily said. "Would you lead us in?"

The small dot hovered before Emily's face. "I would be remiss in my duties if I didn't warn you a final time that this is very dangerous. Are you all certain you don't want to wait for Riza?"

"I wish we could, but they're torturing our friends in there. If we wait for Riza, there's no telling what could happen. They might even kill them."

"I am ready to go in now," Cupid said.

Pegasus bobbed his head up and down.

"As you are all in agreement," Arious Minor said, "I acquiesce to your decision."

The dot led them out on to the main street, the

Strand, and they walked toward the train station. Despite the late hour, the occasional cab drove past them but didn't slow to look at them.

"I wonder if they see a lot of horses in the city," Emily said.

"It is most likely that they are used to seeing strange things in the theater district. I am sure Pegasus could expose his wings and they would not look twice."

That theory was tested when they were approached by a young couple. They were huddled together under an umbrella and nearly walked into Pegasus. Seeing the large white stallion, they simply apologized and walked around him without missing a beat in their conversation.

"This is definitely not New York," Emily said.

"Theater district or not, I do not like being out in the open like this," Cupid said. "I feel like we are being watched."

Emily did too, but she didn't say anything. "How much farther is it?"

"The delivery entrance is just down the street ahead of us," Arious Minor said.

They followed the tiny white dot to a street that

ran beside the large old train station. Most of the street was taken up with brownstone-style homes. Some had gold plaques outside that said they were offices. One plaque even said that Benjamin Franklin had lived there.

"Are you sure it's here?"

"Yes," the dot answered. "It's just ahead at that driveway. The entrance runs under the building."

Emily stopped and took a deep breath. The feeling of being watched was getting worse. A little voice inside her head was telling her to go. Instead she squared her shoulders and walked forward. "All right, let's go."

The driveway turned to the right and descended down a long, dark ramp. It soon split. One way went straight along the road that ran behind the block of brownstones and out onto the next street. The left-hand side took you deeper into the delivery area of the station.

No one was moving in the area, and there were no security guard houses. The only sound they heard was from the heavy machinery of the large ventilation systems blowing air into the station.

Walking to the left along the white painted walls of Charing Cross Station, they approached a tall chain-link fence that blocked the underground entrance. The fence was sealed with a digital security log. Emily was about to use her Flame to burn it open when Arious Minor stopped her.

"Don't destroy it. Let me try." The tiny dot disappeared into the box with the security code numbers. They heard soft bleeping, and then the heavy gates started to swing open.

"That's a handy trick you've got there," Emily said when Arious returned.

"It's better than setting off the alarms."

As they descended deeper, they saw cars parked in bays. These weren't the normal black cars favored by the CRU. Emily thought that these looked more like station employees' vehicles—especially when she noticed a BABY ON BOARD sticker in one of the car windows.

Emily's Olympian night vision also spotted the lens of a security camera hidden in a round ball hanging down from the ceiling. It was scanning back and forth and hadn't made it back to face them yet. "How are you with security cameras?" she asked Arious. "Do you think you could disable that one before it sees us?"

The tiny dot of light followed her line of vision and darted forward. It disappeared into the camera ball. Moments later, there was a flash of sparks and the round cover blew off the camera.

"I'll take that as a yes," Emily said.

The sound of drunken laughter filtered down from the street. Pegasus nickered softly and Cupid nodded. "Yes, we are still very exposed here. We must get inside."

They walked farther along the dark ramp and saw several brick archways with plain gray doors beneath each arch.

"Arious, can you tell us which door to take?"

"I am sorry. The plans I found didn't go into these specifics. I believe any of these doors will take us inside."

"Yes, but which one will lead us down into the CRU part of the station?" Cupid asked.

"That I do not know," the dot answered. "Emily, what do you recall from the vision in Urania's pool?"

Emily thought back. "The way in that I was shown came up through the public bathrooms inside the station, not from out here in the delivery bay. But there must be more than one way in. We can't go through the station itself. It would be too open and dangerous." She looked at each of the doors and shrugged. "This is as good a way as any."

She walked up to the nearest door and was surprised to see there wasn't a keypad security lock, just an old-fashioned key one. She summoned the Flame and her hand burst into a bright fire. Then she placed her palm on the lock. Closing her eyes, Emily intensified the Flame.

Metal dripped to the ground as the lock melted. She reached for the handle and gave a mighty pull. The melted lock and door gave easily. She looked back at Pegasus. "Are you ready?"

When he nodded and nickered softly, Emily walked in. The hall was dark and very narrow. With her Olympian vision, she saw the whole left side of the wall was covered in large electrical piping. The right side had strange metal boxes built into the walls and a framework that helped support the many ventilation ducts hanging down from the ceiling.

Emily looked back and saw that Pegasus could barely fit through. His wings grazed the electrical pipes and gray cement block walls on either side.

"Are you all right, Pegs?"

Pegasus nickered and snorted.

"Perhaps you should wait outside," Cupid suggested.

That set Pegasus off. He responded with a series of soft but angry whinnies.

"It was only a suggestion," Cupid said. "There is no need to lose your temper. I was thinking of you and the damage to your wings."

Emily approached Pegasus and stroked his soft muzzle. "He's been this far with us and seen us through some terrible things. Pegasus stays."

"Fine," Cupid said as he pressed forward and pushed past Emily. "Wait here, then. I'll see how far this goes and if there is any way down into the lower section."

Emily stayed with Pegasus, stroking his muzzle. Cupid was right about one thing. The feathers on his wings were fraying from rubbing along the walls.

"Just ignore him," she said. "It's you and me forever, Pegs. Where you go, I go."

"If you are finished," Cupid called when he walked back, "I have found a set of steps going down. But I warn you, if Pegasus barely fits through the corridor, I will be curious to see how he manages these wooden steps."

Beneath her hand, Pegasus tensed. Cupid was starting to push his buttons. "We'll manage," Emily called back. "Just show us where they are."

They followed Cupid through the tight winding corridor. The metal boxes gave way to large water pipes lining the upper wall. At one point, a gas pipe actually crossed the floor in front of them.

"Mind your step," Emily warned the stallion as she walked over the pipe.

"Here," Cupid said. He stood before a set of wooden steps going down. They looked more like a ladder than stairs. "See, there is no way Pegasus is going down these."

"Well, he's not staying behind," Emily said as she peered down into the darkness. "But I do have an idea."

Emily descended the long set of wooden steps down into an area that looked a lot like the scenes from Urania's well. The ceiling was high overhead and lined with corrugated steel sheets, and the walls were much wider. They were made with much older brick than the concrete block from the floor above and had been whitewashed. This was an original part of the Victorian building.

She looked back up the steps. "Cupid, come down. Pegs, stay there for a moment."

Cupid muttered to himself all the way down the steps. At the bottom, he shook his head. "I am telling you, he will not make it down those steps."

"He won't have to," Emily said. "My powers aren't all gone. Are you ready, Pegs?"

When he nodded, Emily raised her hands, and her power surged as she levitated the large, heavy stallion off the ground. He floated through the tight opening of the stairway entrance and above the steps. She soon lowered him to the floor beside her.

She brushed her hands together and looked back at Cupid triumphantly. "Where there's a will, there's always a way."

Emily looked around. Her eyes let her see a lot in the complete darkness, but not enough. She held up her hands and summoned the Flame. Her palm started to burn painlessly with enough light to drive back the darkness.

"Now where?" Cupid said.

Emily walked forward. This whole area looked similar to what she'd seen in Urania's pool. Ahead of them was a wide, tall corridor with thick brick dividers that made them look like a strange kind of horse stalls. She walked the length. "I wonder what these were for. They look almost wide enough for trains."

Arious appeared before her. "Records show that in the early days of the station, the trains actually did come down this deep. These may be where the tracks were and where the trains were housed at night. Or perhaps this is where they kept the coal for each platform, as the early trains were steam-powered. Unfortunately, the records are scant. However, if this was where the trains were stored, I am sure the CRU would not be beneath us, because the weight of the old steam trains would collapse through the ceiling. The facility must have been built later."

"Or, knowing the CRU," Cupid put in, "they built a very good support system."

Emily looked down at the solid concrete floor. That seemed new, compared to the old brick walls. But there was no telling what the CRU did in the past. It was today she was worried about. Tom said it was a super-facility, which meant it had to be big. Was it just below her feet?

"This way," Cupid called. "I believe I have found something."

Emily held up her hand and saw that Cupid had moved forward and was exploring other parts of the lower level. She rested her hand on Pegasus's neck and followed him toward Cupid, who was standing near the wooden stairs.

"Look." He pointed down into the darkness. "There's a corridor down there that feels strange."

"Strange? How?"

"Follow me. Then you can feel for yourself."

The corridor Cupid found was narrower than the other area. The ceiling was much lower and arched. Once again, the walls were almost too narrow for Pegasus to fit through. But Cupid was right. When

Emily stood in the center of the corridor, she felt a strange, uncomfortable presence.

"Do you feel that?" she asked Pegasus.

Pegasus nickered softly and pawed the concrete floor.

"He does not like it here either," Cupid said.

Emily closed her eyes. Not only could she feel "something," but she could hear it too. "Listen. Do you hear that?"

Cupid tilted his head to the side. "I hear nothing."

"I am not designed to pick up on soft sounds," Arious Minor said.

But Pegasus whinnied and walked forward. His tall white ears were moving constantly, trying to follow the sound as his tail swished back and forth in irritation.

Finally they made it to the end of the corridor, through a tight doorway, and the room opened up.

"This is it!" Emily cried, walking into the wider room. "Isn't it, Pegs? We saw this in Urania's pool."

The room was a good thirteen feet wide and twenty feet long. She held up her hand and saw the fluorescent lighting attached to the ceiling. One wall had an indent that looked like at one time it might have been a large garage door. But now it was all bricked up.

Everything about the room looked as old and unused as the rest of this lower area. But Emily knew it wasn't. There was no dust on the floor or cobwebs hanging down from the ceiling. "This is the entrance to the CRU facility."

"It cannot be," Cupid said. "The walls are solid and old."

"But it is," Emily insisted. She stood in the center of the room. "If you walk back that way through the narrow corridor, instead of going to where the stairs are, turn to the right. You'll find another tunnel leading to a door that heads up into the station's bathrooms. Try it. Tell me what you see."

Cupid did as Emily suggested. He left the room and went down the dark corridor. He returned moments later. "It is as you say."

"I told you, this is the room. We both saw it in Urania's pool." Emily looked back at the garage-door-size indent. "This isn't a wall. It's an elevator."

Cupid frowned and walked up to the indent and knocked on the brick. "But it feels so solid."

Arious Minor left Emily and disappeared into the framework around the indent. When he returned, he reported, "Emily is correct. It is an elevator."

Faced with an elevator that traveled down into the bowels of the CRU facility, Emily looked around with a deep frown creasing her brow. "This doesn't make any sense. There should be guards here and security cameras. We've been to enough facilities to know they are never empty like this."

"I believe we should be on our guard," Arious Minor suggested. "Many times, what is hidden can be infinitely more dangerous than what is shown."

"I agree," Cupid said. He approached the wall. "So if this is an elevator, how do we summon it?"

"I can help with that," Arious Minor said. "The question is where to take it."

Once again, he disappeared into the disguised framework around the elevator doors. They soon heard a soft hum and then the sound of hydraulics.

Moments later, the brick wall before them shifted back and then split right down the middle through the bricks with a parting that none of them had seen. The wall opened to reveal the shiny stainless-steel doors of the elevator. There was a *whoosh*, and the steel doors opened.

Emily looked at Pegasus. "This is a trap, Pegs. Are you ready to walk into it?"

The stallion snorted and walked forward into the elevator. It was large enough to take his size, with room left for others. He turned around and nickered to her.

"Well, Cupid, it's up to you. Do you want to go on or go back?"

The winged Olympian sighed. "I have come too far to turn back now." Together he and Emily stepped onto the elevator.

They were then faced with the decision of where to go. "Wow. It goes down thirty levels," Emily said as she studied the control panel. "This is way bigger than all the others, but which one to choose?"

"It does not matter," Arious Minor said. "Choose any level. When we get there, I shall attempt to enter their computer systems and ascertain where the prisoners are being held."

Emily reached forward and pressed her lucky number, fifteen. The door closed and the elevator started to descend. "It is just me, or do you guys feel really stupid doing this?"

"Oh, I passed stupid a long time ago," Cupid said. "But what choice do we have?"

Pegasus bobbed his head up and down and nickered softly.

Emily looked to Cupid to translate. "He said at least Tom and Alexis know where we are. Should this go wrong, which it most likely will, they can warn the others."

That gave Emily little comfort as the elevator continued down. They felt it slow and then come to a stop. She raised both her hands, preparing to fight whoever was on the other side of the doors. But when they opened, they were all stunned to be faced with a super-modern but completely empty corridor. The lights were dimmed for evening, but as they piled out, they saw the walls were white and sparkling clean. The floor was dark marble tiles, and closed doors lined the corridor.

Arious Minor flew away from the group and approached the nearest door. He disappeared into the keypad lock. They heard soft beeps and clicks and then the door swung open. It was an office—neat, tidy, and sterile. There were no photos on the walls and no keepsakes on the desk. There was nothing to give away the character of the person who worked in here.

But there was one thing they were drawn to, the computer workstation. Emily moved around the desk and sat down in the chair. "All right, Arious. Do your thing."

The tiny dot vanished into the access port of one of the computers. Immediately the screen flashed to life. Just like at the farmhouse, the images on the screen were moving too fast for Emily to understand.

Pegasus was standing before the desk. His nostrils were flared and he was snorting. It sounded more like a sneeze than a snort. Soon he started shaking his head.

"What is it, Pegs?"

Cupid was next to shake his head. He started to sway on his feet. "Do you smell that?"

"Smell what?" Emily said. But as she looked up to Pegasus, her vision started to swim. The air was becoming heavy with a strange medicinal smell, and she started to feel very dizzy.

Alarm bells went off in her head. "Everyone, get out of here. . . ." Emily struggled to get up from the desk, but her legs felt like Jell-O. Pegasus whinnied and collapsed, falling down onto his wings. Cupid was the next to pass out, landing on the stallion.

Emily staggered around the desk. She stepped over Cupid and made it to the corridor. But even outside the office, the hall was filled with the same strange smell. Her eyes caught sight of mist coming out of the sprinkler heads and the smell was strongest from there. Drugs . . . She tried to lift her hands to shoot flames at the source, but she couldn't focus enough to do it.

The elevator doors swished open, and a large group of armed men poured out. Dressed in black and wearing gas masks, they charged toward her. Emily was already falling to the floor, and darkness descended as they reached her.

PAELEN RETURNED TO THE FORGE DRESSED
in human clothes but still wearing his winged sandals. He was surprised to see not only Joel wearing
jeans and a sweatshirt, but also Vulcan. In addition
to the baggy jeans over his artificial legs and the
T-shirt stretched over his broad chest, the strongly
built Olympian also had a large pair of metal wings
with sharp, steel feathers strapped to his back.

"What are those for?" Paelen asked.

Vulcan said irritably, "I hardly think your sandals
could carry the both of us, and though Chrysaor is
strong, he is not strong enough to carry both Joel and
me and reach speed to enter the Solar Stream. How
else am I to travel if not by my own power?"

"I thought you might stay here," Paelen suggested.

Chrysaor squealed and shook his head.

"Stay!" Vulcan boomed. "While my Stella languishes in a CRU prison? Are you mad? I have no intention of staying here and letting you boys try to rescue the best apprentice I ever had."

"But . . . but," Paelen said. "Your wings are metal. They will not work."

"Says who?" Vulcan challenged. He looked at the wings on his back and ordered, "Open." The metal wings did as he commanded and opened. Vulcan punched a grimy finger in Paelen's chest. "Do not ever doubt my ability to create. If I need wings, I make them. If I want to make a metal bull that could rampage through here and knock over Jupiter's palace, I need only build it. Do you understand?"

Paelen nodded his head. "I am sorry, Vulcan. I did not mean to make you angry."

Joel nudged him and whispered, "You can say a lot of things about Vulcan, but never doubt his ability to work metal into magic. You saw what he did with the wheelchair."

"Yes, but . . . ," Paelen said.

"But what?" Vulcan raged. "You think because I am an ugly, deformed man in metal legs and metal wings that I cannot help you? That I am not a skilled fighter?"

"I never said you were ugly," Paelen said.

"Boy, everyone sees me as ugly, except Stella. She never judged me, was never repulsed by my haggard face or misshapen legs. I loved her like a daughter. So it will take more than you to keep me from saving her. Do you understand?"

Paelen looked at Joel and then nodded fearfully. "I am sorry, Vulcan. I did not understand."

"Now you do," Vulcan finished.

"Paelen!" A soft voice arrived outside the forge.

"Uh-oh, Paelen," Joel warned. "Your girlfriend's here."

Paelen turned and saw Lorin running toward the doors. Her long blond hair was loose and wild around her shoulders, she was still wearing her nightdress, and her feet were bare.

"Lorin, what are you doing here?" Paelen asked. "It is early. You should still be asleep."

"I had a bad dream about you. You were on

Earth and being devoured by horrible big monsters with no bodies and terrible, flat faces. When I woke up, I could feel that you are upset and leaving me."

"You could feel me preparing to leave?" Paelen asked.

Lorin nodded. "I always know where you are and what you are feeling."

Paelen didn't know how to take that. Suddenly he felt like he had no privacy from her. "I am not leaving *you*," he corrected. "But I must go to Earth for a short trip."

"When do we leave?"

"We?" Joel said. "Oh no, Lorin, you're not coming with us."

Lorin's stunning blue eyes focused on Joel. "I go where Paelen goes. So if he is leaving here, I am going with him."

"No, you're not!" Joel said, leaning closer to her. "This is our mission, not yours. We don't need a whiny Titan coming with us and crying every few minutes."

Paelen saw the fight brewing between the two.

Joel still held Lorin personally responsible for the changes in Emily. If she hadn't awakened in Tartarus and opened the prison, the Titans wouldn't have escaped and attacked Olympus. Then the disaster in Hawaii would never have happened, and everything would have remained the same.

"It is not just your mission," Lorin said. "If Paelen is going, it is *our* mission. I have more power than you, and I can keep my Paelen safe. You cannot. I am going, and that is the end of it."

Joel shook his head. "You aren't coming! Just get that through your thick skull."

Lorin narrowed her eyes. "And I say I am." She raised her hand, and a ball of flame appeared in the center of her palm. "You, human, had better not try to stop me."

"Lorin, no!" Paelen cried. He pulled her hand down. "Put your Flame away. We have discussed this time and time again. You must control your temper. Never threaten anyone here, especially my friends. Do you understand me?"

"But, Paelen." Lorin pouted. "You said we would always be together. Now you want to leave me."

"I told you, I am not leaving you. But I must go to Earth for a short time."

"This is about Emily. I know it is," Lorin guessed. "She calls and you always answer."

Paelen was tempted to say *That's because at this moment I like her more than you!* But he kept quiet. Lorin was as powerful as Emily, but she had no control over her emotions. When upset, she didn't hesitate to use her powers against the cause of the perceived slight. If he pushed her too far, he wasn't sure she wouldn't turn her powers against him.

"Yes, Emily is in danger," he finally said. "But so is Pegasus. We must save them."

"My Pegasus!" Lorin cried.

"He's not yours!" Joel cried. "When will you get that?"

Lorin narrowed her eyes at Joel again. "I do not like you, Joel. I have never liked you, from the moment we met. The only thing stopping me from showing you how much I do not like you is Paelen."

Joel inhaled, ready to say more, when Vulcan boomed. "Enough!" He placed himself between Joel and Lorin. "If you two want to fight, do it another time. Emily, Pegasus, and Stella are in danger. I will not allow any of you to get in the way of my saving them."

"Vulcan," Joel cried. "Tell her she can't come. She's young and inexperienced. She doesn't understand how to behave on Earth. She'll endanger us all."

Lorin's eyes fell on each of them. She faced Vulcan. "I have power. You know I can help. Besides, you cannot stop me."

"Are you threatening me, girl?" Vulcan said. His voice dropped and he took a step closer.

Lorin backed up a bit. "No, but if you try to leave without me, I will follow anyway." She focused on Joel. "Or, I could go to Jupiter and tell him that Emily has gone to Earth again without his permission."

"You wouldn't dare!" Joel cried.

"She would," Paelen admitted. He'd seen her do it more than once when Emily had said or done something that upset her. Lorin still had so much to learn, including how to get along with others. She was still very much a petulant child.

He looked desperately at Vulcan and Joel. "Lorin does have power. We might need her if we run into trouble."

"You're going to give in to her threats? Paelen, are you nuts?" Joel cried. "For one, if we are lucky enough to even find Emily, they'll start fighting over Pegasus again. Or two, while we're trying to find them, she'll lose her temper and kill us."

"I will not!" Lorin said. "Paelen and Vesta have been teaching me how to control myself."

"Come or do not come, I do not care which," Vulcan boomed as he stormed out of the forge. "But one way or another, I am leaving right now."

Lorin's expression softened. "Please, Joel, let me come. How can I learn to be a better person if you do not let me help? If Pegasus is in danger, I must go to him."

Joel looked at Vulcan and then to Paelen. Finally he inhaled deeply. "All right, all right. If the others say you can come, I won't stop you."

Lorin's grin spread across her beautiful face. "Paelen, please, let me come with you."

Every nerve in his body said this was a big

mistake. But Paelen nodded. "All right, you may come. But you will do everything that I tell you to."

Lorin clapped her hands and jumped up and down. "I will, I promise."

Vulcan shook his head at all of them. He commanded his metal wings to open and take off. "So let us go," he called as he climbed into the night sky. "Londinium awaits."

"PSYCHE, WAKE UP."

Emily felt someone gently patting her face. "You must wake up now, my beloved."

Her eyes opened and she saw Cupid's face hovering before hers.

"Yes, Psyche, wake up. You are safe."

As Emily's head cleared, she wondered why Cupid was calling her Psyche. Wasn't that one of his many girlfriends on Olympus? "Cupid?"

"I am here, my love. Just be calm. You are safe."

Arious Minor whispered softly in Emily's ear, "Play along with him. The CRU do not recognize you as Emily. Cupid told them Emily was dead."

"Where's Pegs?"

The stallion nickered, and his muzzle gently brushed her brow.

Emily sat up and stroked him, more to reassure herself than him. They were in a large, dimly lit cell with heavy bars. At the front of the cell, she saw Earl and Frankie standing together, looking at her curiously. Stella was sitting on the edge of another bunk in the middle of the cell. Her face was a picture of pure terror as her frightened eyes lingered on Pegasus and Cupid.

Emily realized that the Stella from this time line had never seen anything like the Olympians before, and the sight of them terrified her.

A third bunk was against the opposite wall. Emily saw the saw the still form of Agent B lying there. His eyes were swollen shut and his face appeared even more bruised than she'd seen from Urania's pool. She could hear his steady breathing. He was alive.

"What happened to us?" Emily asked.

"I am uncertain," Cupid said. "I myself awakened a short time ago, as the agents delivered me here. I fear they may have done something to us while we were unconscious." He lifted her arm to show a bandage.

Emily pulled it away and saw a tiny pinprick of blood. "They've taken our blood."

Cupid nodded. "At the very least."

"There's no tellin' what these dirty dogs have done to any of us." Earl walked over. "Howdy, miss. My name is Earl. I don't think we've had the pleasure."

"I—I am Psyche," Emily said. It was difficult not to greet her friend with a hug.

"This here's my son, Frank," Earl said as he invited Frankie over.

"Hello, Frank." Emily was stunned by how grown-up he was. It hadn't been that long since she'd seen him, but now he looked to be sixteen or seventeen. He still had the bright, curious eyes and red hair, but he was now heavily built. This was further proof of the time difference between Olympus and Earth.

"How long have you been here?" Emily asked.

Frankie shrugged. "I don't know. It's kinda hard to tell the days here."

Earl patted Pegasus on the neck. "Boy was I surprised to see you when they brought you in here. I thought for sure Emily would be with you."

Cupid nodded. "Sadly, Emily was killed in Hawaii. We have suffered a great loss."

"I heard about the disaster in Hawaii," Frankie said. "But the TV news said it was the Diamond Head volcano that started to erupt."

"It was actually a fight between the Olympians and the Titans that caused the eruption of the volcano."

"Titans!" Earl cried. "I thought all of them were locked up in prison."

"They were, but they escaped and came after Olympus. The fight ended up here. It was terrible," Cupid explained. "Emily gave her life saving us. She used all her powers to send us home but then died in Diamond Head."

It felt very strange to hear Cupid talk about her like she was dead. Emily remained silent as he gave the details of her "death" to their friends.

"I'm so sorry, big fella," Earl said to Pegasus. "You two were as close as peas in a pod. We all loved Emily dearly." As he said that, Earl looked at her again with a strange expression on his face. "At least these CRU monsters can't never hurt her again."

"That is true," Cupid said.

"Are Joel and Paelen with you?" Frankie asked. "Have they taken them, too?"

Cupid shook his head. "No. Things have not been the same since Emily died. They do not even know we are here."

"Why did you come? That was a really stupid thing to do," Frankie said.

Cupid sighed. "I know, but it was Emily's fault. She changed me and made me care." He looked at her and smiled. "Psyche and I were out walking when Pegasus found us and told us you were in danger. After everything we have been through together, we could not let you remain a prisoner of the CRU. But unfortunately, without Emily, we have failed in our endeavor to free you."

Emily rose and patted Pegasus softly on the neck. She crossed the cell and knelt before Stella. "Hello, my name is Psyche. Who are you?"

"I am Stella."

"Are you all right?"

Stella looked up at her, and Emily could tell she'd been crying. "I'm frightened. I don't understand why I am here or what you are."

Emily ached to take Stella in her arms and hold her. Like Frankie, she too was older. She had a lovely face and a flash of long dark hair. But sitting there, she seemed so vulnerable.

"Is that a Greek accent I hear?"

When Stella nodded, Emily patted her hands. "Surely, then, you recognize the Great Pegasus of Olympus, and that is Cupid." Emily looked back at Cupid. "Would you open your wings to show Stella?"

Cupid did as Emily asked and extended his wings. Stella gasped at the sight. "This is impossible. Those are just myths. That can't be Eros. He is not real."

Emily remembered that Stella knew the Olympians only by their Greek names. "Yes, it is, believe me."

"I am very real," Cupid said.

Stella's eyes opened wider. "Then you are Psyche, the real Psyche? Wife of Eros?"

That tidbit of information was something that Cupid had failed to tell her. She didn't know that he was married, let alone to Psyche. She looked sharply back at him and he shrugged.

"Yes, Stella, Cupid is my husband," Emily said tightly.

"Will Zeus come to rescue us?"

Emily shook her head. "I hope not. He and his brothers have ferocious tempers and have no love for these people. If they find out what they have done to us, they may lose their tempers and Earth will suffer greatly. The best thing that could happen would be for them to release us immediately."

"I doubt that's gonna happen," Earl said. "Don't know exactly how long it's been that we've been here, but it's been long enough. I don't even know where here is."

"You are in Londinium," Cupid said.

"Where?" Earl said.

"London," Emily corrected. "London, England."

Stella gasped. "London? How? Why? Who are these people that murdered my parents and brought me here? I ask, but they never tell me."

"What?" Emily cried. "They killed your parents?"

Stella lowered her head. "We were on a dig in Crete. My parents are, I mean, were, archaeologists. The men came for me. My father tried to stop them, but they . . . they . . ." Stella stopped speaking and started to weep.

Emily sat on the bunk, stunned into silence. Stella had helped the Olympians win the first war against the Titans, and this was the price she paid for her help. Finally Emily put her arm around the Greek girl. "I am so very, very sorry. I promise you, Stella, we'll get you out of here, and I'll take you to Olympus, where Zeus himself can thank you."

"For what?" Stella wept.

"Yes, Psyche, what does Zeus have to thank Stella for?"

Emily hadn't heard the agents entering the cell block. She hadn't felt them either, which was further proof of her diminished powers.

Three CRU agents stopped before the cell while another four stood with weapons raised, farther down the corridor. Two of them had dark hair styled back, while the other—the one who had spoken—was blond, with curly hair that refused to be tamed. He had a strong English accent and a cold, calculating expression. He looked to be in his late thirties.

Pegasus whinnied and charged up to the bars.

"Tell your horse to calm down or we'll tranquilize him again."

"He is not a horse," Cupid snapped as he joined Pegasus. "This is the great stallion Pegasus, son of Neptune, and you will show him respect."

"He's a flying horse," the agent said dismissively. "I've seen plenty of them in my time and don't care that he's the original."

That comment struck fear in Emily. This English agent had seen other winged horses? Had he visited the Area 51 facility, or were there more clones around the world? Either way, it was all bad news.

Emily left Stella and walked to the bars. "If you know who we are, you might consider releasing us before the others get here."

"Let them come," the agent said. "We're ready for them. . . ." He leaned closer to the bars. "Especially Emily and Lorin."

Emily looked at Pegasus and Cupid in shock.

The agent smiled. "If you think for one minute we believe that ridiculous story that Emily died in Hawaii, you are sadly mistaken. Emily can't die because she isn't alive. She, and Lorin, we believe, are nothing more than sentient energy. It can't be killed, but it can be contained."

"You are a fool," Cupid spat. "Even if Emily were still alive, she would not come here."

The agent laughed without humor. "Of course she would. They'll both come because of him." He moved closer to the bars and pointed to Pegasus. "We know from Hawaii that Lorin wanted him as much as Emily. He's just the bait we need to get them here. They'll do anything to protect him, especially when they feel his pain."

Pegasus shrieked in rage and reared up. He kicked the bars with a sharp, golden hoof and dented the heavy steel. They actually bent outward after a second kick.

The four guards raised their weapons and prepared to fire, but the blond agent held up a restraining hand. "Not yet. Stand down." He focused on Pegasus. "Try that again and I'll let them shoot you. I know it won't kill you, but it will hurt."

He looked back at the four armed men. "Keep an eye on them—especially the Olympians. If they try anything at all, shoot one of the humans."

The three agents left the corridor, but the four armed guards remained, positioned outside the cell with their weapons at the ready.

Emily stood beside Pegasus, stroking his mane. Arious Minor was still in her ear, hidden like a hearing aid. His tiny, high-pitched voice said, "Emily, I believe they mean it. They will kill the humans if you try to escape."

"I know," Emily whispered. She made it look as though she were speaking to Pegasus. "Can you get inside their computer system again? Find out where we are and if there's a way out for all of us?"

"I will. Walk closer to the wall near Agent B. I don't want them to see me."

Emily gave Pegasus another pat and then walked over to the bunk containing Agent B. She knelt down beside him and brushed a lock of long curly black hair out of his eyes. She couldn't feel Arious Minor leave her ear, but she saw the flash of light as he darted down to the floor and through the wall.

"Don't worry, Agent B," she said softly. "We'll get you out of here."

"Do you know this man?" Earl asked quietly as he came to stand beside her.

"It's complicated. I know of him. He's a CRU agent."

"I kinda figured that by the way he was dressed. But he must have done something mighty awful to get these folks riled enough to do that to him. They've all but beat the stuffin' out of him." Earl knelt down and dropped his voice. "And if you wanna convince these folks that you're really an Olympian, you'd best start speakin' more formally like they do and stop calling your friend Pegs. You did that when you first woke up. If they heard you, they'd figure it out. There's only one gal in the universe who calls him that, and we all know it."

Emily's eyes went wide as she looked at him.

Earl winked. "Good to see you again too." He stood up, walked to the bars, and called to the guards, "So when's lunch? I'm starvin'."

The guards weren't impressed. They stiffened and motioned with the guns. One ordered, "Sit down."

"You ain't the friendliest bunch of people I ever met," Earl said as he left the bars and walked back to Pegasus. "How you doin', old friend?"

Pegasus nickered and pressed closer to Earl.

Still kneeling before Agent B, Emily looked around. There were cameras suspended outside their cell pointing in. There was one door and thick steel bars. From the sound of it, they were the only prisoners on the floor.

She had more than enough power to open the cell door but forced herself to wait. She needed to know what Arious Minor would find. They were a large group with two incapacitated members. They had to know exactly where they were going before they attempted any kind of escape.

Emily walked back to Pegasus. The stallion was quivering and pawing the ground. A nerve twitched in his shoulder. It was obvious he was still feeling the same dark presence they'd all felt in the elevator area. Only now that they were farther underground, whatever it was, Emily knew it was that much closer.

"I feel it too and it is not good." Emily looked over at Cupid and could tell by the expression on his face that he was aware of it also.

"It is evil, is it not?" Emily said formally to him, trying to speak like Diana.

"It is," Cupid agreed. "A great evil, pulsating and alive." He paused, and his face became haunted. "I do not believe it is part of this world."

"What are you talking about?" Frankie said. "What's evil?"

"There is an evil presence in this facility," Emily said. "We can feel it, but it is not from this world. The CRU have been capturing aliens and anything out of the ordinary for a very long time. I fear they may have captured something particularly bad and it is being held here. What I feel is powerful and very dangerous."

"Or they created it," Cupid suggested. "Remember the clones."

"What you'll feel, Psyche, is a bullet," one of the guards said. "Unless you shut your mouth and sit down."

She studied the guard's face closely. Despite his bravado, their words were getting to him. He and the other guards had to know what their commanders were doing and what they might have created. But Emily didn't push it. With their fingers on the triggers, one mistake could be a disaster. Instead, she sat back down beside Stella.

As the hours ticked past, the guards changed and food was delivered to the cell. Emily was surprised to see that among the Earth food, the CRU had also returned the large bags of ambrosia cakes, nectar, and her Xan food hat.

This was another clue that something was very different about this capture. First, why were they all kept together? For safety reasons, they should have been separated and locked on different levels. Now they return their ambrosia? Food they knew would keep the Olympians strong. What was going on?

Emily reached into the bag and pulled out several cakes. She didn't need to give any to Earl or Frankie, as they had already consumed plenty of it when they'd visited Olympus after the Area 51 incident. Whether the CRU knew it or not, they were now as immortal as the Olympians.

She carried a cake over to Stella and whispered, "This is ambrosia. You know the myths and you know what will happen if you eat it. We are in danger here. This will help protect you."

Stella shook her head. "They have taken everything from me—my home and my family. Why would I want to survive or live forever?"

Those words cut Emily deeply. She could feel the

pain and despair from her friend. She reached for her hand. "Stella, I wish I could explain this to you right now, but I cannot. I beg you to trust me. You have a special place in Olympus, with many powerful Olympians who care a great deal for you."

"How can this be? I have never been to Olympus. Until today, I didn't believe it existed."

"I will explain everything to you when we are free," Emily said. "But for now, please eat the ambrosia."

To illustrate that it was safe, Emily took a bite of the cake. She moved it around her mouth to see if the CRU had sabotaged or drugged it. But it tasted the same.

Stella reluctantly took a bite and frowned. "It's so sweet."

Emily nodded. "Nectar is even sweeter." She held the cup of nectar out to her and was relieved when Stella took a drink. Emily looked over to Agent B. Somehow they had to get ambrosia and nectar into him.

"Keep eating," Emily said softly. She rose and carried a piece of ambrosia and the cup of nectar over to the sleeping agent.

She gently lifted his head and pressed the cup to

his mouth. A tiny amount of precious nectar touched his lips, and immediately Agent B's tongue licked the sweet syrup.

"Yes," Emily coached. "Try some more. . . ."

Little by little Agent B responded and drank the nectar. With the Olympian drink in him and Emily touching his head, her power set to work and his wounds started to heal. Seeing this, Emily pulled her hand away. She couldn't let the CRU see that she could heal him. They knew that healing was one of Emily's powers.

But their brief touch had been enough. Agent B's eyes fluttered open. They were sore and bloodshot but the same blazing blue that she knew so well. His eyes landed on Pegasus, standing above him.

"What the . . . ?" Agent B forced himself up into a sitting position. "What's going on here? Who are you?" His lips were cracked and swollen, and blood had dried in a corner. His black suit jacket was torn and tattered, and there were bloodstains on his shirt. The CRU had been vicious with him.

"I am Psyche," Emily said calmly. "This is Pegasus, and that is Cupid."

Agent B moved back farther on the narrow bunk. "What . . . what have you just given me?"

"It is all right," Emily said gently. It saddened her most that he didn't remember who she was or what they'd been through together. "This is nectar. It will help you heal."

"Nectar?" Agent B said. "That's an Olympian drink. It will change me."

"Yes, it will heal you. Please, eat this cake. It is ambrosia and will also help."

"No!" Agent B swatted her hand away. "It will make me immortal. I don't want that."

His words echoed what he'd said so long ago when a Shadow Titan had broken his arm in ancient Greece and her powers couldn't heal him until he ate the ambrosia. Back then, she'd threatened him into it.

"Benedict Richard Williams," Emily said softly but sternly. "You listen to me. You will eat this right now or I will force it into you. Believe me, I can."

Once again, his eyes shot around the cell. "How do you know my name? Who are you?"

"I told you, I am Psyche, and I know more about you than you know about yourself. The CRU have betrayed you. They have tortured you and locked you away, but you have done nothing and they will not tell you why. I know why. If you eat the ambrosia I will explain everything."

It stung to see the anger and distrust in his eyes. But if she had to, she would force him to eat it.

Agent B reluctantly accepted the cake and started to eat it. He spat crumbs at her. "I am doing this under protest."

"I know," Emily said. "Just like last time."

He was about to say something when one of the guards came closer to the cell. "Well, well, well, look who's awake."

Agent B's expression hardened. "L, you come in here and I'll show you who's awake and who remembers what you did to me."

"You're hardly in a position to threaten me, B."

"That is not a threat; it's a promise!" Agent B winced when he moved, pulling his wounded ribs. "I demand to speak with the commander. You can't just torture me and keep me in here with these monsters."

Every word he spoke reminded Emily of the old Agent B. The one before they'd journeyed into the past—the one she'd hated. It would take time to draw out the better man in him. But did they have that time to wait?

Emily rose and stepped back, then said to Pegasus, "Let's leave him alone for a while."

Cupid walked up to her and whispered, "This is your precious Agent B? He is a Gorgon to have spoken to you like that."

"He doesn't remember me or what we went through," Emily whispered back.

"If he does not remember soon, he will have me to deal with." Cupid looked out at the guards. "No one speaks to my wife like that!"

Emily cringed. She wasn't sure if Cupid had done that for her sake, or to tease her. With him, she could never be sure.

Time dragged on as Emily settled down to wait for Arious to return. They had to know what the CRU planned before they made their move. Until then, they could do nothing.

Two more mealtimes came and went before Emily saw the dot of light again. Arious came creeping along the wall at the floor line. She looked outside the cell and saw one of the guards also following the small ball of light. He nudged his partner and pointed.

When they walked closer to investigate, Arious Minor flashed a blinding light at the guards, knocking them off-balance. "Olympians, use your powers; we must get out of here right now!"

Pegasus whinnied and reared. His front hooves came crashing down on the cell door and smashed the lock and hinges. When the door flew open, the enraged stallion charged into the corridor and attacked the nearest guards.

One guard managed to fire his weapon at the rampaging stallion, but the bullet did nothing other than infuriate Pegasus further. Before the guard could shoot again, Cupid ran out of the cell and punched him into the wall. He then took on the other guard.

Earl and Frankie were next out of the cell. But Emily stayed behind with Stella. "I know you are paralyzed and cannot walk. Let me carry you to Pegasus."

Stella's eyes were wide as Emily lifted her up. "How did you know that?"

"It is a long story."

Pegasus dropped his wing to let Emily hoist Stella onto his back.

"Hold tight to his mane. He won't mind."

"What about him?" Earl said, pointing at Agent B as he gathered the weapons from the fallen guards.

Emily nodded. "I will get him. Just be ready with your weapons when more come for us."

"Hurry," Arious Minor said. "We must get out of here. You haven't fooled *them*. They know who you are—they can feel you."

"Who does?" Emily called as she ran back into the cell.

"The evil that lies below!"

Emily made it back to Agent B, but he shied from her touch. "Don't touch me. Just go!"

"Trust me, Agent B. You stand a better chance of surviving with me than you do if you stay. You're a CRU agent. Think. What will happen once they realize you're not needed anymore?"

"I haven't done anything!" he spat. "They know that."

Emily shook her head. "Yes, you have. You just

don't remember. We're the closest of friends. Somehow they've discovered this. That's why you're here. *You* were the bait to capture me."

"I don't know you," he insisted as he tried to rise. "Why do you care what happens to me?"

Emily reached forward, put her arm around his waist, and half carried him to the stallion. At her touch, he continued to heal, and his strength started to return. But the damage the CRU had done to him was extreme, and he couldn't walk yet.

"I'm Emily Jacobs and I care for you more than you'll ever know. You just don't remember because it happened a long time ago. Now shut up and get on Pegasus!"

"Emily Jacobs!" Agent B cried. "That's impossible. I've seen photos of Emily. You look nothing like her."

"Yeah, I hear that a lot these days," Emily said. She didn't give him time to question her further as she hoisted him up onto Pegasus's back. "Hold on to Stella, but be careful. She's paralyzed below the waist and has no leg control. You must help keep her stable."

Agent B slipped his arms around Stella's waist. "This is insane!"

"It's about to get much worse," Emily said. "Just hold on tight and, please, trust me like you used to."

"Come. It's this way!" Arious Minor called as the dot flashed down the hall. "The elevator is over here. I can override the control."

Earl and Frankie held their guard's weapons high as they ran down the corridor. Seconds ticked by like hours as they waited for the elevator to arrive. When the doors whooshed open, Emily raised her hands to defend against anyone who came out. But the elevator was strangely empty.

"Where are the guards?" she asked suspiciously

"I don't care," Earl said. "Let's just get the heck outta Dodge!"

They piled in and pressed the uppermost button to take them up into Charing Cross Station. It was only when the doors started to close that Agent B shouted, "Wait! Stop. Don't let the doors close. This is a trap!"

Emily's hand flashed out to stop the doors, but they kept closing. She had to snatch her hand back to keep from being caught. She tried her powers and commanded the doors to open, but they wouldn't.

"Cupid, grab the other side. Help me pry them open!"

Emily and Cupid each held one of the doors, but despite their Olympian strength, they would not open even a fraction.

"It feels like someone is holding them," Cupid panted.

Moments later the elevator hummed to life. Instead of taking them up toward the exit, it started to descend.

"We're going down," Cupid cried.

Pegasus whinnied and pawed the floor.

Arious Minor vanished into the control panel. A moment later he reappeared. "I can't override it. Emily, try your powers again. We must not go down there."

Emily held up her hands and focused on changing the direction of the elevator. She could feel the powers flowing from her core, yet despite her best efforts, other powers, greater than hers, were drawing them down. "I can't stop it," she cried, "no matter what I do. There's something fighting against me."

"Keep trying," Arious Minor commanded.

Everyone looked up to the number panel high above the door and watched the numbers descend like a deadly countdown to the bottom floor, sub-level thirty. But when they expected the elevator to stop, it didn't.

Agent B looked around. "This isn't possible. This facility doesn't go down below thirty levels."

"Yes, it does," Arious Minor said. "And what is in the bottom pit is more horrible than anything I've ever seen before. Emily, try again. We must not go down to them."

"Flame, get us out of here. I can feel the evil," Cupid cried. "We are getting closer."

Emily felt it too. The deeper they descended, the worse the sense of malevolence became. She held out her hands again and put everything into stopping their descent. Sweat broke out on her brow, and her head was pounding from concentration. But still the elevator descended. "It's not working. I can't stop the elevator!"

"This is bad," Arious Minor said. "Very, very bad."

"What's down there?" Earl asked.

"Living evil," Arious Minor said.

Agent B held out his hand to Frankie. "Give me a weapon."

"You? No way," Earl said. "Emily may trust you, but I don't."

"Give me a bloody weapon!" Agent B spat. "Look what they've done to me. They'll kill me, too, if they get the chance."

Emily looked at Frankie. "He's right. Give him one of the guns. Whether he likes it or not, he's with us now."

Earl nodded to Frankie, who reluctantly handed over one of the weapons. "You try anything funny and you're a dead man."

"I'm already a dead man, thanks to you," Agent B said darkly.

The elevator started to slow and then stopped completely. The doors didn't open right away, and Arious Minor said, "Emily, prepare your laser flame. You're going to need it."

The moment the doors opened, Stella started to scream. Pegasus whinnied, and Cupid's mouth hung open in terror.

Emily charged forward and fired at the creatures

closest to her. Gunfire echoed behind her, and she felt more than saw Earl, Frankie, and Agent B shooting at the creatures.

"What are they?" Cupid cried as more of the terrifying creatures came at them. Some looked like large walking turtles; others looked almost like the Minotaur, while another type were black with wings and looked almost like armored ravens.

"Shadow Titans!" Emily shouted.

9

THE SHADOW TITANS SWARMED DOWN ON the group in numbers too high to count. The futile blasting of gunfire filled the air until all the bullets were expended, but not one Shadow Titan had fallen as a result. After guns, the others used hand-to-hand combat, but they didn't stand a chance.

As had happened long ago, only Emily's flames could destroy the hollow, leatherlike warriors. But no sooner would she blast one into oblivion than more would descend. Despite her best efforts, Earl was captured by the creatures, followed by Frankie, and finally, Cupid. Pegasus was subdued, but Stella and Agent B were allowed to remain on his back.

What was different from the past was the Shadow

Titans did not kill her friends. Instead, they held them captive, binding their arms but doing no harm.

"Emily, you cannot win against us," a bodiless male voice boomed. *"Surrender now or we will kill the others. . . ."*

"Don't do it!" Earl cried.

"We mean it, Emily. Surrender now, or your friends will die."

Emily had no choice. She knew the horrors of the Shadow Titans. The others didn't. She held up her hands. "All right. You win. I won't fight you."

"Flame, no!" Cupid shouted. "Leave us. Get out of here!"

The moment her hands went up, two large Shadow Titans grabbed her. Their grip was firm but not painful.

"Bring them in," the voice said. *"We have waited long enough."*

"Yes, yes, bring them to us . . . ," another voice called.

The presence of evil was smothering like a blanket on a hot summer night. Emily and her friends were completely surrounded by Shadow Titans as they were led forward. They moved down a long corridor. At the end, they descended a ramp into an area that opened up into a massive room much larger than the train station high above them.

Many cages lined the walls of the room, and Emily was horrified to see that the occupants of some of the cages were beings she'd never imagined possible.

"Those ain't Olympians, are they?" Earl asked softly as the passed before the pitiful-looking gray-skinned creatures.

Cupid shook his head. "No. I have never seen their likes before."

"I think they're aliens," Frankie offered. "Look at their big black eyes. They're just like in the reported sightings."

Other occupants of the cages were all too familiar to Emily—winged horses, Dianas, Cupids, and Paelens reached out to her. Just like at Area 51, they seemed to know that she was important and that they needed her.

Pegasus reacted to the clones and whinnied loudly. At his call, the two winged horses also responded and kicked the doors of their stalls. Pegasus started to quiver, and his tail flashed out.

Several more Shadow Titans moved closer to the

stallion and caught hold of his mane to keep him down on the ground.

"Don't fight them, Pegs," Emily warned. "They are too dangerous for you."

"Ah, so you remember our Shadow Titans," the voice called.

"I'll never forget them," Emily said. "How can this be? We destroyed them thousands of years ago. And the clones? We rescued all of them from Area 51."

"You didn't destroy all the Shadow Titans. Some remained on Earth. As for the clones, these are not the Area 51 clones," the voice said. *"You cost us dearly there, Emily. But luckily, we were doing the same thing here."*

"Why?"

"Come forward and see for yourself."

"Yes," a female voice offered. *"Come and see what you have created."*

There was something in the way she said it that sent a chill down Emily's spine. They moved past the room with the captives and into another corridor. At the end they saw two tall, sealed steel doors.

"Come forward, Flame of Olympus. Come to us. . . ."

The Shadow Titans led them onward. At their

approach, the doors slowly opened. The room ahead was dimly lit, and it took a moment for the humans' eyes to adjust. But for Emily, Pegasus, and Cupid, their eyes saw the horror that lay before them immediately.

Pegasus whinnied, Cupid cried out, and Emily's hands ripped free of the Shadow Titans and rose to her mouth as she tried to stifle her scream.

This was followed by Earl's, Frankie's, and Stella's outbursts of complete terror. Even Agent B cried out at the creatures that lay before them.

"Closer," the heaving masses commanded as one.

There were three of them. They were either lying side by side or they were connected. Emily couldn't tell. Her mind was incapable of grasping the horror of their existence. They were like giant jellyfish, the kind that sometimes washed up on shore, or clear balloons filled with a thick, slimy liquid.

Grotesque faces lay in the center of each of their undulating masses. They each had large, unblinking, bulbous gray eyes, nostrils with no nose, and thin lips on tiny mouths. Each creature stood almost twenty feet high and the same in width.

If they were even alive, they were living pools of gelatinous goo.

"My God," Earl cried. "It's 'The Blob!'"

Words could not come to Emily's mouth as she beheld the horrors before her.

"What's the matter, Emily?" the female voice said out of the tiny, moving mouth of the middle creature. *"Don't you like what you see? You created us, Mother. Behold, we, your special children!"*

Only one other time in her life had Emily felt such blood-chilling terror. Back when she first met the Gorgons. The two sisters of Medusa had caused a similar reaction in her. But now she realized these three monsters were infinitely worse.

"Cat got your tongue, Emily?" the third new voice teased. It was lighter than the others, but certainly male. *"And yes, Emily, we did know it was you from the very start. Your change of body could not fool us like it did our gullible agents."*

"What do you mean *your* agents?" Agent B demanded.

"Ah, yes, the wonderful Agent B," the female voice said. *"Hero of the Titan War. You, Stella, and Pegasus*

are almost as responsible for our existence as Emily is."

"What are you talking about?" Agent B spat.

"Why, sister, he doesn't remember us," the first voice said. *"Perhaps we should remind them of their crimes."*

The grotesque creatures pulsated, and colors flashed through their clear, liquid bodies like lightning.

Emily felt their powerful minds enter her brain. She started to scream as they accessed the memories of the other time line. Further and further back, leading all the way to the Titan War and their place in it. Once they had her memories, the monsters shared them with everyone in the room.

Emily also saw the war from other perspectives. She learned that while she, Pegasus, Joel, and Agent B had fought in one part of the battle, Stella and elderly Paelen had worked with Vulcan at the mobile forge in another. She saw things she'd never known had happened. How much Stella had cared for Paelen and Brue, and suffered when she'd witnessed their fiery deaths. Nothing was held back.

Beside her, Pegasus's head flew back, and he whinnied as his mind filled with visions of the past—including seeing his own death as a frail old stallion. His anguished, pain-filled cries mixed with the others as they all received the memories. When the pain finally stopped, Emily collapsed to her knees.

Pegasus was breathing heavily and nickered softly. He pawed the ground and shook his head. When his eyes found hers, they were filled with compassion.

"You saw all that?" Emily asked.

When Pegasus nodded, Emily looked over to Cupid. "Did you see it too?"

He was panting and rubbing his temples. "I never realized it was so bad. . . ."

Stella had passed out from the sudden dump of information. Agent B caught hold of her before she fell off of Pegasus. He laid her gently forward on the stallion's neck. Like everyone else, his breathing was heavy and his brows furrowed with pain. Agent B looked at Emily with absolute recognition in his face. "I remember it all now," he said softly. "I remember you. You came back for me."

"I promised I would."

"How sentimental," the female voice said. *"Feel the love. . . ."* But then her voice became hard. *"But it won't*

last. We have waited millennia for this moment, Emily. The time has come for you to pay for your crimes against us."

"What crimes? Who are you?" Emily demanded.

"*Don't you recognize us?*" the first male voice said. "*You should. After all, you created us.*"

"Stop saying that!" Emily cried. "I didn't do anything."

"*Of course you did,*" the female accused. "*Cast your mind back. Saturn had you trapped in his energy void, but somehow you escaped. You and your dog made it to the cell block to free Joel and Prometheus. When we came in to stop you, you used the powers of the Xan against us. . . .*"

Emily remembered the fight on Tartarus. She'd wounded Saturn, his brothers, and several of his top leadership. But her powers had also vaporized three others. She instantly remembered Riza's sad voice saying, "Oh, Emily, what have you done . . . ?"

"*I believe she's starting to recognize us now,*" the female said. "*Yes, Emily, we are the three Titans you vaporized but couldn't destroy.*"

The thoughts were too terrible to consider. "It's not possible," Emily said.

"*After that blast, we were all but destroyed, but still*

conscious. We witnessed everything—Stella creating the flame-swords that defeated the Shadow Titans and the end of the battle, with Agent B's valiant sacrifice. We saw you destroying Saturn's weapon and changing the time line. We witnessed it all, alive but not living."

Emily was shaking her head at the horror of it all. Back on Xanadu, Riza's father had spoken to her of the damage she had done that hadn't been realized yet. Was this it?

"Yes, Emily, Riza's father meant us. He knew what you did on Tartarus and what you created with the power of his people," the female said, reading her thoughts. *"Now do you understand?"*

"B—but how did you survive?"

"How?" the first voice said. *"By sheer willpower. You left us wounded and bodiless. After the war we combined what was left of our powers and fled to Earth. We buried ourselves deep under the ground of this small, cool island, where our wounds could heal. But no matter what we tried, we could not restore our bodies. Instead, we fed on anything we could catch."*

Emily didn't want to hear any more. It was all too terrible.

"But you will listen to us," the first voice said. *"We fed and we grew. But humans weren't enough to restore us. So as humanity developed technology, we controlled some weak-willed men and created the agency that you now know as the Central Research Unit."*

The female took over speaking. *"Our agency has been hunting extraterrestrials and anything with power for a very, very long time. Each and every life form we absorbed added to our power, but as you can see, it changed us."* She started to laugh with mirthless humor. *"Can you imagine their surprise if the agents of the CRU ever discovered that they had been serving the very things they have hunted and despised?"*

"That's not possible," Agent B said. "The CRU was set up to find aliens and study their technology to serve the world and keep the peace."

"You blind fool!" the female said. *"All those aliens and people of power did was feed us! And very soon, thanks to Emily, we shall soon rise from this pit and get back to Olympus. Imagine the power we'll amass when we have consumed genuine Olympians and not just their clones. Finally, we will move on to Titus and devour those who betrayed us."*

The third voice laughed. "*The great Saturn will kneel before us and beg for mercy as we absorb his people. Then, when those worlds are gone, we will make our way to Xanadu. Riza, the last Xan, will sustain us for a very, very long time.*"

Emily was sickened to realize that the clones and aliens in the cages they'd seen in the other room were nothing more than food to these terrible monsters. "You've completely lost your minds," she cried. "Whether you've been down here too long, or absorbed too many innocent species, you're all insane and filled with evil."

"*We are what you made us!*" the female said. "*And now, after all this time of watching and waiting for you to be born and meet Pegasus, after all the adventures you've had, it is time for you, Emily Jacobs, to feed us!*"

The third voice cackled. "*The power of the Xan within you will finally free us from this pit. You, Emily, will grant us the power to devour your beloved Olympus!*"

"Emily, kill them!" Cupid cried, struggling against the Shadow Titans. "Use your powers and destroy them!"

"*Yes, Emily,*" the male voice teased. "*Kill us before we absorb you.*"

Emily screamed as invisible hands wrapped around her and lifted her off the floor. She struggled in their grip as she was slowly dragged toward the hideous creatures. But no matter what she tried, she couldn't break free.

"Feed us, feed us, feed us . . . ," the three mutant Titans cried as one.

Emily summoned her powers, and flames shot out of her hands toward the gelatinous creatures, but the laser shot right through them and burned through the wall on the opposite side of the large chamber.

"Yes, yes," the female cried. *"Do that again. Summon all your powers against us. You will taste so much sweeter!"*

Pegasus shrieked and the others screamed as Emily was drawn closer to the nearest of the three.

"No!" she howled. But for all her remaining powers and strength, Emily could not break free of the invisible grip. Higher and higher she was lifted until she was suspended directly above one of the creatures. It opened its thin, quivering lips and mewed in anticipation.

"Feed us, feed us, feed us . . . ," the Titans chanted.

Emily screamed a final time as she was drawn into

the gaping, clear, toothless mouth and swallowed whole by the demented Titan. She took a final gulp of air as she passed through the mouth and then down the throat of the grotesque Titan. Invisible muscles pushed her steadily down toward its stomach. As she moved, she peered out through the clear mucus that composed the creature to the blurry images of those outside it. Pegasus was rearing and screaming as he watched her move.

She focused on tearing the body open or trying to draw herself back out of the monster. But it was as though she had no powers at all. The Titan somehow countered everything she tried. Even firing the flame back up did nothing. The laser flame shot through the liquid like a hand cutting through water. But with each blast, she felt the muscles contract as the creature laughed.

Down, down, down she descended. When she entered the creature's stomach, her skin started to burn in a way she'd never felt before. In Hawaii, the lava of the Diamond Head volcano never touched her. But now she felt like she was swimming in clear, burning lava. She held up her hand and saw the skin starting to peel and her clothes melt from the stomach acids. She quickly shut her eyes as the gel of the creature's stomach started to dissolve them.

The booming voice of the creature howled in delight. *"She is part Xan! I can taste her power—soon it will be ours!"*

"Emily," Arious Minor cried in her ear. "You are being digested! Hurry, you don't have much time left. Focus your thoughts and use the ring Riza gave you. Use it now before it's too late!"

Every inch of her body burned like she was on fire. She wanted to scream, but that meant opening her mouth to more pain. With her thoughts fragmenting, she struggled to raise a dissolving arm. She balled her hand in a fist, opened her eyes, and pointed the ring at the blurry image of Pegasus.

As her mind faded, she called one name. "Riza!"

PAELEN CARRIED LORIN AND FOLLOWED
beside Joel on Chrysaor while Vulcan used his impossible metal wings to speed toward the Solar Stream.
Moments later they entered the swirling vortex of
light and headed toward Earth.

The sounds around them made speech impossible. But when Lorin hugged his neck and kissed his
cheek, he knew speech wasn't necessary. He looked
at her and saw the triumph sparkling in her eyes.
She had played him. He knew it. But for reasons he
couldn't understand, he just couldn't say no to her.

As they traveled through the Solar Stream, he
couldn't shake the feeling that something was very,
very wrong. Perhaps it was because he was with Lorin

and not Emily. All he knew was that he dreaded what they would find when they arrived.

When they burst through the other end of the Solar Stream, they were in the bright blue Earth sky. Vulcan immediately took the lead. The way he was moving with those strange metal wings made Paelen certain that Vulcan didn't care if he and Joel were with him or not. He was desperate to get to the girl, Stella.

In all his life, Paelen had never seen Vulcan so concerned for one person—especially a human. But there was something about that other time line that had made everyone who'd been there so secretive and obsessed with it.

Emily rarely spoke of it, apart from mentioning Agent B. But when he pressed her for details, she wouldn't say anything other than he had been very brave and had given his life for the others.

They came down lower in the sky, passing through billowing clouds. Below them they saw an expanse of water.

"Any idea where we are?" Joel called to Vulcan.

Vulcan reached into his pouch and pulled out a

small device. "We are over the North Atlantic." He pointed to the left. "Londinium lies that way— follow me."

They changed direction and flew together for most of the day. As they neared their destination, the weather turned and the sky darkened with storm clouds. It was dusk when they reached the English shoreline.

Passing over land, they saw fields mostly empty of crops. But on more than one occasion, farmers saw them in the sky and pointed. Cars on roads stopped, and their passengers climbed out to stare at them.

"Vulcan," Joel called. "We should fly higher. We're being seen. It won't take long for the police or even the military to find us."

"Let them come," Vulcan boomed. "I will not be stopped."

Joel looked over to Paelen. "He's gone crazy."

"You can tell him that," Paelen said. "But I would not."

"I will tell him if you like," Lorin offered. "Vulcan, Joel says you are crazy," she called. "We should fly higher."

Vulcan shot a look at Lorin that would have withered Paelen. Instead she shrugged. "He is a fool not to listen to us." She looked at Paelen. "But do not fear. I will protect you if the soldiers come."

"Thank you, but I hope you will protect all of us."

"Would it please you if I did?"

"Immensely," Paelen said.

"Then I will."

As more time passed, Paelen found it increasingly disturbing that given the number of people who had obviously seen them, there were no military helicopters or any other vehicles chasing them. Even when they reached more populated areas and they were being seen by thousands, they kept moving without opposition.

He maneuvered closer to Joel. "Why has no one come for us? We have been seen. There must be many reports."

"I've been thinking the exact same thing," Joel called. "I have a bad feeling about this."

After a few more minutes they saw a large city looming ahead.

"There it is," Vulcan called as he pointed forward.

"Londinium! It has changed greatly since my last visit." He looked back at Paelen. "Command your sandals to take us to Charing Cross."

Lorin was gazing around with wide, excited eyes. "It is so interesting down there. Can we stop to look around for a while?"

"Maybe later," Paelen said. "Right now we must focus on finding Pegasus." He was careful not to mention Emily or the others. Lorin would help if Pegasus was in danger. He doubted she would lift a finger to save Emily.

He called down to his sandals, "Take us to Charing Cross Station."

Paelen took the lead as the sandals followed his command. Eventually they stopped and hovered high above the large train station. He called over to Joel and Vulcan, "We are here. We should land away from it and walk back."

"Do it," Vulcan called. "And be quick. If my Stella is down there, I want to see her."

Paelen directed his sandals to take them away from the station and to land on a quiet backstreet.

When they alit, he set Lorin down on her feet.

"Stay with us. I know you want to see the city, but for now we have a job to do."

Lorin nodded. "Just as long as we see it after Pegasus is safe. There is so much to see and I have such little time left."

Paelen frowned. "We have all our lives. I promise I will show you Earth after Pegasus is safely home."

She grinned at him. "Yes, we have all our lives. . . ."

The sun had set some time ago and it seemed London was even busier at night. They followed along the narrow street where they'd landed toward the Strand. Vulcan was storming through the crowds and shoving people aside without caring that everyone he encountered could see his large metal wings.

Lorin was just the opposite. She was stopping in front of every shop window and peering at the items inside, squealing with each new discovery.

"Lorin, come on," Paelen cried, trying to drag her along.

"But I want to see," she protested, pulling back.

"Fine," Paelen finally snapped. "Stay here and see all you want. But I am going to the station to save Pegasus and Emily!"

He pushed past her and stormed forward.

"Paelen, calm down!" Joel said as he jogged to catch up with him.

"What is wrong with them?" Paelen said. "Vulcan is rampaging through here like the Minotaur with a toothache, not caring who is around us or what they are seeing. And all Lorin wants to do is go window-shopping. They are both driving me mad!"

"I know," Joel agreed. "But look around. This isn't like New York. We're out in the open and no one seems to care about us. Look, they hardly even notice Chrysaor!"

The winged boar looked up at Joel and snorted in agreement.

There were some curious glances at Chrysaor, but not enough to draw a crowd.

"And that is another thing," Paelen said. "Where are the soldiers or CRU agents? Why are we being left alone? This is not right, especially as we are so close to a large CRU facility."

They gazed around at the masses of people on the busy street. Up ahead a couple of well-dressed men stopped Vulcan to ask where he'd bought his wings. When he answered that he'd made them, they gave him their card and asked him to get in touch, explaining that they had an art gallery and would be interested in seeing what else he had made.

"I don't know," Joel said, glancing around. "Something's not right. No one seems to be watching us, but I have the feeling that we *are* being watched."

Paelen also looked around. Joel was right. He too had the distinct feeling they were being watched. It was then that he noticed Lorin moving away from a shop window. There was a frightened expression on her face, and her wide eyes were darting around.

"Paelen . . ."

"What is it?"

She huddled closer to him. "I do not know. But something feels very wrong. I think we should all leave here, right now."

"Wrong? How?" Joel demanded.

Paelen knew Joel didn't like Lorin. But he respected her powers because they were just like Emily's. If she said she felt something, she did.

"I cannot explain it," Lorin said, frowning. "But it started when we arrived on this big street. With each step we take, it grows. I do not like this. I really think we should go before it is too late."

"No!" Vulcan spat. "I have come this far. I will not leave until I know everyone is safe."

"But there is evil all around us."

"I feel it too, but I am ready for it." Vulcan reached into his sack and pulled out a sword.

"Vulcan, no!" Joel cried. "Put that away. You can't draw a sword in the city. That's a surefire way to call the police. Look, when we're at the forge, I do everything you tell me to because you have way more experience than I do. But here on Earth, I'm more experienced with the modern world. I know what will happen. Please, put that thing away."

Vulcan grumbled, but he reluctantly stowed his weapon back in the bag. "I will bow to your experience, Joel. But I hope you are right."

"So do I," Joel muttered.

With the rain falling heavily and the crowds in London increasing, the short trip to Charing Cross seemed long. But finally they stopped across the street from the station.

"Well, there it is," Joel said.

Paelen shook his head. "I still cannot believe the CRU has a super-facility right here in the middle of this large, busy city. What were they thinking?"

Vulcan rubbed his chin. "From what I am feeling, whoever is in there has been here longer than this city has."

"All right," Paelen said. "So now that we are here, how do we get in?"

Lorin pointed. "We could walk in, just like all those people."

They followed a steady stream of people entering the busy train station. Large red buses stopped in front and more people disembarked and also walked into the station.

"It looks like it is rush hour," Joel offered. "Maybe we should wait for later."

Standing opposite the large station, the group wasn't aware that the crowds around them had changed. No longer was it a mix of working men and women trying to get home. Suddenly they were completely surrounded by people wearing black, with grim expressions on their faces.

"No, Joel," one of the men said as he came up

behind them. "How about we all go in right now. Just stay calm and no one gets hurt."

They turned and saw a man standing with his weapon drawn. The others behind him also had their guns pointed at them. It was only then that they realized they were completely surrounded by at least fifty agents.

"You know the drill, boys, and you know we're not afraid to shoot out here on the street. So nice and easy—just cross the street and go into the station."

"Who are you?" Vulcan demanded.

"I'm shocked that you don't recognize us by now. We're the CRU. Welcome to London."

EVERY PART OF EMILY'S BODY WAS BURNED as she was dragged through the Solar Stream. Her eyes felt like they were about to burst, so she kept them shut tightly. She prayed that the power of the ring was enough to take her and the others out of the clutches of the mutant Titans and away from the danger.

The length of the journey could not be measured, as Emily was in too much pain to pay attention. But for her, it seemed endless. Eventually she felt herself slowing and then crashing down and sliding across a cool metal surface.

"Emily!" Riza cried. The tall Xan ran to her side and knelt down. "Don't open your eyes or move. Rest for a moment and let me heal you."

Emily felt a cool, fine-boned hand lightly touching her forehead. The pain started to fade. "Just be calm. It will be over shortly."

Moments later, she heard the best sound in the world, Pegasus's soft nickers. Emily opened her eyes and saw his white muzzle at her face. Then her eyes landed on the beautiful Xan.

"Riza," Emily choked. She tasted foulness in her mouth and spit out some thick, slimy liquid that had come from the Titan's stomach.

"Just settle down for a bit," Agent B's soft English accent said. "Let Riza finish healing you."

"Agent B?" Emily lifted her head and saw the CRU agent kneeling on the opposite side of Riza. He was draping his torn jacket over her. He was left wearing only his white shirt, and Emily could see the blood and other evidence of the beatings he'd taken. Cupid stood behind him with concern showing on his face.

When she was healed, Riza offered Emily her hand and helped her stand up. The Xan touched Agent B's jacket and it vanished. Emily was now standing in the same lovely white flowing robes that the Xan wore.

"Not that I'm not thrilled to see you all," Riza continued. "But by the state of you, and the fact that Stella and Agent B are here, I'd say you found yourselves in some trouble." She put her hands on her hips. "And you didn't wait for me."

"It's a nightmare," Emily said. She looked around and saw Stella still seated on Pegasus, but there were two missing. "Where are Earl and Frankie?"

When no one spoke, she turned to Agent B. "What happened back there? Where are Earl and Frankie?"

"I'm not sure, but they were standing farther away from us. My guess is, when you used that ring, they weren't included."

"They didn't make it?" Emily cried. "We must go back! We can't leave them there with those monsters."

Riza shook her head. "I'm sorry, but we can't go anywhere right now. Look around you. See where we are. This is a world on the verge of complete destruction."

Emily looked past Pegasus. They were in what looked like a large control room with metal paneled walls and an immense window that seemed to encircle the whole room. It actually looked at lot like

Arious's control room on Xanadu except for the window that revealed a sky full of flashing colors of red, yellow, and gold.

She gasped when her eyes landed on several strange-looking people standing on the opposite side of the room. There were huddled together and staring curiously at them, whispering softly using clicks and burrs. They almost looked human, but their skin was silver and their long hair was lavender.

"Don't be alarmed. They're a very peaceful people," Riza said. "Unfortunately, they don't speak any Earth languages, but they are capable of learning them. It will just take time."

"Where are we?" Emily asked.

Riza grinned, showing her pearl-white teeth. "Welcome to Rhean—at least, that's the closest translation I can give you."

"Rhean?" Emily repeated. "I've never heard of it."

"Of course you haven't. It's on the other side of the universe."

"What?" Agent B cried. "That's impossible! I'm remembering a lot from the past—mind you, but I don't seem to remember either of you looking like that, or being separate. What I especially don't remember is this kind of space travel."

"Oh, how I have missed you, Agent B." Riza laughed. "You were always so resistant to change. First you didn't believe in time travel until we all went back to ancient Greece. Then you didn't believe you could make a difference in the war, when your actions saved us. Now you can't believe that Emily and I have been separated, or that Emily has changed. But we have. And believe me, we have crossed the universe."

"Riza, we must go back," Emily pressed. "We have discovered something really terrible. . . ."

They explained everything they'd been through to Riza, including the grotesque Titans living under Charing Cross Station and how they'd created the CRU to serve their evil plans.

"They've been eating the clones," Emily finished. "That's why the CRU created them. They weren't for an army to take over the world. They were growing them for food."

"But I do not understand why," Cupid said.

Riza's eyes were unreadable as she said, "My guess is to absorb their power. They told you they intend to devour Olympus and Titus. So it's logical to assume that each time they absorb someone with power, they absorb the power as well and it becomes theirs. We must also assume that in creating the clones, they were hoping that Olympian powers would be replicated. But only their physical strength was. They will need more power if they are to break free of their pit and enter the Solar Stream."

"Their ultimate goal is to absorb you," Emily said. "They want the power of the Xan."

Riza's face was filled with peace. Her elliptical eyes were calm and her iridescent, pearly skin smooth and unwrinkled. It gave nothing away. But Emily knew that Riza was part of her. Even if she didn't show her full emotions, they were there and she was very angry.

"Well, they can't have me," she finally said.

Cupid came forward. "Please, you must send us to Olympus. There is no avoiding it now. Jupiter must be told about those Titans. Even if it means the destruction of Earth, they must be stopped before they escape."

Riza shook her lovely head. "You know I care for

Earl and Frankie and all the Olympians very deeply, but I can't leave here yet. It is taking all my powers just to create a shield to hold back the destructive rays of the sun as it turns supernova. Should I leave, or even divert a bit of power to send you back to Olympus, millions of lives would be lost."

"But they'll kill Frankie and Earl," Emily said.

"I don't think so," Riza said. "From what you tell me, they need to absorb beings of power. Humans don't have that kind of power. They are more valuable alive, knowing that you care and will come back for them."

Agent B shook his head. "This all seems so impossible, ancient Titans living under Charing Cross. We've crossed the universe and I'm surrounded by aliens."

"These are the Rheans, and technically speaking, *we* are the aliens here," Riza corrected. "This is their home. Or at least it was." She pointed out the window. "Look out there and you can see their dying sun. Most of the planets in this system have already been destroyed. The survivors have moved here, to the outermost planet." She looked at Emily. "It's kind of like everyone leaving Earth and going to your system's outer, dwarf planet, Pluto, to escape your sun. When we are ready, I will bring all the survivors back to Xanadu."

She looked at Agent B. "This is what my people did for many, many millennia. We rescued the survivors of dying worlds and gave them sanctuary on Xanadu."

"That is astounding," Agent B said. He looked over at the silver-skinned people and nodded.

They nodded back.

"But what about Olympus?" Cupid asked. "Once those Titans escape their pit, they will devour it. They already have a lot of power. More than Emily has. She could not stop or even harm them."

Riza frowned, and it creased her perfect face. She turned to Emily. "Even the Flame?"

"It passed right through them," Emily said. "Nothing I tried worked. I'm sure it won't take much more power for them to get out of there."

Arious Minor appeared out of Emily's ear. "But it doesn't mean that they will reach Olympus."

"Arious!" Riza said. "What are you doing here?"

The dot of light buzzed in front of Riza. "Well, since you couldn't go, I had to. I couldn't let them face the CRU alone. But what we encountered is more horrendous than anything we've ever seen before. I've been inside their computer's mainframe. The human CRU agents have no idea they have been serving monsters. I fear should the Titans escape, they will spread their poisonous evil throughout the universe."

Riza walked to the window and peered out into the swirling colors of the approaching supernova. "I can't abandon this world. Without me, everyone will perish—the people, wildlife, flora—everything will be lost." She paused. "But there is another way."

"What?" Emily cried. "Tell us."

Riza came up to Emily and grasped her hands. "Those mutant Titans are still trapped in their pit under Charing Cross. They need the power of the Xan to escape it and enter the Solar Stream. But with you and me here, they won't have access to that kind of power."

Pegasus nickered and snorted.

"What am I suggesting," Riza said to him, "is that you all stay here and help me." Her eyes landed on

Emily. "Especially you. If we combine our powers, we may accelerate the rescue of these survivors. The moment we get them to Xanadu, we can then deal with those evil Titans once and for all."

Emily looked back at the silver-skinned people. The danger the Titans posed was immense. But the danger these people faced was more imminent. "You're right," she said. "Tell me, what can I do?"

"YOU!" VULCAN CHARGED AT THE AGENT. The weapon the agent carried discharged, but the bullet only lightly grazed Vulcan's skin. It was enough to enrage him further. Vulcan reached for the lapels on the agent's coat and easily hoisted him over his head. "Where is my Stella? Bring her to me!"

The agent shook his head while another agent charged forward and pointed his weapon at Joel. "Drop him right now or we'll shoot Joel. I'm sure he's still human enough to be hurt."

Chrysaor squealed and charged two of the agents threatening Joel. The angry boar knocked them over, and his sharp tusks cut into their legs. He turned to charge at the others.

"Stop him," an agent cried, "or I swear we'll open fire!"

Joel knelt down to Chrysaor and placed his hands on the boar's head. "It's all right. Please stop. They'll hurt you. They'll hurt all of us."

Chrysaor calmed slightly and squealed softly at Joel.

Joel looked up at the agent. "He's very protective. If you threaten me again, there's no telling what he'll do."

"Then you'd better keep him under control, or we will."

Vulcan dropped the agent onto the wet ground. "I am warning you, humans, if any of you dare touch the boy, you will have me to deal with!"

The agent who'd been dropped rose shakily to his feet. He rubbed his neck and slowly recovered his breath. "That was a mistake, old man. Who do you think you are?"

"I am Vulcan. Joel and Stella are both my apprentices and under my protection. Now you will bring Stella to me or you will face my wrath."

"If you want Stella, you will come with us."

Vulcan looked at the others and nodded. "Agreed."

"Fine, we'll take you to her. But be warned, if you try any of those Olympian tricks, we won't hesitate to start shooting."

"And that," Vulcan said darkly, "would be your first and last mistake."

Several agents ran into the road and stopped traffic as the large procession crossed the Strand and made their way toward the busy entrance to Charing Cross Station. They walked through the entrance alcove and into the spacious terminal. Despite the numerous CRU agents, the station was packed with travelers.

Information boards before them announced the arrival and departure of trains, and other signs directed travelers to the London Underground. High overhead there was a glass ceiling in a Victorian framework.

Paelen and Joel looked at each other but said nothing. This was unlike any other time they'd been captured by the CRU. Nothing about it felt right.

"This way," one of the agents called.

The other agents were holding the public back

as they streamed through the busy station. Directly ahead they saw a sign indicating that the restrooms were on the next level down. When they started to descend the stairs, Paelen looked back at the agents. "Thank you, but I do not need to go."

He received a shove in the back in response. That upset Lorin, who summoned a flame in her hand. "Never touch my Paelen again, do you understand!"

Paelen caught hold of her arm. "Not yet," he said while eyeing the agent. "Let us wait a bit, and then you can set them all on fire."

That comment raised a spark of fear in the young agent's eyes.

"This is Lorin of Titus," Paelen explained. "You might have heard of her from the disaster in Hawaii. You know that incident at the volcano when it erupted? Or perhaps you heard of the events at the zoo when she took on Pele, goddess of the island. Do you really wish to make her angry now?"

"Shut your mouth, Paelen," the senior-looking agent said. "We've been briefed on all of you. I know about the trouble you like to cause. Your threats mean nothing to us."

"Who said they were threats?" Paelen finished.

When they reached the bottom of the stairs, the agents pushed them forward. To the right they saw the signs for the men's and ladies' restrooms, but past those was a plain-looking gray door at the end of the hall.

The first agents punched a code into the keypad and the lock clicked. They pushed through the door.

"This way," they ordered.

Paelen took hold of Lorin's hand as they passed through the doorway into another corridor. Joel and Chrysaor were close behind, followed by a grumbling Vulcan. They were led to an extra-large elevator.

"What do you need it so big for?" Joel said. "Elephants?"

The agents around them said nothing as they waited for the elevator. When it arrived, the doors opened and Vulcan peered inside.

"What is this?"

"Don't ask questions. Just get in the lift," he was ordered.

Vulcan peered in again. "What lift? I see nothing to lift any of us."

Joel said, "He means for us to get inside. This is an elevator. It's like a giant box on cables. It transports people to other levels so they don't have to use the stairs."

"What is wrong with stairs?"

"Just get in!" one of the agents said as he shoved Vulcan brutally against his metal wings.

Vulcan turned on him. "You touch me again like that, boy, and I'll have your head."

The agent backed off, but his face remained hard. Then the senior agent came forward. "If you really want to see Stella and the others again, you'll get inside—now!"

"It's all right, Vulcan," Joel said. "I've used elevators many times before. They're normal."

"Nothing about this ridiculous world is normal," Vulcan grumbled as he followed Joel into the elevator. "The sooner we get back to Olympus, the better."

Ten agents piled into the elevator with them. The senior agent leaned forward and pressed the sublevel twelve button.

Vulcan jumped as the elevator doors closed and they started to move.

"I do not like it here," Lorin whined as she squeezed Paelen's hand. "There is a bad feeling and it is getting worse."

Paelen felt it too. As they descended, the feeling intensified.

Everyone on the elevator watched the numbers flash above the doors, increasing in negative value as the elevator descended down into the lower levels beneath the station. The lead agent frowned when they reached twelve and didn't stop. He pressed the button again, but they still kept descending.

He quickly pressed fifteen, but the elevator kept moving. The same thing happened when he pressed twenty. The agent held up his weapon. "Okay, whoever is doing that, you will stop it right now."

"Doing what?" Paelen said.

"Taking us down."

"It is not I," Paelen insisted. He looked at Lorin and saw the fear sparkling in her eyes. "Are you doing it?"

"No," she whimpered. "They are."

"Who?" the agent demanded.

"Those that live below—the evil ones."

"Don't be ridiculous. There's nothing down this deep but holding cells, and they're all empty."

"No, they are not," Vulcan said. "Lorin is correct. There is something very sinister down here."

"Stop it!" cried another agent. "You're just trying to spook us."

"Look at Lorin," Vulcan commanded. "Does she look like she is trying to spook you? She has more power than all of us and senses more. She is terrified."

"They know I am here," Lorin whimpered, clinging to Paelen. "I do not want to see them!"

"See who?" the senior agent demanded. His face was reflecting the same fear as all the agents in the elevator.

"Lorin, use your powers," Joel cried. "Stop this elevator. Take us back up."

"I have tried. It does not work!" Lorin cried desperately. She physically touched the steel wall and closed her eyes. The whole elevator trembled, and the cables groaned in protest as she poured more power into stopping them, but they continued down. "They are stronger than me. I cannot stop it."

The numbers were just reaching thirty. "We're at

the bottom," the agent said. But before he finished, the elevator kept descending. "Wait. This is impossible. The facility doesn't go down below thirty."

"Yes, it does," Paelen said as his heart started to pound. "And there is something very evil at the bottom of it."

Vulcan opened his bag and pulled out one of the swords. The agents around them raised their weapons to his head.

"Put those things down, fools. This is not for you. It is for those at the bottom. And if you are very smart, you will be ready to fight when we stop."

The agents looked to their superior.

"He's right. Something isn't right here. Get ready."

Vulcan removed another sword from the bag and handed it to Joel. He gave another to Paelen.

"What about me?" Lorin whimpered.

"You have your Flame," Joel said. "Be prepared to use it."

With no numbers to guide them, they had no idea how deep they were going. Eventually the elevator slowed and then stopped. The doors remained closed for a good full minute before opening.

Vulcan was first to react when they finally swished open. He gasped. "Shadow Titans!"

Paelen's voice croaked when he saw the monsters waiting for them outside the elevator.

Vulcan roared and charged forward, swinging his sword at the nearest creatures. His blade cut through the leather and chopped pieces off the Shadow Titans. But even with missing limbs, the hollow creatures kept coming.

"Paelen, Joel, go for their heads!" Vulcan commanded.

Paelen quickly joined the fight and so did Joel, slashing away at the Shadow Titans with their swords. But it seemed there was a limitless supply of the creatures coming after them.

"Lorin," Vulcan shouted. "Use your Flame. You have the power to destroy them!"

Lorin stood back in the elevator, her eyes wide with fear as the others fought. The agents used their guns but soon discovered they were useless against the attacking swarm.

"Lorin, burn them!" Paelen cried.

Snapped out of her terror, Lorin raised her hands

and started to fire blasts of flames at the monsters. With one shot, she could destroy more than the others put together.

Emboldened by her success, Lorin came out of the elevator and fired at the Shadow Titans going after Paelen.

But for all their success, they were being swamped. The agents were the first to be subdued, followed by Joel and then Paelen. It took many Shadow Titans to knock Vulcan over and get him down to the ground and even more to keep him down.

Lorin tried to blast the creatures away from Paelen, but her aim was off and she hit him in the chest. He howled in pain and collapsed to the floor, clutching his burned chest.

"Paelen!" Lorin shrieked. She stopped firing and tried to run to him, but the leather creatures quickly captured her.

"Lorin, keep fighting!" Joel shouted as he struggled against the creatures holding him.

"No!" a strange female voice sounded. *"If Lorin continues to fight, we will have our Shadow Titans finish Paelen off."*

"No!" Lorin cried. "You will not harm him."

"Then you will stop fighting us," the female voice ordered.

"Bring them to us," a high, male voice said.

The Shadow Titans pulled Paelen to his feet. The wind had been knocked out of him and he hadn't felt pain like that in a very long time. Looking down, he found his shirt was burned away and the skin of his chest was black and blistered.

"Paelen, I am so sorry," Lorin wept.

He looked back at her and saw the tears and horror shining in her eyes. "It is all right," he said softly to her.

Lorin shook her head slowly. "No, it is not. It will never be all right again."

They were led through a long corridor and down a steep ramp at the end. The area opened up into a large room filled with cages. Many of them contained the same type of clones they had encountered at Area 51, but other cages held stranger beings. At the very end, they saw one cage containing two people they knew very well.

"Joel, Paelen!" Earl called. "You shouldn't have come here."

Two Shadow Titans crossed to the cage and opened it up. Earl helped draw Frankie out and over to them.

They immediately noticed that something was very wrong with Frankie. His eyes were haunted and his face was gray. He didn't react to seeing them, and Earl had to keep his arm around him to get him to move.

"Is he all right?" Joel asked.

Earl shook his head. "He's in shock. He ain't spoken a word since them monsters in there ate Emily."

"What?" Joel cried. "What happened to Emily?"

"It was awful. There're these big Titan blobs down here. They're the ones that started this whole CRU business, not these dumb agents. This whole thing, all of it, has been a trap for Emily because she's part Xan and they want her power. When they had her, one of them blobs swallowed her whole. But then she blasted a hole through it and everyone disappeared 'cept Frank and me."

Earl looked at the agent prisoners. "Yes, you stupid morons, the CRU is a lie. You are nothing but slaves to Titans."

"That's not possible," the senior agent said.

"You're dumber than a bag of hammers, ain't ya?" Earl continued. "Look around you, boy. Do these leather monsters come from around here? No, they're with the Titans."

"But what about Emily?" Joel cried.

"She's gone and took the others with her."

"What about Riza?" Vulcan asked.

"She wasn't here."

"Enough talk," one of the male voices boomed. *"Bring them in. I grow impatient to leave this pit. Bring them now!"*

They were roughly shoved forward out of the room and through another long corridor. When they reached the silver doors at the end, Frankie started to scream and claw at the Shadow Titans.

"No! I won't go back in there!"

But the more he shrieked and struggled, the harder the Shadow Titans handled him.

"Leave him alone!" Earl and Joel shouted together. But the Shadow Titans wouldn't listen. Finally one of them struck Frankie on the head and knocked him out. When he fell to the floor, Earl picked him up. "Just leave him be, you dung-eatin' escapees from a shoe factory!"

The silver doors whooshed open, and everyone gasped when they saw what lay behind them.

"Yes, Vulcan, come in and see us," a voice teased.

Paelen's pain vanished and screams were stolen from his throat as his eyes landed on the horrors before him. They couldn't be Titans. In all his life, he had never seen anything like them.

"They are from my dream . . . ," Lorin gasped.

"You dreamed about them?" Joel cried.

Lorin covered her face with her trembling hands. "We are all going to die."

"No, we are not," Vulcan said as he broke free of the Shadow Titans and fearlessly stormed into the room containing the Titans. "Who are you?"

"Don't you recognize us?" the female said coyly. *"Granted, it has been a few thousand years, but have we really changed so much?"*

The Shadow Titans shoved everyone else into the large dark chamber and then stood back by the doors, blocking the only exit.

"I do not know you," Vulcan challenged. "But if you try to harm anyone here, you will answer to me."

"Brave words from an Olympian failure," the higher

male voice said. "*Trying so hard to fit in when everyone laughs at you. Your mother, Juno, rejected you at birth, and even your own wife, Venus, will have nothing to do with you. The only one who ever cared about you is Stella. But she herself is too broken to realize what you really are.*"

"You speak cruel words," Vulcan said. "But do you have the courage to tell me who you are? You, who claim to know so much about me."

"*We know more than you would imagine. When the monster, Emily, murdered us in Tartarus, she also created us. And thus we grew in strength and power.*"

"Emily couldn't have murdered you," Joel said. "She doesn't do things like that. . . ."

"*Ah, yes,*" the female voice said. "*The famous Joel—love of Emily's life. You know so little about her. But don't worry. We'll tell her how you died, right before we absorb her!*"

"You are the ones who are going to die," Paelen spat.

"*Don't think we don't remember you, too, Paelen,*" the male voice said. "*A decrepit old man, surviving off the scraps of Vulcan's forge. The only bravery you've ever*

shown was at the end of your pathetic life, when you sacri-
ficed yourself to save Vulcan and Stella."

"You do not know what you are talking about," Paelen spat.

"No, you don't. But now, at the end, you will learn. You will see it all, as Emily saw it and we did."

Paelen's head burst with pain as his mind was suddenly filled with memories that weren't his own but contained him. He saw himself through Emily's eyes as a very old man sitting on a creature that looked a lot like Brue of Xanadu. But the large, two-headed purple creature had changed. She was ferocious, with long, sharp teeth and tearing claws. He also saw Pegasus, looking old and frail, being protected and cared for by Emily. Then he saw Joel, Stella, and Agent B fighting together against the Shadow Titans and real Titans. All the stories Emily had told about the other time line and more now flashed in bold, living color in his mind.

When the visions ended, Paelen collapsed to the floor. Joel fell beside him, panting hard. Chrysaor squealed softly and shook his head.

Paelen looked over at his friend and saw the

haunted expression in Joel's eyes. They had seen all of Emily's memories from the time, including how close she and Joel had become—and heard Joel tell Emily how much he loved her. That he would always be with her, no matter what.

It was one thing to hear the stories of a strange time that had never happened for them, but it was something else to actually see the horrors they had experienced and their part in the ancient war.

The Titans started to chuckle, and the female said, *"Now do you see what Emily did for you? What she surrendered when she destroyed Saturn's weapon? How do you feel now, Joel, knowing you turned away from her when she needed you most?"*

"Shut up!" Joel shouted as he climbed to his feet and charged the Titans. "You don't know anything about me or how I feel about Emily!"

"Of course we do," the female said. *"We saw it all in your mind. How you won't see her or how you've hurt her because you're just an insecure little boy—frightened that you're not good enough for her now that she has changed so much. You can't believe that someone so special could ever love you, or that you would even deserve her love. You are*

quite right, Joel. You aren't good enough for her, and you don't deserve her love. . . ."

"Shut up!" Joel shouted again.

"I think we have struck a nerve," the male Titan said. "Yes, Joel, we have seen everything in your mind, and we'll let Emily know just how much you loved her, right before we absorb her."

"You won't absorb her, do you hear me? You won't. Emily is going to stop you!"

"Such brave words from one about to die," the female said.

"So, who first?" the light male voice asked. "They all look so delicious."

"The Olympians," cried the other male Titan. "Let us each absorb one and share in the feast! We can save Lorin for last!"

Paelen screamed as he was suddenly lifted off the floor by an invisible force. He kicked out his legs and fought against the grip that held him, but nothing worked. Vulcan and Chrysaor were both hoisted off the ground with him.

"No!" Lorin shouted. "Let them go!"

"Stop!" Joel cried. "You can't do this!"

"Watch, Lorin. Watch and see the fate that awaits you!"

"Lorin, do something," Joel cried, running up to her. "Kill the Titans!"

Lorin summoned the Flame and destroyed the Shadow Titans running toward her. Then she charged at the three Titans and fired a steady stream of Flame at them. But her flames shot right through their clear bodies without doing anything at all apart from burning a large, smoldering hole in the wall behind them.

Paelen kept struggling to break free, but there was nothing he could do. He was raised higher above one of the creatures and closer to its mouth. He looked up to the ceiling and saw the old brickwork.

"Lorin," he shouted. "Go for the ceiling. Bring the station down on us. Kill the Titans!"

"Yes," Vulcan shouted. "Forget us. Destroy the building. Bring it all down!"

"Do it!" Joel agreed. "Do it now!"

Lorin raised both her hands and fired a full blast of flame at the ancient brickwork over the heads of the Titans. The moment the intense flame struck the bricks, large chunks of ceiling exploded and came crashing down onto the clear creatures.

"Keep going!" Paelen cried. "Destroy it all!"

The Flame that Lorin shot at the ceiling intensified. "Release the others or I will bring it all down!" she cried.

"Stop," the female Titan shouted. *"Or we will all perish. If you surrender to us, we will release your friends!"*

Paelen cried, "They are lying. Do not do it! Destroy the building!"

Moments later, Paelen, Vulcan, and Joel began to scream as the invisible hands started to crush them.

"Let them go!" Lorin cried.

"Stop your Flame and we will!"

The breath was being squeezed out of Paelen, keeping him from calling out to Lorin. But when the pressure increased, he started to see stars before his eyes, and he knew he was suffocating.

Lorin screamed and finally stopped the shooting Flame and left only fireballs in her palms. "Release them now, or I promise you, I will destroy us all."

"You would kill your precious Paelen?"

"He will die anyway," Lorin said. "But I will make the trade with you. If you release everyone, you can have me."

The pressure stopped as quickly as it started and Paelen could breathe again. "What?" he rasped. "Lorin, no . . . We can defeat them. Bring the ceiling down!"

"She can't defeat us and she knows it," the female Titan cried. *"She contains some power of the Xan but not enough to destroy us. But if she surrenders to us, you will all live."*

"So you will trade my life for theirs?" Lorin asked.

"Yes," the three Titans said as one. Paelen, Chrysaor, and Vulcan were lowered to the floor of the room. *"Everyone is free to go, but only if you stay."*

Paelen staggered over and put his arms around her. "Lorin, no, you cannot sacrifice yourself for us."

Tears rimmed her eyes. "I must. They are stronger than me and will kill you if I do not. You are all that matters to me, Paelen." She reached out and gently touched the wound on his chest. "I am sorry I hurt you."

Like Emily, Lorin still retained her healing powers. At her touch, the deep burn on his chest healed.

"No," Paelen wept. "Please, do not do this. Do not leave me."

"I am not leaving you, not really. I will always be

with you in here. . . ." She pressed her hand to his heart as tears sparkled in her eyes. "I love you, Paelen."

"No. I will not let you do this."

Lorin pulled him close and whispered in his ear, "Paelen, I am dying—each day I have been getting weaker. When I asked Riza, she confirmed it. I have very little time left. Let me give up that time to save you."

"What . . . ? Dying?"

She nodded. "I was never meant to live. But you gave my short life meaning. I love you, Paelen. I have always loved you. . . ."

Lorin kissed him with such intensity that Paelen felt his heart breaking. When she released him, he whispered, "I love you too. . . . Please, give me your final days, not them. We can do this."

She stepped back and shook her head sadly, then looked over to Joel and then Vulcan. "Keep my Paelen safe and tell Emily and Pegasus that I am sorry."

She raised her hand and used her powers to lift everyone, including the CRU agents, off the ground. They were carried over the heads of the remaining Shadow Titans and through the exit doors.

"Lorin, no!" Paelen shouted as he tried to run back in. But her powers held him firm.

"I love you, Paelen. I will always love you. . . ."

Paelen watched Lorin turn away from him and face the three creatures. She dropped her hands, extinguished her Flame, and lowered her head as she surrendered herself to them.

The last thing he saw before the doors slammed shut was Lorin being lifted off the floor and brought closer to one of the mutant Titans.

The final thing he heard through the doors was Lorin starting to scream.

"LORIN!" PAELEN SLAMMED HIS FISTS
against the doors, trying to get back in. Somehow
he could feel her—her love for him, her pain, and
finally, her death.

"No," he howled as he collapsed to the floor.

From behind the doors they heard cheering and
celebration. These were suddenly followed by the terrible screams of the higher-voiced Titan, as though he
was in great pain.

"She's getting away!" Joel shouted.

"No. Lorin is dead," Paelen wept.

"Then what's going on in there?" the senior agent
asked.

"I don't know, and I don't wanna know," Earl

said. "Let's just get outta here before them monsters change their mind and decide to have us for dessert."

"Paelen, I'm so sorry," Joel said softly as he knelt down and put a comforting arm around his best friend. "Please, we can't help her now. Come on. We must go."

"I cannot move." Paelen sobbed. He raised his tear-filled eyes to Joel. "Lorin was dying. She gave up her remaining time for us."

Vulcan put his hand on Paelen's shoulder. "No, Paelen. She gave it up for you, so that you would live. You do not want to dishonor her sacrifice by remaining here and being destroyed by them."

"He's right," Joel agreed. "We can't waste this opportunity she's given us. If we wait much longer, those things will come after us again!"

"What about them?" one of the CRU agents asked as he pointed at the cages of clones and aliens.

"Leave them!" the senior agent said. "Let's just get to the lift while we still can!"

Vulcan rose to his feet. "No!" he howled. "I will not leave them here to be devoured by those creatures. Set them all free!"

The agents looked from their senior officer to

Vulcan. Moments later, they followed Vulcan's command and started to open the cages.

"I said leave them!" the senior officer cried. "Leave all the Olympians down here! This is their war, not ours!"

"You fool!" Vulcan cried. He charged over and caught hold of the man. "What is wrong with you? This fight involves all of us. Those creatures in there do not care whether they kill humans or Olympians. Your only hope is the Olympians, and our only hope is to get back to Olympus so that Jupiter and his brothers come here to stop them. So for once, put your prejudice against us aside and work with us, not against us!"

Vulcan threw the agent down and looked at the others. "Can you not see this?"

The senior agent got up. "You're lying. This is your fault. . . ."

Before he could finish, Paelen rose to his feet and punched the CRU agent with enough force to send him flying across the vast chamber. "My beautiful Lorin died so that we may live. We either work together or we die together. Which is it to be?"

The other agents turned from their superior and nodded. "Work together."

It didn't take long to open the cages. But as the large group ran from the cage room through the corridor and to the elevator, they realized they had another problem. There were no stairs and only the one elevator. It was large but not large enough to carry them all.

"All right, Vulcan," the senior CRU agent challenged, rubbing his bruised chin. "You seem to know so much. Now what? There's only the one lift, and we all can't fit in it."

Paelen looked back at the large gathering of clones and even stranger creatures. There had to be at least thirty Dianas, Cupids, and Paelens, plus two large Pegasus clones. Their frightened, innocent eyes looked to them in hope.

Vulcan came forward and poked his finger in the chest of the senior CRU agent. "You will take your human agents and anyone here that cannot fly into that metal box and get back up to the surface. Set off your alarms. Warn the others what is down here and get everyone out. You were never an agency of science. You were set up and used by those demented

Titans to escape this pit. Because of you, they now have the power they need to get out. Soon they will be free to destroy us all."

"That's a lie," the CRU agent said. "We didn't serve them!"

"You're too stupid to live," Joel spat. "Of course you did. But now the CRU are finished!"

The ground beneath their feet rumbled and started to shake as though there were an earthquake.

"Do you understand now?" Vulcan raged. "In absorbing Lorin, they have the power to free themselves! Get in to that metal box and take everyone out of here."

The intensity of the rumbling increased, and the sound of deep cracking started. The sickening laughter of the Titans filled the underground area.

"Go!" Vulcan roared at the agents.

The agents piled into the elevator with the Diana and Paelen clones. Several small, gray-skinned creatures with large black eyes also followed them on. The gray creatures turned back to Vulcan and nodded in gratitude.

"Earl, Frankie, go with them," Joel said.

"No way!" Earl said. "We're sticking with you no matter what."

Paelen leaned in to the elevator and pressed the button for the top floor. "Do not stop. Get out of here now!"

The doors closed, and the whine of the elevator started as it carried its strange cargo away.

The rumbling in the ground increased as Earl shook his head. "They won't do it, you know. Them CRU agents will stop at one of the agency floors and try to lock up them poor clones again."

Paelen was filled with so many emotions—grief, guilt, and loss—but hearing Earl's comment caused a burning rage to rise to the surface. "Oh no, they will not! If I have to push that elevator all the way to the top, they will not keep those clones!"

He stormed forward and used his Olympian strength to pry open the outer elevator doors, exposing the wide shaft, and peered up. The elevator was still climbing. "I will follow them to make sure."

"Good idea," Vulcan agreed. "We will all fly up right beneath them. If they try to stop, we will push them up!"

Just as the first cracks in the ceiling appeared, Joel

ran up to the Cupid clones. "All right, you guys, I know you can understand me, and I know you can fly. So you are going to use your wings to follow us up. Two of you are going to carry Earl and Frankie, and the rest will do as we do. When we say push, you will push. Do you understand?"

There was fear in the innocent eyes of the Cupids, but they all nodded their heads.

Just as they prepared to move, a large chunk of the ceiling crashed down near where they were standing. There was an even deeper rumbling as the chamber holding the Titans started to collapse.

"They're getting out!" Earl cried.

"Move!" Vulcan commanded as he ordered his metal wings to open and fly.

Joel climbed onto Chrysaor, and the boar squealed as he charged into the open shaft, spread his stubby wings, and started to fly up.

"Go!" Paelen ordered the Cupids. He then ran back to the Pegasus clones. "I hope you can understand me. Follow us if you wish to live!"

The stallions' eyes were wide with terror, and they whinnied.

"Paelen, come on," Joel cried from inside the shaft. "This whole place is coming down!"

More of the ceiling collapsed, and dust filled the corridor as the ground shook violently. There was a strong sense that they didn't have much time left before the whole place was destroyed.

"Come!" Paelen shouted at the Pegasus clones. He leaped into the elevator shaft and commanded his sandals to take him up.

The tall, dark shaft was filled with the sound of beating wings as the large group started the long, vertical climb. Paelen stole a look down and was grateful to see that the two Pegasus clones had figured out this was their only means of escape. As they winged their way up, the sounds of the Titans' triumphant roars mixed with the cracking of the ground around them.

Halfway up the long shaft, Earl started shouting. "There's the elevator, but it ain't moving fast enough. This shaft will collapse before it reaches the top!"

"Everyone, push the bottom of the metal box!" Vulcan commanded. "We must help them up!"

Paelen commanded his sandals to move faster. He

soon joined the group of Cupids and Vulcan pushing the bottom of the elevator. "Harder!" Paelen grunted.

The cables screamed in protest as the heavy elevator was forced to move faster than it was designed to go. Beneath them the sounds of collapse intensified.

Faster and faster the group of winged Olympians carried the elevator up. Vulcan punched an arm through the floor of the elevator. "How much farther?" he called.

One of the agents shouted down to them, "Just eight more levels. Seven, six, five . . ." He counted down until they reached the top. "We're here! Stop pushing."

They heard the scuffling of the people in the elevator. The senior agent's face appeared at the hole. "You've broken the lift. The doors won't open!"

Vulcan punched a second and then third hole in the elevator floor. His reached up and started to peel back the box's framework and metal. The hole was too small for anyone to fit through except for one.

"Paelen, you can make it through there," Joel said. "Teach the others what you need them to do. Open the elevator doors and get everyone out."

It had been some time since Paelen had used his powers to stretch out his body. He focused his thoughts on what he wanted to do. Soon his hands, arms, legs, and torso started to stretch. Paelen winced as his bones snapped out of their joints and his muscles elongated until he was thin enough to fit through the hole in the floor of the elevator.

Two agents reached for his arms and finished pulling him up. When he was safely inside, he painfully returned to his natural shape.

"I'd heard you could do that," one of the agents said. "But I never believed it. Does it hurt?"

"No, it tickles," Paelen said sarcastically. He pushed through the clones to the elevator doors. "You," he said to a clone of himself. "Do as I do. Help me pry the door open."

In the past, whenever Paelen encountered one of his clones, his instinct was to fight it. This time, he saw the innocence shining in the eyes of his mirror image and he felt nothing but compassion. Had Lorin changed him so much?

The clone nodded and followed his every move as Paelen forced his fingers into the crack of the closed doors and started to pry them open. Soon the inner elevator and outer security doors were pried open, and everyone ran out.

From deep below the ground the sounds of rumbling increased and the whole upper level of Charing Cross Station shook violently.

"Everyone is safe," Paelen called below. "Push harder. Lift the elevator higher and you can get out."

Working from the outside, Paelen and three of his clones caught hold of the bottom edge of the elevator and helped to heave it up higher to free those from beneath it. Slowly it rose up to their knees, waists, and then to almost over their heads.

"Go!" Vulcan ordered the others in the shaft. "All of you get out!"

Paelen and his clones helped Joel and Chrysaor climb out. They were followed by the Cupid clones.

When they were safe, Vulcan pushed the elevator even higher. "Get the two stallions out of here."

Paelen peered down into the shaft and saw the two Pegasus clones. They were using their wings to hover in the shaft but were too frightened to climb any higher.

"Take me down to the stallions," Paelen ordered his sandals. Immediately he was lifted off the ground and carried back down into the dark shaft. Flying past Vulcan, he could see the muscles in his arms quivering with the strain and the metal wings struggling to support the weight of the massive elevator.

"Hurry!" Vulcan commanded.

Paelen reached the clones and placed himself between the two. "Fly with me," he ordered. The two stallions whinnied in fear, but as Paelen moved, they started to follow behind him.

"That's it," Joel called from above. "Keep coming. Keep coming!"

Frankie appeared at the entrance. "C'mon, boys, you can do it," he called softly.

The moment Frankie started calling the stallions, they flapped harder and climbed higher in the shaft, neighing and whinnying.

"That's it, boys," Frankie coaxed. "Come to me!"

Soon the two stallions flew past Paelen and out of the shaft.

Just as they were clear, explosions started from below. Paelen looked down and could see flames flashing into the shaft. The collapse had reached the lower floors of the CRU facility and was taking out its power plant.

"Paelen, get out!" Vulcan shouted.

Paelen ordered his sandals to move. Just as he flew free of the shaft, the whole building, heaved with the ferocity of a great explosion from below.

The elevator shaft groaned, shifted, and bent. Everyone standing was thrown to the floor.

"Vulcan, come out of there!" Joel cried, climbing to his feet again.

The Paelen clones were struggling to hold the elevator from the outside of the shaft. But when the building heaved a third time, they were thrown free. Vulcan was left holding the full weight of the enormous elevator.

"I cannot hold it!" Vulcan roared.

"Give me your hand," Joel cried. "Get out of there!"

The elevator dropped several feet as Vulcan's strength gave way. "Forget me. Get back to Olympus!" he shouted. "Warn Jupiter and the others. Tell them . . ." Before he finished, the building rocked again and the elevator shaft buckled completely. Cables snapped, and the heavy elevator started to fall, taking Vulcan with it.

"Vulcan!" Paelen shouted as the elevator whooshed past them and free-fell down into the dark abyss.

"Vulcan!" Joel cried. "No . . . !"

The sounds of explosions intensified as the top of the elevator disappeared into darkness. Moments later, a rush of roaring flames shot up through the shaft. Paelen had to pull Joel free to avoid being burned alive.

"Vulcan . . . ," Joel whispered.

"He is gone," Paelen said softly. "Just like my Lorin. He gave his life for us."

The horrible sounds of laughter from the Titans was now all around them and booming louder than they'd imagined possible.

Paelen looked back and saw all the clones and the aliens waiting for them. Frankie was back with the two Pegasus clones, and Earl was with the Dianas. But all the CRU agents had gone. The ground was now shaking constantly and the floor beneath them starting to crack.

"We must get out of here," Paelen warned. "This whole place is coming down!"

"I can't leave him. He might be alive!"

"Joel, Paelen!" Earl shouted. "We gotta go. Vulcan was right. We gotta tell Jupiter and his brothers about them Titans. They plan to devour Olympus!"

Paelen could feel Joel's grief at losing Vulcan, and he shared in it. Both Vulcan and Lorin had sacrificed themselves so that they might survive. "Come," Paelen said, catching hold of his best friend. "We will not serve Vulcan or Lorin if we are killed in here. We must go."

"Boys!" Earl cried. He was holding open the door that led to the restrooms and the stairs going up into the open station.

The ground beneath them split open as the sounds of people screaming filtered down from the station just above. Suddenly a large part of the upper section of the station came crashing down into the restroom area.

With no time to grieve or even think, Paelen and Joel ushered the large group of clones forward while Earl and Frankie kept to the back, making sure they all got out. Black smoke billowed into the area from the elevator shaft, choking them. They coughed and picked their way through the rubble toward the stairs.

They arrived at the concourse level to complete chaos. Sirens and alarms were blaring while an automated voice ordered the full evacuation of the station. People were leaving their luggage and running for their lives in every direction.

The panicking crowd hardly glanced at the new arrivals. If they even saw the Cupids with their wings, they paid no attention. The appearance of the two winged stallions was actually ignored.

"This way!" Paelen called, leading his large group forward. "Earl, Frankie, get on the stallions if you can. We are going to have to fly the moment we leave here. If we are lucky, they will fly with us." He moved back to the Cupids. "All of you, I want you to carry the Dianas and Paelens. Stay close to us. This is going to be very dangerous."

The clones nodded and paired up. Joel climbed onto Chrysaor's back. "The exits are all blocked with people." He pointed in the opposite direction toward the turnstiles and train tracks. "Let's get out that way.

You can see daylight down at the end of the tracks. They lead out of the station."

Paelen nodded. He looked back and was glad to see Earl and Frankie had been accepted by the winged stallions and were now seated on their backs. "Everyone, fly. Follow me!"

Commanding his sandals into the air, Paelen lifted off the ground. Chrysaor and Joel were next, followed by the clones. This time the panicking people did stop long enough to scream and point at them.

"Don't stop. Just keep going!" Joel shouted.

Just as they gained height in the station, they heard the most horrendous roars from outside it. *"We're free!"*

The ground shook and the building heaved, causing the glass ceiling of the station to shatter. Most of the larger pieces were caught by the pigeon netting high above the concourse. But smaller shards of glass rained down, cutting victims and making the ground slippery for the fleeing people.

"Let's get outta here!" Earl shouted.

They flew faster over the heads of the crowd and toward the turnstiles. Soaring easily over the top, they approached at least fifteen train platforms. Some trains were moving to get out of the damaged station, while others were blocked with falling rubble and debris.

"That way." Joel pointed. "Follow that train out!"

The Olympians and clones chased a train evacuating the station. People stood in the rear carriage, pointing and taking pictures of the group of flying creatures following directly behind them. The moment they came out from under the cover of the station, Paelen climbed higher in the sky. He looked back and gasped.

Charing Cross itself was still standing—somehow. But it was hanging on the edge of a vast precipice that went down into the depths of the Titans' pit. It was wider than the station and had swallowed half the block across from it. Buildings that had stood there for years were now missing, with only a large hole in the ground to mark where they'd been.

But the worst sight of all was the two massive Titans. Now free of their dark pit, they were no longer clear liquid. Instead, rainbow colors flashed and pulsed in their heaving bodies as they poured themselves like thick nectar along the streets of London.

The two Titans roared in delight as they shot

tendrils of themselves out and crushed double-decker buses and cars on the roads. Instead of remaining on the street level, one of them slid up the side of a building until its hulking weight brought the building crashing down.

"We are free!" the female Titan screeched. *"Soon you will all feed us!"*

"Where's the third one?" Joel called from the back of Chrysaor. "I only see two."

"They devoured it!" a voice boomed from behind them.

Paelen and Joel turned back and saw Vulcan flying toward them. His metal wings were bent and severely damaged, but somehow they still worked. His clothes were burned and smoldering, and his hair was singed short.

"Vulcan!" Joel cried. "You're alive!"

"Barely," Vulcan said. "I had to follow those two monstrosities out of their pit to escape the collapse. I saw what was left of the third Titan after they devoured it. They have absorbed all of its power. With it and Lorin combined, they have enough to enter the Solar Stream and make it to Olympus."

"If they got the power, why ain't they leavin'?" Earl called.

"They are too heavy to launch from the ground," Vulcan explained. "They must climb to the highest peak and cast themselves off it to achieve flight. Only then they can enter the Solar Stream."

Down on the ground, the Titans were moving toward two of the many bridges that crossed the river. In the distance, on the opposite shore, was one of the tallest buildings in the area. It had a massive pyramid at the top and looked large enough to support their hulking weight.

"That is where they will launch from," Vulcan warned.

The roar of military jets sounded overhead as they flew toward the two Titans.

"I never thought I'd be glad to see them," Joel said. But his enthusiasm vanished the moment the jets opened fire on the Titans. Their rockets passed right through their heaving gelatinous bodies and exploded on the ground beneath them.

Despite the damage around them, the Titans kept moving toward the bridges. As they went, they appeared to take pleasure in knocking down smaller buildings and destroying any vehicles within reach.

The first mutant arrived at Waterloo Bridge and slid its shifting hulk onto the crossing. The second moved farther down to Westminster Bridge, right beside the Tower of Big Ben. As they flowed onto the bridges, they left flattened cars, trucks, and buses in their wake.

Once the Titans arrived at the center of the bridges, the jet fighters launched aggressive attacks. Rockets blasted the foundations and tore into the decks, exploding on contact. Both bridges were destroyed in seconds and collapsed into the River Thames, taking the two mutant Titans with them into the cold water.

"I hope they dissolve!" Frankie cried.

But their hopes faded when the two Titans floated on the surface like balls of grease and made their way to the opposite shore. Further attacks achieved nothing but the destruction of the city around them.

"What if we get the jets to destroy the tall building?" Joel called.

"They will only find another," Vulcan said. "Come. It is time we left this place. There is nothing we can do to save it. Only the Big Three stand a chance of defeating them. We must get back to Olympus."

Paelen shook his head. "No, Vulcan. You go, and take the clones with you. Get to Olympus and tell Jupiter what has happened. We are going to Xanadu. We must find Emily and Riza. If the Big Three cannot stop them, perhaps they can."

Vulcan nodded and swooped closer to the Cupid clones. "Come, children of Olympus. Follow me. I will bring you home." Vulcan led the Cupid clones higher in the sky, and the military helicopters and jets actually moved out of their way to allow them to pass. Paelen looked over to Joel. "Why are they not shooting at us? Do you think the CRU have told them to leave us be so we can inform Jupiter?"

"I don't care," Joel called. "As long as they leave us alone, this world stands a chance. Without us, it's doomed."

Paelen nodded without saying he believed the world was doomed anyway. Instead he looked back at Earl and Frankie on the Pegasus clones. "Stay close and follow us. We are going to Xanadu."

Paelen took one last look back at the two Titans

tearing through London. As he watched, they slithered onto the opposite shore and moved toward an enormous Ferris wheel with large passenger pods. They laughed maniacally as they pushed it into the river.

"I will be back for you," he said grimly. "You will pay for what you did to my Lorin. You will pay for it all!"

With a rage he'd never felt before burning inside him, Paelen called down to his sandals, "Take me to Xanadu!"

EMILY WAS WORKING WITH RIZA IN THE central control room on Rhean to help bring more of the people and wildlife together. They had created an area of protection that was larger than the whole of the United States, and it was here that people, animals, and plants were being delivered from around the rest of the dying planet, in preparation for transport to Xanadu.

Pegasus was at Emily's side, gazing out the large window at the flashing reds of the dying sun.

Agent B and Cupid arrived in the control room with a group of the silver-skinned people. They were all covered in dirt and brushing mud off their hands.

"Well, that was fun," Agent B said, grinning.

"Not what I could call it," Cupid complained. "Look at the state of me. I am filthy and my feathers are caked with mud. I need to bathe, but there is no water to spare."

"A little dirt never hurt anyone," Agent B said. He looked at the silver-skinned people and nodded. "Right?"

They smiled and nodded back and did the closest approximation to the sound "right." It was obvious they had no idea what he'd just said.

"What happened to you?" Emily asked, coming over.

"We've been putting young trees in travel containers," Agent B said. "There are some amazing plants here. We're saving all we can."

"But it is heavy and dirty work," Cupid said.

Emily looked at Cupid approvingly. "Hard work and dirt suit you. You should show your *wife*, Psyche, when you get back to Olympus."

Cupid grinned at her. "I might just do that."

Emily tilted her head at Agent B. "It's going to be hard to go back to your old life on Earth after you've seen all this."

He shrugged. "No, it's not, because I'm not going back to Earth. After all those memories of the past coming back to me, and seeing all of this, I can't. There's nothing there for me. I'm hoping Jupiter might let me stay in Olympus. Or better yet . . ." He looked over to Riza. "Maybe Riza will let me stay on Xanadu to help these folks get settled."

Riza turned and nodded. "I would be grateful for the help. You are most welcome to stay on Xanadu."

"That's settled, then," Agent B said.

Across the large control room, laughter rang out. Stella was with a group of young silver-skinned girls. They were using a lot of animated gestures to try to communicate. The one thing they all had in common was the ability to laugh. The young Rheans didn't take notice that Stella couldn't walk. There were more than enough of them offering to carry her around.

Emily also noticed that the Rhean teens had managed to help ease her grief over the loss of her parents. When this was over, she felt certain that Stella, too, would find a new home, either in Olympus with Vulcan or with the Rheans.

"Another group has just arrived," Arious Minor reported as he popped out of the mainframe computer on the primary consul. "They are settling in sector C right now. There are reports of extensive burns and radiation sickness, but they are being treated."

"Very good," Riza said. "Just a few more to come and we'll be ready to leave."

Emily watched in amazement as Riza and Arious Minor worked together like a well-oiled machine, each anticipating what the other needed or would say. In so many ways, Riza was just like her—a wild, fun-filled free spirit. But as she worked to save an entire civilization, Emily had a glimpse of what the Xan really were: a sensitive, intelligent people dedicated to preserving life. She felt privileged to call Riza her friend.

As she gazed around at everyone, Emily realized for the first time in a very long while that she was at peace. Agent B, Stella, and Cupid were safe, and Pegasus, her beloved Pegasus, was by her side. And even though Earl and Frankie were still in danger, she realized Riza was right. They were too important to the Titans to kill.

Emily was also struck by the sudden realization that she had finally found a purpose to her life. Working with Riza to help save the Rheans was what really mattered. It suddenly seemed trivial to worry so much that she had changed and looked like Diana or that Joel wasn't interested in her anymore. In that single polarizing moment, Emily knew this rescue was the start of something much bigger. After they dealt with the Titans under Charing Cross, there would be many more such rescues.

As though reading her mind, Riza looked over at her and smiled. It lit up her whole, pearly face. "I like working with you too," she said, winking at her.

Emily was about to say something when she felt a terrible pain tearing through her chest. It was unlike anything she'd ever felt before, as though something were being physically ripped out of her body. As the pain intensified, she was driven to her knees, gasping for breath.

Riza howled, clutched her chest, and collapsed to the floor.

"Flame!" Cupid cried as he rushed to Emily's side.

Emily was panting heavily and in too much pain

to speak. Beside her, Riza was helped up by Agent B and two of the Rheans. When she looked over at her, Riza was weeping—with cream-colored tears streaming down her cheeks.

"What was that?" Emily gasped. "It's like I felt Lorin or something."

"You did," Riza wept. "We both felt her die."

Pegasus whinnied loudly and shook his head while everyone demanded to know how.

Riza was leaning heavily on Agent B. "Lorin was a part of us and we were part of her. All of us connected. But that connection has been violently severed. . . ."

Emily was helped up by Cupid. She stood, holding on to Pegasus for support. The stallion was pressing his head to her in sympathy. "How is this possible? I don't feel Lorin anymore, but I still feel her power."

Riza started to shake. "This is terrible. . . ." She focused on the dot of light. "Arious, we're out of time. We can't wait to gather everyone together here. Send out a warning to the other outposts on the world. Tell them that we have to transport the whole planet to Xanadu."

"Riza, you can't!" Arious Minor cried. "You don't have the strength for this. If more of the Xan were here, yes, but alone, it will take too much out of you."

"We don't have a choice. We can't leave anyone behind to perish when that sun goes. But we must get back to Xanadu immediately. Those Titans must be stopped."

"Riza, Emily, please, you're scaring me," Stella said. "What's happening?"

Riza shook her head. "You have good cause to be frightened. We all do. I do not know how it happened, but somehow, Lorin has been killed by the Titans under Charing Cross. They have absorbed her powers. She is dead, but her power lives on, in them."

Cupid gasped. "That means . . ."

Riza started to nod. "Yes. They now have the power they need to escape their pit."

Pegasus whinnied and pawed the floor, while the others gasped in shock.

Riza nodded to him. "Once they are out of there, they will head straight to Olympus. If they absorb the Olympians and gain their powers as well, there will be no stopping them!"

The preparations on Rhean were manic as everyone did their part to ready the world for transport. Emily and Pegasus stood outside the control room on the red, sandy ground of the dying planet. There were no structures to be seen. It looked more like a dry desert than a living world. Riza explained that the people had known about the supernova for many years and had moved everything, including the plant life, underground to survive the heat.

Somehow, the air around them even smelled burned. Above them, the flashing colors of the sun blazing outside the protective energy field were blinding. Despite the shield, the heat of the impending supernova was blistering and increasing by the minute. Emily was reminded of what it felt like to sit in a car with the windows closed in the middle of the summer. Though the air was breathable, it was becoming difficult to inhale.

Thousands of the silver-skinned people were gathered around them. There was no mistaking the collective fear on their faces. They all knew what was at stake.

"There is nothing more we can do," Riza said,

"other than hope that this works. But I will not lie to you. What I am proposing to do is very risky. However, I won't be doing it alone."

"I do not understand," Cupid said. "There are no other Xan here."

"True," Riza agreed. "However, Emily contains part of the Xan. Also, you and Pegasus have great powers."

"We don't," Stella said. She was seated on the stallion's back and holding on to his white mane.

Riza nodded. "Yes, you do. Every living being generates energy. For most, it's imperceptible. But for others, like the Olympians, Titans, and Xan, we have more and can use it. My hope is if we all hold hands, it will connect us and I may be able to summon all our powers together and focus them to transport this planet into a safe orbit around Xanadu."

"That sounds great in principle," Agent B added. "But what about an atmosphere and gravity?"

"That is where I will come in," Arious Minor said. "I have already warned Arious Major. When we arrive, we will generate a field around the world to create a supporting gravity and atmosphere. It won't last indefinitely, but with luck, the planet's core and orbit should start to generate its own. If we move the plants to the surface again, they could ideally create a self-sustaining environment. This world could become a moon or even a sister planet to Xanadu."

"That's a bold idea," Agent B said.

"It is," Riza agreed. "And there is no guarantee it will work. But we have little choice. Would you leave these people behind to burn up when their sun dies?"

Agent B looked over to the large gathering of Rheans. "Of course not."

Emily asked Cupid, "What about you? Would you abandon them so we could go fight the mutant Titans before they attack Olympus?"

Cupid hesitated for a moment, and then his wings drooped. "No, I would not."

"They're both important," Stella offered.

"Indeed they are," Riza agreed. "So moving this world is the only possible solution. Now, this is going to be a touch uncomfortable. But I have to reach out to every living being on the planet and tell them to touch one another. The power must flow through all of us, unbroken."

Emily nodded. "We're ready."

"Then let us begin. Take my hand. Everyone, start touching."

Emily took hold of Riza's finely boned hand and reached out to touch Pegasus with her other hand. Stella reached down to hold on to Cupid and Agent B, who then reached out to the nearest Rheans. One by one, the gathered masses started to take hold of one another.

"Here we go," Riza said. "I'm about to make the call and tell everyone to touch."

Riza closed her eyes and tilted her head back. Instantly, Emily heard Riza's voice blasting in her mind as she telepathically told everyone on the world to take hold of one another and form a single mass connection. It was the same voice she'd heard in her head for so long.

Emily winced as the pain in her head intensified. She opened her eyes and saw her friends also showing signs of distress. Pegasus nickered and shook his head, and Cupid was moaning. But as the minutes passed, Emily felt the strangest sensation, like a soft tickling on her skin, raising the hairs on her arms.

"That is the power of unity," Riza said, reading her mind. "The people of this world know what's at stake. They will do everything they can to save their planet and each other."

Riza soon stopped broadcasting the call to touch. "It is done. We are all connected."

Agent B shook his head. "That's wasn't a sting. It was a sledgehammer."

"I'm sorry, but it was necessary to get everyone connected."

"Do you mean everyone alive on this planet is now holding hands?" Cupid asked.

"Hands, paws, claws, wings, and leaves . . . ," Riza said. "If it is alive, it is connected. I just hope it is enough power to move us into the Solar Stream and then get us out again when we reach Xanadu."

"It is time," Arious Minor said. "Everything is prepared. Arious Major is waiting to receive us."

Riza looked down at Emily. "I really need your help, Emily. You are the only other being alive with Xan in you. I must call upon that power to get us moving."

"I understand." Emily leaned over and gave

Pegasus a kiss on the soft muzzle. "Whatever happens, Pegs, you know that I love you."

Pegasus nickered softly and nodded his head.

"He loves you too," Riza said.

Emily didn't need Riza to tell her that. She already knew. After everything they'd gone through, their bond was stronger than ever, and she could feel his love like a comforting blanket.

"All right, let's begin." Riza took a deep breath, closed her eyes, and once again, tilted her head back. Instantly, Emily felt the drawing of power coming from deep within her core.

At first nothing happened. But then everyone felt the first tremors from beneath the ground. These increased as Riza started to physically move the entire planet.

It was the strangest sensation and almost reminded Emily of the Staten Island Ferry, which she used to take with her parents. On the ferry, she could feel the deep, steady rumbling of the large engines as the boat pulled away from the dock. At first it didn't move very fast, but the feeling belowdecks promised greater speed. This was almost the same. The feeling that there were great engines starting and soon the planet would move a lot faster.

Emily wasn't wrong. Before she finished the thought, she felt the rumbling increasing. The swirling colors above the protective field started to spin even faster. But the sun wasn't moving—they were!

Faster and faster the entire planet shifted as they pulled away from the blazing heat of the supernova and into darker space. The temperature dropped with each second as they left the sun's influence.

Before Emily could say anything, she felt a sudden, wrenching whoosh and saw the blazing light of the Solar Stream surrounding them. The Rheans around them clicked and growled in terror. It was obvious they'd never seen the Solar Stream before.

As always, it was impossible to gauge time and how long they had been in the Solar Stream. But after what seemed an eternity, Arious Minor started to scream. "Riza, slow us down. We're approaching Xanadu too fast!"

Emily looked over to Riza. Her head was still back and her eyes were clenched shut in concentration.

"Riza!" Emily shook the Xan's hand. "Slow us down!"

She tried to pull her hand free but discovered they were fused together. Nor could she break her connection with Pegasus. The collective power that had helped them move the planet was now keeping everyone bound together.

"Riza, wake up!" Emily shouted again. "You must stop us now!"

The small dot of light appeared before Emily's face. "Emily, she's unconscious. It's up to you now. Summon your power if you can. You must stop us if we are to survive. Do it now before we reach the end of the Solar Stream and are obliterated!"

Emily's heart was racing. She had allowed the ancient Xan complete control of her powers to move the planet. But now that Riza was unconscious, there was no one but her to pull them free of the Solar Stream. Emily shut her eyes and started to focus her thoughts. She summoned every ounce of power she had left to stop the planet.

Harder and harder she concentrated, until she felt a tearing in her head and burning in her whole body.

"Stop!" she shouted. With a final, heaving push, a hidden door in the deepest depths of her core flew open and unleashed an explosive power she'd never imagined possible. It was like a living thing, pouring through every cell of her body.

"I said stop!" she commanded with her mind.

As her power swelled, she heard dreadful scream-ing and howling from the others around her. Pegasus whinnied louder than she'd ever heard before. They were dying. She'd failed, and because of it, they were all dying. These were the final thoughts flashing through her mind as darkness overwhelmed her.

15

PAELEN BURST FREE OF THE SOLAR Stream high above Xanadu. The sun was just starting to set and the sky was a stunning crimson red. Joel, on Chrysaor, appeared right beside him, followed by Earl and Frankie riding the two Pegasus clones.

"This is Xanadu?" Frankie asked.

Joel nodded. "It is a beautiful place."

"It's a wonder," Frankie said as he gazed all around.

"You haven't really seen it yet," Joel said. "Wait till you see inside the Temple of Arious."

Paelen heard the exchange but was in no mood to add to it. His heart was heavy and he couldn't shake the feeling that somehow he'd betrayed

Lorin. He should never have let her come along. She was dead because of him.

Flying in silence, he led the group to the clear landing area outside the temple. He touched down and, without waiting for the others, stormed into the temple. "Emily? Pegasus? Riza?" he shouted.

Receiving no answer, he ran for the stairs and moved down deeper into the temple until he reached the chamber of Arious. Without knocking, he stormed in and heard the distinct hum of the Xan computer. "Arious, where are Emily and Riza? I need to see them immediately."

"Paelen, I am so glad you are here," the computer answered. "There is terrible trouble."

"I know. The Titans under Charing Cross murdered Lorin and stole her power. Now they are free."

"I'm not talking about that. I meant with Riza."

"Riza? What about her? Is she with Emily and Pegasus?"

"Yes, they are all on the remnants of Rhean."

"Where?"

"Rhean. It was a dying planet on the other side of the universe."

"What's she doing there?" Joel cried as he entered the temple.

Earl and Frankie were walking closely behind him. When Frankie's eyes saw Arious, he gasped and approached the main consul of the supercomputer.

"The Rhean sun is going to go supernova, and Riza went there to gather the survivors to bring here. But then Emily arrived with details of what happened on Earth. Both she and Riza felt Lorin die and know her powers are now within the mutant Titans."

"So what is the trouble?" Paelen asked.

"There was no time left to gather all the planet's survivors together to bring here. Instead, they decided to bring the whole planet. It is in the Solar Stream right now."

"They what?" Joel cried. "Can Riza actually do that?"

"I fear not," Arious said. "My counterpart, Arious Minor, is with them and tried to warn them. But Riza had to try. She joined with Emily, and they have united all the survivors together, hoping the combined energy would be enough to get them here. Riza managed to move Rhean into the Solar Stream. But it is doubtful that she can pull it out again."

"So what will happen?" Joel asked. "They'll be trapped inside the Solar Stream and just keep circling around in it?"

"No. Once they fly past Xanadu, they will reach the end of the Solar Stream. The planet and everything on it will be destroyed."

"No, that's not possible!" Joel cried. "They can't be destroyed, not now, not after everything we've been through."

The computer spoke softly. "Riza has great power, but she is a single Xan. Attempting this alone was beyond her abilities."

Paelen watched the pain rising on Joel's face and shared in it. He didn't think he could ever feel any worse after losing Lorin. He was wrong. His heart clenched with pain and fear for Emily.

"What can we do?" Paelen asked. "There must be something."

"There is little any of us can . . ." All of the lights on the Arious consul started to flash. "No, no, it's not possible . . . ," the computer cried. "Keep trying. You must wake her up!"

"What is it?" Paelen demanded.

"The strain is too much for Riza. She has fallen unconscious. She can't stop Rhean or free it from the pull of the Solar Stream!"

Just as Arious finished speaking, there was a peal of thunder so loud, it shook the whole temple, perhaps even Xanadu. Everyone in the computer room was knocked down to the floor with the violence of it.

"What was that?" Paelen cried.

"They are here," Arious cried. "Emily did it!" The computer consul started to hum even louder, and then a high-pitched siren sounded.

Paelen put his hands over his ears. "What is happening?"

Arious shouted back, "I am settling them in a safe orbit and sending out a gravitational field to protect the planet and give it an atmosphere."

The pitch and volume rose and drove everyone from the control room. They ran full speed through the immense temple and climbed the stairs two at a time. When they reached the clearing outside, the siren was still blaring but it no longer hurt. The all looked up and gasped.

A planet much bigger and closer than the three moons of Xanadu was now in orbit high above them. The setting sun's rays reflected on the surface, making the planet appear like a brilliant red ruby in the sky.

Moments later, a blazing beam of light shot up from the temple toward the planet. When it reached the surface, they saw the light beam split apart like a giant spiderweb and completely envelop Rhean in a protective field.

Joel collapsed to his knees. "I'm seeing it, but I just can't believe it. They moved a whole planet!"

"Look, Joel. Look at what Emily and Riza have achieved," Paelen said. "You must not let your own insecurities diminish her. They have saved a world. Who else but our Emily would attempt something so foolish and make it work?"

They gazed at the new addition to the Xanadu sky, hardly believing it was possible. As the night slowly descended, Rhean passed into shadow. They could no longer see its details, just the large black outline it cast, blocking the stars behind it.

Soon the sounds of the jungle around them changed. Gone were the birdsong and insects, replaced by the stranger calls of night animals as they started to wake. Not long after dark, the noisy sound of crashing through the trees started. Paelen recognized it and rose to his feet.

"Brue," he called as the large, two-headed, purple-furred Mother of the Jungle arrived. She trumpeted excitedly and started to dance on her feet like an excited puppy at the sight of Paelen.

After seeing the images of an older version of himself seated on her back, Paelen's feelings toward Brue had changed. He realized they had a bond that ran deeper than he imagined possible. Paelen opened his arms and embraced the massive animal. "I have missed you, my friend," he said into her long fur.

Brue responded by licking him all over with her two black tongues. For once, Paelen did not fight or protest the obvious show of affection.

Frankie looked up in stunned wonder at the Mother of the Jungle. "Wow. Is that really Brue?"

"It is, but you're safe. She won't hurt you," Joel said. "She lives here and is guardian of the jungle. As you can see, she really loves Paelen." He also climbed to his feet and greeted the large creature.

After everyone came forward to meet Brue, Earl looked back up at the world now in darkness. "So, you boys got any suggestions on how we get up there?" Earl asked.

"I was hoping they'd come down here," Joel answered.

The sound of urgent whinnies came from just inside the temple.

"That's Pegasus!" Paelen turned back to the temple entrance. "They have found a way to return."

Across the clearing, the two winged stallions reared and called a challenge to Pegasus.

"Oh no, not again!" Joel cried. "Everyone get inside now. We can't let Pegasus out here to fight those two."

Paelen stopped to listen to Pegasus calling. "He is not coming out," Paelen shouted as he started to run. "He is calling us in. He says we must hurry. Riza and Emily have collapsed."

Pegasus was already back inside by the time Paelen and the others entered the temple. They followed him down the stairs and deeper into the bowels of the ancient building and to the control room.

Cupid and a CRU agent were kneeling down on the floor, cradling Emily and Riza. A girl was seated beside them. When she saw them, she pointed. "I remember you—you are Paelen and Joel!"

Paelen's eyes flew open as the memories from the Titans returned. "And you are Stella." He looked at the agent. "And you are Agent B!"

"Boys, get over here!" Agent B said. He was cradling Riza's head. "They're both alive, but moving the planet was too much for them."

A small dot hovered over Riza's face and spoke in a high-pitched voice. "Riza used too much of herself to save Rhean."

Paelen approached the dot. "Who are you?"

"That's Arious Minor," Agent B said. "He's part of Arious here, like a satellite."

The dot started to buzz. "She is in grave danger and must be supported."

Behind them a wall panel opened and a bed slid out. "Agent B," Arious Major said. "Please place Riza on the bed. I will take care of her."

The CRU agent lifted Riza off the floor and carried her to the bed. When she was settled, the bed slid back into the panel.

"What about Emily?" Joel demanded. "How is she?"

"She is just unconscious and will recover," Arious Major said.

Joel knelt down and reached for Emily. "I've got her," he said to Cupid.

Cupid's eyes turned hard, and he refused to surrender Emily to him. "Now you have her? After ignoring her and leaving her alone? You are no friend, Joel. You proclaimed your love for her, but when Emily needed you, you abandoned her. She felt she had to go on this quest alone. Now look at her. She used herself up to pull us out of the Solar Stream."

He shoved Joel away. "You do not deserve the love she holds for you. My only hope is when she wakes, she sees you for what you really are—a selfish, weak human."

Rage rose on Joel's face, but it soon faded. He

sighed and lowered his head. "You're right. I've been a mega idiot. But why did she face the Titans without us? Why didn't she come to me?"

Pegasus nickered softly and shook his head.

Paelen also lowered his head as he translated. "Pegasus says she felt she couldn't ask us. I was too busy with Lorin, and you hid yourself away in Vulcan's forge. She knows you do not love her anymore."

Joel looked at Emily and reached for her hand. "But I do love her. I love her more than anything."

"Why did you not tell her?" Cupid asked.

"Because I was stupid, all right?" Joel said, almost shouting. "Look at her. She's beautiful, wonderful, and does all these amazing things. Why would she ever choose someone like me, just a dumb human who works in a forge, when she could have anyone?"

"Because she loves you," Agent B said.

"But she's changed completely. She doesn't need me."

"Emily has changed yet again," Arious Minor said. "Will you walk away when you discover how?"

Paelen and Joel looked closely at Emily as she lay in Cupid's arms.

"I do not see any changes," Paelen said.

"Not all changes are on the outside," Arious Minor said.

"What has happened to her?" Agent B asked.

"It is not for me to tell. When she wakes, I will inform her. After that, she may decide to share this knowledge with you or not."

Once again, Arious Major made an electronic sound, and the room hummed. A second panel opened and a bed slid out. "Put her on it. She needs to rest and recover from the strain."

Cupid lifted Emily and carried her over to the bed. He lay her down and kissed her softly. "I will be waiting for you outside," he said.

"All of you will leave now," Arious Major said, "except Pegasus."

"Why does he get to stay when I have to go?" Joel protested.

Paelen put his arm around him. "Come, Joel. Leave her to rest. We will all wait outside."

Paelen, Joel, and the others watched as the bed slipped into the panel, taking Emily away with it.

EMILY WOKE IN DARKNESS AND INSTANTLY panicked. She reached up and felt the tight walls that confined her. She had no idea where she was or how she'd gotten there. Had she been buried alive? Was she trapped in a box and being taken somewhere? The last thing she remembered was holding Riza's hand and fighting to slow Rhean down enough to escape the Solar Stream. What had happened?

"Welcome back, Emily," a voice said.

"Arious? Is that you?"

She heard a soft hum and was relieved to see the light pouring into the tight cubicle as the door at her feet swished open. The bed beneath her started to move, and she was freed from the dark enclosure.

Emily sat up and gazed around, realizing she was on a recovery bed in the chamber of Arious.

Pegasus whinnied excitedly and pressed his head in closer to her.

"I'm all right," she said softly as she stroked his soft muzzle. "Just a little dizzy. I'm sure it will pass."

Emily climbed off the bed and leaned against Pegasus. She gazed around and saw they were the only ones in the chamber. "Where is Riza? Is she all right? What about the Rheans? Did we save them?"

Arious didn't answer for some time. Finally he said, "Riza is in stasis."

"What's stasis?"

"It is a kind of suspended animation. She hurt herself badly when she moved Rhean. It was too big for her."

Fear gripped Emily. "Is she going to be all right?"

"I do not know," Arious answered softly. "She is within me, and I am doing all I can to support her. But it will take time for her to recover—if she recovers."

"She has to," Emily said. "I need her. We all do."

"She knows how much you care. I am sure if she

can recover, she will. In the meantime, Emily, there is something important you must do."

"Is it about the Rheans? Did we fail?"

"No. Just the opposite. Because of you and Riza, they are in a safe and stable orbit above Xanadu. I have set up an artificial atmosphere and gravity. Initial scans suggest that this may work. Before long, they will not need my support and their environment will recover naturally. You both did well."

"So they'll live?"

"Yes, Emily, they will, and I am certain they will thrive."

Emily rested her head against Pegasus, grateful for the good news. With everything else going wrong, it was a relief to know that at least one thing they'd tried had worked.

"Emily, please step onto the platform. There is a message waiting for you."

"Can it wait? I want find out how the Rheans are and the latest on the mutant Titans."

"No, it cannot wait. Please step up on the platform."

There was something in Arious's voice that left

little doubt that this was important. Emily gave Pegasus a gentle pat. "I need to do this. Remember not to touch me when I'm inside. I don't want you hurt."

Pegasus nickered and nodded. He walked beside her as she made her way to the docking consul.

"I'll be right back."

Emily stepped forward and placed her two hands on the receiving ports. It was here that she could connect directly with Arious and the archives of the ancient Xan. Almost immediately she felt the tight link setting up. Images of the past flashed through her head. She closed her eyes and waited to receive the message.

"Emily," a voice called. "Open your eyes, please."

Emily did as she was told and looked around. She was on the surface of Xanadu. The jungle looked as it always had but was strangely silent. When she turned to look back at the temple, she saw Riza's father.

"Emily, my child," he said, coming forward.

When he stopped, he stood above her, almost nine feet in height. His beautiful Xan face was pearly white and shone with iridescence. It was filled with peace.

His eyes, just like Riza's, were like living pearls. He reached out his long, fine-boned hands to her.

Emily took hold of his hands. "Sir."

He actually smiled, and it brightened his serene face even more. "Of course, I never did tell you my name. And I doubt my daughter would have either. I am Yird."

"Yird," Emily repeated. "Am I dreaming, or are you really here?"

This time Yird actually chuckled. "Neither. But I doubt you would understand. I am here, but I am not. However, I do know that you have completed the next stage of your metamorphosis. I must tell you what is to come."

Emily knew the word "metamorphosis" meant "change." A caterpillar went through metamorphosis to become a butterfly, but she had no idea what it meant in regard to her. "I'm sorry, I don't understand."

"Child, you and Lorin were never meant to exist. That you did was an accident caused by Riza when she tried to follow us into the cosmos. In her failure, everything changed. She destroyed herself, and pieces of her remains were cast out into space. The heart of the Flame, as you knew it, crashed on Olympus and fed its powers to the Olympians. The core was then hidden in a human child and passed through the ages. But along the way it changed. It changed and it became you."

This was what Emily understood about her powers and how she'd come to be the Flame of Olympus.

"But it was more than that," he said, reading her mind. "Riza's spirit entered you as well. Another large part of my daughter crashed on Titus and entered Lorin—though she remained unconscious until you summoned her."

"I didn't summon her."

"You did," he said. "You just didn't know it. You two were tightly connected from the very beginning because you came from the same source. That connection sealed when you touched on Diamond Head."

"Yes, but it kinda destroyed us. That's why you had to give me this new body."

His lovely head nodded. "Yes, I did. But there was something I failed to tell you, because knowing would serve no one."

Emily felt the first tremors of fear. "Yes . . . ," she said softly.

Yird smiled again. "Do not fear. You are safe—now."

"Now?"

He nodded. "When I removed most of the powers of the Xan from you and Lorin, I knew I was condemning you both to death. You were born with it and needed it to survive. But I had to remove it. You were both too young to handle such power."

Emily could barely breathe. "So, I'm dying?"

He shook his head. "Not anymore. My daughter saved you when she slipped some of herself into you. She thinks I didn't see, but I did. However, Lorin received no such gift. Had the mutant Titans not killed her, she would have died soon anyway."

"Did she know?"

"Yes. When she started to feel unwell, Riza told her the truth and suggested she savor each day she had left. But she gave up her remaining time to save the others. Her sacrifice must be remembered."

"I will tell everyone," Emily said. "But it may not help. If you know what happened to Lorin, you know the mutants are free. They will destroy us all."

"They may, but then again, they may not."

"How can we stop it? I don't have that kind of power anymore. Lorin is dead, and Riza is very sick. I'm frightened she's going to die too."

He smiled gently. "She will not die—she cannot die. But she does need time to recover."

"Then will you stop the Titans?"

"I cannot. I no longer possess the power."

Emily lowered her head in shame. "I caused all of this. I should never have used my powers against the Titans in Tartarus. You said my actions had consequences, and you were right. Now the Olympians and Titans will die because of me."

Yird's brows came together in a light frown. "I do not understand something. You knew the Olympians were in danger, yet you offered what little power you had to Riza to save the Rheans. Why would you do that?"

"Their sun was dying."

"True. But you were prepared to use yourself up to save them instead of waiting to save the Olympians. Why did you choose one over the other?"

"I didn't choose one over the other. Their need was more immediate. I couldn't let their sun kill them if I had the power to help stop it. It was the only thing to do. They deserved a chance to live like everyone else."

"Even though they are nothing like you and there was nothing to be gained by doing so?"

"You're wrong. There was everything to gain—their whole world, their cultures, and all the wild-life. All of that would have been destroyed if we didn't try."

"What about the Olympians? What will you do now?"

Emily shrugged. "I don't know. But I must try something. The Titans were turned into those monsters because of me. I did that. So if I have any power left, I'll use it to stop them from destroying Olympus and Titus."

"You wish to save both worlds even though Saturn tried to kill you?"

"Well, yeah. I can't let those monsters kill the Titans any more than I'd let them kill the Olympians."

"Why?"

"The truth is I always hoped that one day they would make peace with each other. I mean, they are all one family."

The Xan nodded his head. "Very true."

"So please, Yird, can you help us? Even a little bit of your power is a lot more than we have. You could end this whole thing in a second."

"I told you, I have no power left." He paused and tilted his head to the side. "I gave it all to you."

Emily frowned. "No, you didn't, because I can hardly do anything!"

"Believe me, child, I did. But I hid it from you. Only now is it starting to awaken. You felt the first change when Riza was unable to stop Rhean from being destroyed in the Solar Stream. You called upon the power and it was there for you."

"I don't understand."

"You, Emily, stand on the threshold of a new beginning. But the choice must always be yours. When I was building your new body, Riza shared with me all that you had both been through. She said you were young but you were growing. She believed you could control your powers and use them for good. She had absolute faith in you and told me you were worthy of them. I must admit, I did not hold such faith in you.

"But as there was only one opportunity to do this,

Riza begged me to try. While you slept, I put all the powers that I possessed into you. But I locked them away behind two psychic doors. In your fear for the Rheans, you broke down the first door and accessed some of the power."

"I felt it!" Emily said. "When we were in the Solar Stream, I really felt it."

"Yes," he said, and then frowned again. "I still find it perplexing that you did not use those powers to save yourself on Earth when the Titan consumed you. But you did when the Rheans needed you most. Your concern for their safety over your own convinced me that you are ready."

"Do I really have your powers?" Emily asked softly.

"Some, but not all are available to you yet," he said. "There is one more door yet to open. But the moment you do, you will change irrevocably. You will no longer be Emily of Earth, or even Emily of Olympus. You will truly be Emily—a full Xan. You may look as you do now, but nothing of you will be the same. You will become as Riza is. You will have all the powers of the Xan at your command. But you will be expected to take up the duties of the Xan. You will work with my daughter to protect Xanadu and to seek out dying worlds and bring their inhabitants here. This is an enormous responsibility, Emily, and not one to be taken lightly. Once you agree, there will be no going back."

Emily inhaled deeply. "Do I have to decide now?"

He smiled gently. "I would rather you didn't. This is too large a decision to be made hastily. But if you decide you do not want this, you must tell Riza. She and Arious know what they must do to neutralize the power."

"Will it kill me?"

"No. Riza will see to that. But should you choose to accept this offer, the second door will not be opened so easily. You must ask for it. I have set a special lock in place, a lock that can be opened only in time of great need. Then you must call out your mother's full name and tell her to open the door. She is the guardian at the door to eternity. She is the one who will free the power and set you on your course of final metamorphosis."

It all seemed so impossible to take in. Emily looked at the Xan before her, standing so calm, as if they had been talking about the weather on a sunny afternoon and not the monumental decision she had to make.

He smiled at her a final time. "It is time for you to go back," he said lightly. The tall Xan leaned down and kissed Emily on the top of her head. "I am sure you will make the right decision."

When he straightened, he gazed up. "We are finished, Arious. Cease communication."

Emily staggered backward out of the consul. Pegasus was waiting for her and came forward. He nickered softly.

"I—I'm fine," Emily said. She walked over to the computer. "Arious, did you hear all that?"

"Yes, Emily."

"May I tell the others?"

"You are not forbidden to. But as you know, ultimately, the decision must be yours."

Emily walked back to Pegasus knowing she could never tell the others. This was too big to put on them, and it would only confuse her. But there was one that she knew she could always trust with everything. As she gazed up into the stallion's beautiful eyes, she smiled. "Pegs, I really need to tell you something. . . ."

EMILY AND PEGASUS WALKED OUT OF THE chamber of Arious. The moment the large door opened, she found Joel, Paelen, and Chrysaor waiting in the corridor outside it. Joel jumped to his feet and ran over to her.

"Em, Em, I'm so sorry. I've been such a jerk and I hurt you. Please forgive me. It doesn't matter what you look like—tall, short, fat, slim—just as long as you're okay. That we're okay."

Emily was stunned by his reaction and could see the sincerity in his eyes. "You hurt me, Joel," she said softy. "You turned away from me just because I changed. Do you have any idea how that felt?"

"I know, and I feel terrible about it. The problem

was with me, not you. I've been so insecure that I just didn't handle the change very well. When I saw the new you, I thought I lost you because you were so much better than me. Beautiful and powerful. I didn't think you would care for me anymore."

"So you decided to hurt me first and push me away before I could hurt you—as if I ever would." Emily knew this wasn't the time to confront him with all the bigger issues happening. But somehow, all the hurt came pouring out. "What would you do if I changed again? Give in to your insecurities and walk away?"

"No, never. I know I've been stupid." He looked over to Paelen. "Actually, I had a lot of help being shown how stupid I've been. Paelen and Cupid were right. How you've changed doesn't matter. What does is that you are still the same wonderful person. It's *you* whom I love. Not just your pretty face."

"You what?"

"I know I should have said this long ago. . . ." He paused. "Actually, I did say it a very long time ago, but I should have kept saying it. I love you, Emily Jacobs. I love you more than anything in my life, and I couldn't bear to lose you. Please, please forgive me."

Emily hesitated. "I—I don't know, Joel. After everything we've been through, you turned away from me just because I physically changed."

"I know," he cried. "It was dumb and selfish and stupid, and I'll regret it for the rest of my life. But please, Em, please forgive me. It was a terrible mistake. . . ."

"You hurt me, Joel," Emily repeated. "Badly."

"And I'm going to spend the rest of my life making it up to you."

Paelen cleared his throat. "And speaking of that life, it may not be very long if the Titans have their way."

"Emily, listen to me," Joel implored. "We are going into our biggest fight yet. But I can't face it if I don't have you with me. Please don't leave me. Not now . . ."

Emily looked back at Pegasus and he looked away—telling her the decision was hers alone. Finally she reached forward and slapped Joel hard across the face. "Joel DeSilva, if you ever do that to me again, I swear I will send you so far across the universe that not even Riza could find you!"

"I swear I won't!" Joel promised. "Does that mean you forgive me?"

Emily sighed. "All right, all right. I forgive you."

Joel's eyes flew open wide, and he scooped her up in his arms. "I love you, Emily Jacobs, and I don't care who knows it!"

Emily put her arms around him and felt all the hurt and anger melting away. When he released her, she frowned. "But, Joel, how do you know about the past?"

"Those mutant Titans showed us—they showed us everything."

"But how did you know about them?"

Paelen started to speak. "After the silver beach, I felt so bad for what happened I went to see you. Tom told us where you had gone, and we had to follow you. But we never expected to find what we found under Charing Cross. Those creatures were terrifying."

"What about Earl and Frankie? Are they all right?"

"They're here," Joel said. "We freed everyone, including the clones."

Joel and Paelen went in to details of their time

under Charing Cross Station. Emily was shocked to hear that Vulcan had gone as well. "Is he here? Has he seen Stella?"

Joel shook his head. "He took the clones and went back to Olympus to warn Jupiter. We came here to see if you were all right. Arious told us about Rhean." He grinned at her. "My Emily, superhero and savior of worlds."

Emily shook her head and smiled. "Not quite."

"So we're all right?" he asked hesitantly. "I mean, you and me?"

Emily could feel his guilt and shame for turning away from her. But she wasn't going to make it easy for him. She turned to Paelen. "Should I forgive him everything?"

Paelen nodded. "Please. He will be impossible to live with if you do not."

"Hey," Joel protested.

Emily smiled at him. "All right, I'll forgive you, but only to save Paelen."

Joel grinned and pulled her close. When they parted, Emily turned to Paelen. "I'm sorry about Lorin."

"She gave her life for me," Paelen said softly. At the mention of her name, tears sparkled in his eyes, but he refused to let them fall.

Emily took both his hands in hers. "She loved you. I know that. But I must tell you something that I hope eases your pain." Emily wondered how best to tell him. Finally she said softly, "Paelen, Lorin was dying."

He nodded. "I know. She told me . . . at the end."

"What?" Joel cried.

"When Riza's father removed most of her Xan powers," Emily started, "her body couldn't cope. Mine couldn't either, but Riza gave some of herself to me, so we could be sisters, and it saved my life. Lorin didn't receive any and had very little time left. She gave up what she had to save you."

Joel lowered her head. "She was dying and I was so mean to her."

"Me too," Emily said. "I should have tried harder to be friends."

Paelen dropped his head. "She was jealous of you because of Pegasus—she did not want to be your friend. But even so, I loved her. . . ."

"I know you did." Emily reached for Paelen and held him tight. She whispered in his ear, "I also know you'll find someone special who will see you for the wonderful person that you are."

Paelen shook his head. "No. I think I have had enough of love. Right now, all I want to do is destroy those Titans who killed Lorin."

"And I'm going to help you," she said softly. "We just have to figure out how. They have so much power. They nearly absorbed me. If it hadn't been for Riza's ring, I would be dead too."

"Lorin's Flame couldn't hurt them," Paelen said.

"Mine couldn't either. Nothing I tried worked. If I'm honest, I'm not even sure they can be destroyed."

"Perhaps the Big Three can do it."

"I hope so," Emily agreed. "I did kinda have another idea, but it's a really bad one. But fighting those mutant Titans is like trying to wrestle with a bag of water. We're going to need all the help we can get."

"What's your idea?" Joel asked.

Emily walked over to Pegasus for reassurance. "Now, don't hate me for suggesting this. But we know those three Titans—"

"Two," Paelen corrected.

"There were three mutant Titans under Charing Cross."

"Yes, and when one of them consumed Lorin, the other two consumed it to take his power and Lorin's. They are even more powerful now."

Emily dropped her head. "Then my bad idea may be the only one left to us."

"Emily, stop waffling and tell us," Joel said.

"All right, we know those two mutant Titans exist because of me. If I hadn't fired on them in Tartarus, they would never have been created."

"And . . . ," Paelen said.

"And I think we should go talk to Saturn to find out who they were and if he can help us."

Joel nodded his head. "You are so right. . . . That's the worst idea ever! Saturn is the one who started the war, remember? He wants us dead. Now you want to go ask him for help?"

"Yes," Emily said. "Look, those mutant Titans aren't really Titans anymore. They're monsters. Creatures that have absorbed so many beings they don't even have real bodies—just that gelatinous goo. They told me their plan. They are going to absorb all the Olympians and then go after the Titans. Individually we can't defeat them. But maybe united we can. It's in everyone's best interest to work together."

"She's right," Agent B said.

Joel turned back to him. "That is just like a CRU agent! Creeping around and spying on people."

"I'm not spying, Joel. I came for an update on Emily and Riza." He approached Emily. "I'm relieved to see you up and around. How is Riza? Is there any news?"

Emily nodded. "She's recovering; it's just going to take time. Maybe more time than we have, considering the three Titans are now two and that much more powerful."

Agent B nodded. "I heard."

"How was the arrival at Xanadu? Were the Rheans all right?" she asked.

He laughed and combed his fingers through his long dark curly hair. "It was a bumpy ride, that's for sure. But thanks to you and Riza, we all made it. Arious transported us down here."

"What?" Emily cried. "Arious can do that?"

Agent B nodded. "Very quickly too."

Emily stormed up to the supercomputer. "Arious, is it true? You can transport people?"

"Yes."

"Why didn't you tell me?"

"Technically, you never asked."

"Em, if you're still thinking of going to Titus to speak to Saturn, you're crazy. He'll kill you."

"No, he won't." She paused and frowned. "At least I don't think so. Pegasus and I saw him in a magic well that Urania has on Mount Helicon. It showed Saturn sitting all alone in his throne room. Urania says she's been watching him. He's changed. They all have. The Titans are more focused on living than attacking the Olympians."

"What makes you think Saturn can help us?" Agent B said.

"You saw him from my memories. He's Jupiter's father and has a lot of power. If we can get him to agree, he might join with his sons. With all the Olympians working with the Titans, there is a chance we could defeat the mutants."

"There's also a chance he may attack us."

Emily nodded. "I know. But we have to risk it."

"There is one other problem," Paelen put forth. "Riza's father banned all travel between Titus and Olympus. Even if Saturn agreed to help us, he could not come to Olympus to do it. Nor could the Big Three go to him."

"Oh, that's right," Emily mused. Then she remembered. She held up her hand with the ring. "Arious, this ring that Riza gave to me, it had the power to transport us across the universe. Does that mean you can create gemstones to open the Solar Stream like the ones we used to have?"

"This is not something I should be doing," Arious said. "Yird was very clear on that."

"Who's Yird?" Joel asked.

"That's Riza's dad," Emily said. She looked back at the supercomputer. "But you know what will happen if we don't get the Titans to help us. Please, tell me. Can you create the gemstones for the Solar Stream?"

"Theoretically, yes, I can. But I dare not make them portable. I will make a deal with you. . . ."

"Wait," Joel said. "You're a computer that makes deals?"

"I am more than that," Arious said.

"He is," Emily agreed. "So, what's the deal?"

Sometime later, they walked out of the temple toward the camp. Earl, Frankie, Stella, and Cupid were seated before a fire. Brue was standing over Frankie, washing him with her two tongues.

Emily ran forward and embraced her friends. When she hugged Earl, she said, "I can't believe you guessed it was me. How soon after we arrived in the cell did you know?"

Earl grinned and walked over to Pegasus. "I knew from the moment you opened your mouth. You might have changed on the outside, but on the inside, you are still the same."

"So you knew right away it was me."

"Course. Any kinda fool could see that."

Emily shot a look at Joel and raised her eyebrows.

"I know, I know," he said. "So shoot me!"

"Don't tempt me," Emily said.

The two Pegasus clones whinnied loudly to Pegasus. Emily looked at Pegasus and then to the clones. All of the stallions had flared nostrils and wild, angry eyes.

"Oh, no, Pegs, not again!" Emily warned. "You know they're just clones. Ignore them, no matter what they say to you."

Emily crossed the clearing and approached the two winged stallions. "Both of you will stop that this moment!" she chastised. "He is not your enemy."

The two clones' nostrils continued to flare, but the whinnying stopped. They snorted, pounded the ground, but stayed where they were.

"Don't know how long that truce will hold," Earl said. "Them stallions sure wanna tussle."

Frankie joined Emily by the two clones and started to pet their muzzles. "Calm down, boys. Just calm down."

Emily raised her eyebrows at him.

"That boy sure has some talent," Earl said. "If it ain't computers, it's critters. Even big old Brue likes him."

"I like animals," Frankie called back.

"That's a great thing," Emily said. "Please, would you keep them calm if you can?"

"So," Earl said, rubbing his hands together. "What's the plan?"

"Emily's come up with a suicide mission," Joel said.

"It's not suicide," Emily said, walking back to the fire. "And you don't have to come if you don't want to."

"Oh no. I nearly lost you once. Never again!"

Paelen stepped forward. "Emily would like us to speak with Saturn to ask for his help going against the mutant Titans."

"What?" Cupid cried, jumping to his feet.

"Saturn? Ain't he the one that started the war?"

"Yes!" Joel cried. "See, Em, it's a crazy idea."

"No, it ain't," Earl said. "Them blobs plan to attack the Titans as well. The more of them we have on our side, the better."

Emily stuck her tongue out at Joel. "See? Now who's crazy?"

"He will never side with us," Cupid said. "He will celebrate our demise."

"Not if we tell him they're next," Emily insisted.

Stella was seated on a long fallen log. "Shouldn't we tell the Olympians the plan so they don't start fighting the Titans again?"

Emily looked at Stella and remembered what a

good strategist she was. "You're right. We should. Besides, Arious is going to give us two gemstones that must be mounted in Olympus and Titus to allow travel between the two worlds—so half of us could go to one place and the rest to the other."

"Fine," Agent B said. "Emily and I will engage the Titans. Cupid, you and the others can go back to Olympus."

"What?" Joel cried. "You aren't seriously going to do this? It's insane. I agree with telling the Olympians the plan. It is their world. They should have some say. We can't just go to the Titans and invite them to the party without asking Jupiter first."

"All right," Emily said. "Will it make you happy if we talk to Jupiter first?"

"Yes!" Joel cried. "It will make me ecstatic."

"Me too," Cupid agreed. But then he frowned when he and Joel looked at each other, realizing they were both on the same side.

"All right," Agent B said. "Olympus first. But let's get moving!"

Earl leaned in closer to Emily. "Hope you don't mind, but I think Frank and me'll sit this one out."

He nodded toward Frankie, who was still with the Pegasus clones. "He ain't doin' so hot after seein' them blobs eat you and then Lorin—can't say I blame him. But bein' here is doing wonders for him—especially with those two big boys over there."

Emily and others looked over to Frankie standing with the stallions. "That's fine, Earl," Emily said gently. "Stay here with him. You can tell Riza what's happening when she wakes. Until then, I can leave some extra food for you. If you need anything else, just ask Arious."

"Remember," Cupid warned. "This is a world of peace. Do not kill anything here. Not a plant or even an insect. They will not harm you, so you must not harm them. If you are uncertain about anything, ask Arious."

"Will do," Earl said.

The team made their way back into the temple and down into Arious's chamber. Inside, the supercomputer opened a large drawer that held two gleaming brick-size black gemstones.

"These are the stones," Arious said. "They must be mounted against a solid wall. You will approach them and call out your destination. The Solar Stream will open for you." The computer paused. "Emily, remember what Yird said. This is a test of your respon- sibility and trustworthiness. It is part of your meta- morphosis. Please do not betray our faith in you."

Emily looked at Pegasus and nodded. "I under- stand. You can trust me."

"Then you may take the stones."

As Emily lifted the stones from the drawer, Joel came up to her. "What metamorphosis? What's he talking about?"

"It's complicated," Emily said. "I'll tell you later."

Joel didn't look satisfied, but he simply nodded. "We're all right, aren't we?"

Emily smiled. "Yes, we are. But right now there's a lot happening. If we survive this, I promise I'll tell you everything."

"If?"

She nodded. "If."

"Well, on that cheery note, I think we should be going," Agent B offered.

Emily went up to the computer console. "Arious Minor, are you coming?"

The small dot appeared. "I thought you would never ask!"

Back on the surface, Paelen approached Stella and knelt before her. "I remember you," he said to her. "We were once good friends. It would be an honor to carry you to Olympus."

Stella actually blushed as he lifted her into his arms. "I remember you too. But you didn't look the same. You were very old."

"I am not old now."

Stella's cheeks turned brighter red as she put her arms around his neck. "No, you're not."

Emily climbed up on Pegasus. Agent B settled behind her and slid his arms around her waist. "Just like old times," she said to him.

"Very true."

"When this is over, remind me to give you your journal back."

His dark eyebrows rose. "I forgot about that. You didn't read it, did you?"

Emily grinned at him. "I might have glanced at it . . . once or twice."

"We'll have to have a talk about boundaries later," he said sternly.

"That is definitely like old times." She laughed.

Earl and Frankie came over to say their final good-byes. "Y'all be careful," Earl said.

"We will," Emily promised. She looked down at Frankie. "You'll take care of the two stallions, won't you?"

He nodded, and looked back at the Mother of the Jungle. "And Brue, if she'll let me."

"She will," Paelen said.

Emily leaned forward on the stallion's back. "This is it, Pegs. Let's go home."

Pegasus whinnied and pawed the ground. He started to trot and entered a full gallop before opening his white wings and soaring into the sky.

THE MOMENT THEY BURST THROUGH THE
Solar Stream and into the bright skies above
Olympus, they could see that something was ter-
ribly wrong. The parts of Olympus that had been
rebuilt now lay in ruins again, and fires burned and
smoldered within the rubble.

"Please tell me this is damage from the old war
and not from the mutant Titans," Agent B said.

Emily shook her head. "It's the mutants; they're
here."

She wasn't the only one who could feel their presence. Pegasus whinnied and started to tremble. The
feeling of malevolence was much stronger here than
at Charing Cross. Fear clutched her heart as she

gazed down on the swath of destruction. Everyone she loved was here: her father, her aunt, and all the Olympians. How many had died?

"Emily . . . ," Paelen said.

"I know they're here," she said. "And they're so much stronger. Paelen, ask your sandals to take us to Jupiter. We must find him."

Cupid swooped in close to Pegasus. "I am not going to Jupiter," he called. "I must find my mother first and make sure she is all right."

"I understand," Emily said. "When you do, meet us back at Tom and Alexis's cave. That may still be safe."

Cupid nodded and flew harder in the direction of his home.

Emily looked at Paelen. "Lead on. Take us to Jupiter!"

Paelen called down to his sandals. Immediately they circled around in the sky and headed in the opposite direction.

Beneath them, the crisscrossing trails of destruction were everywhere. Emily couldn't see any dead or wounded on the ground. She didn't see anyone at all. Had the mutants actually devoured everyone they encountered?

"Where are the wounded?" Agent B mused aloud, as though reading her thoughts. "I can't imagine a people as strong as the Olympians being defeated."

"That's what scares me," Emily agreed.

They continued through the ruined landscape away from the central city. Soon they arrived at Mount Helicon. Once again, the damage seemed absolute, with not a building left standing.

Not only was there damage to the buildings, but it seemed the mutant Titans were devouring all life in their path. Emily saw huge areas of bare, open ground with no trees, plants, or animals of any kind.

"They're eating everything!" Joel cried. "Look, there's nothing but black dirt down there. They're even eating the grass!"

Paelen dropped lower as his sandals took him down toward the side of Mount Helicon. They alit on a sharp outcropping that was barely large enough for Pegasus and Chrysaor to land. At first it appeared deserted, but when Emily slid off the stallion's back, she spied a small cave opening.

"Jupiter, are you in there?"

The opening widened and Jupiter limped out. "Emily child, you're alive!" He embraced her tightly. "We feared the worst. Come in, come in. The council is here. We are trying to work out a strategy against these monsters."

At her touch, Jupiter's many wounds started to heal. He inhaled deeply and thanked her. Then he waved his hand in the air. The entrance widened further until it was large enough to allow Pegasus through. Once they were in, he shut it again.

Inside the spacious cave, Emily was relieved to see many of her favorite Olympians who made up the war council. Pluto and Neptune rushed forward. "Thank the stars," Neptune said as he embraced Emily and then Pegasus.

The centaur, Chiron, was there. His bare chest bore the scars of battle, and he was grateful to be healed by Emily. Behind him was one of the giant Hundred-handers. He had to crouch down to fit into the cave.

Athena, Juno, and countless other Olympians came forward to welcome them. Their clothes were in tatters and looked like they had been caught up in a ferocious battle. Emily greeted them all, but as she searched among their ranks, she couldn't see her father or Diana.

"Jupiter, where's my dad?"

"I do not know," he answered gravely. "He and my daughter fled in the opposite direction when those strange Titans attacked. We have all scattered across Olympus, trying to escape their onslaught—so many have already fallen to them."

"How bad is it?" Agent B asked as he slid down from Pegasus.

Jupiter's eyes widened in surprise. "Agent B, you're back!"

"Yes, and I'm so sorry. I'm partly responsible for this mess. If the CRU hadn't imprisoned me, Emily would not have tried to rescue me."

Emily shook her head. "No, it was me. I created those monsters when I used my powers against Saturn on Tartarus. They were the ones who started the CRU and were using them to gain more power."

"Blame is irrelevant," Jupiter said. "What we need is a way to stop them."

"Can't you?" Joel cried. "You're Jupiter, the strongest Olympian there is. You must be able to destroy them."

Jupiter shook his head. "Their powers are beyond me and continue to grow with each victim they absorb. I have used my most powerful lightning storms without success. Even dropping huge chunks of buildings does nothing to slow them. It passes right through them as though they had no substance at all."

"They are beyond all of us," Pluto added. "Nothing we try works against them."

"How is this possible?" Paelen asked. "You are the Big Three! You have more power than all of us."

Jupiter nodded his head. "We have, but it makes no difference. Those creatures have no bodies to harm, no minds to manipulate. No amount of lightning, flood, or death seems to touch them. They are consuming our world, and we are helpless to stop them."

Joel looked at Emily with haunted eyes. "You were right. It's the only way."

"What is?" Jupiter demanded. "What can be done? Is Riza coming?"

Emily shook her head and quickly explained that

Riza was in a coma and couldn't help. Then she told them about her idea to engage the Titans in the fight.

Jupiter shook his head. "Asking my father is madness. He would rather see us destroyed than lift a finger to help."

"Is it any crazier than doing nothing?" Agent B asked. "Jupiter, you're a smart man. You must realize that you're as good as defeated by those blobs. What more could Saturn do to you that these monsters haven't already done?"

"B is correct." Vulcan emerged from the back of the cave. He was covered in bruises and his face had a deep cut. His artificial legs were missing, and he stood unsteadily on withered, deformed limbs that lifted him no taller than Jupiter's waist. But despite his height, he was still an imposing sight.

"Vulcan!" Joel cried in greeting. "What happened to you?"

"Those filthy blobs nearly had me. They caught me by my golden legs and tried to eat me. I had to cut myself free to escape being absorbed."

Emily reached forward and touched Vulcan's arm, healing his wounds. But no matter how strong her healing powers were, she could do nothing to restore his deformed legs.

"Vulcan?" Stella called. She was frowning as the memories surfaced. "Vulcan, I remember you!"

Vulcan looked up and peered around Pegasus. When his eyes landed on Stella in Paelen's arms, his face brightened. "My Stella, how I have missed you!" He struggled over to Paelen and pulled her down from his arms to embrace her tightly. His hard eyes went up to Paelen. "Why did you bring her here? It is not safe!"

"Nowhere is safe," Emily said. "That's the point. Unless we find a way to destroy those two mutants, they will devour Olympus and then go straight to Titus. We must make a stand against them now, before this whole world is devoured."

"Jupiter, please be honest," Joel said. "Does Saturn have more power than you?"

Jupiter glanced at his two brothers. They looked beaten and defeated. He dropped his head. "Individually, yes, he absolutely does. But together we are equal to him."

Emily mused, "So if we could convince him to join

this fight, and if you all united your powers against them, it might be enough to defeat the mutants."

Neptune shook his head, and his blue eyes were dark as a stormy sea. "He will not do that. Our father will celebrate our demise, not help to stop it."

"Even if he knew Titus was next?" Paelen offered.

Jupiter looked to his brothers, then to the rest of the war council. "You have been with me from the beginning. We have seen off two Titan wars and a Nirad invasion. But now, I fear, this could be our undoing. Tell me your thoughts. Do we seek the assistance of the Titans, or try to evacuate Olympus?"

Emily shook her head. "I am sorry, Jupiter, but evacuation won't work even if you could get everyone to Earth or Xanadu. Those mutants will follow you. They already have their sights set on Xanadu after Titus. Then Earth. After that, who knows where? They must be stopped here or there will be no future for any of us."

Vulcan was holding Stella and nodded gravely. "Emily is correct. I have seen their power up close. They are unlike any enemy we have ever faced before. None of us can stand against them, and no weapon can stop them—it is like using a sword to fight the sea. We are actually feeding them with each and every Olympian they absorb. Soon they will grow too large for any of us to defeat."

"What are you suggesting we do?" Jupiter asked.

Vulcan shrugged. "The only thing we can do—appeal to Saturn for help. I would rather sit in Tartarus, if that is what he demands, than watch Olympus be devoured."

Agent B came forward. "Come on, Jupiter, you know this is the only solution. Those blobs are eating Olympus alive. I for one don't want to see the same thing happen on Earth. And we all know it will."

"We have to give this plan a chance," Pluto said. He looked at Emily, and his dark eyes were filled with sadness. "Go to Saturn. Tell him I will surrender myself to him if he helps us defeat these monsters."

Neptune lowered his head. "I will do the same. I too will hand myself over to him in exchange for his help."

There were grumblings of agreement from the full war council. Finally Jupiter nodded. "It is agreed, then," he said softly. "Go to Titus and ask for our father's help. Tell him we will accept whatever terms he sets. But he must save Olympus."

"Do you want to come with us?" Emily asked softly.

Jupiter shook his head. "No. I must stay here and fight, or at least die trying."

"Don't do anything stupid. That's what those blobs want," Agent B warned. "You and your brothers are very powerful. If they absorb you, there's no telling how big or strong they'll become."

Jupiter chuckled, and it was filled with irony. "A human is telling me what to do. . . ."

"Yes!" Agent B said. "Because right now your emotions are ruling you. You are seeing your world imperiled and are paralyzed by it. Stop it! Get mad and start to fight like you did thousands of years ago. I was there, remember?"

Jupiter nodded and looked at the whole war council. "It is up to us now. Emily needs time to reach Titus and enlist Father's aid. We must remain here and fight to stop those creatures, or at least slow them down until help arrives." His sad eyes landed on Emily. "It grieves me that you must face my father alone."

"She's not alone," Joel said as he laid his arm across

Emily's shoulders. "We'll be with her, all of us, her team: Pegasus, Chrysaor, Paelen, me, and Agent B, just like it's always been and always will be."

Emily breathed a great sigh of relief. It was just like long ago. Her whole team was back together. And together they would be unstoppable.

"Just promise me you will be careful," Jupiter said. "My father is tricky."

"I remember. It's just like . . ." Emily stopped midsentence and her heart started to pound. She looked back to the cave opening "They can feel me. I am leading them here." Emily leaned forward and kissed Jupiter on the cheek. "We must go now. Please, find my father and keep him safe until we return."

"I will," Jupiter promised.

As they prepared to leave, Vulcan handed Stella back up to Paelen. "Take my girl to Titus and keep her safe."

"I will," Paelen promised.

Stella shook her head. "No, I am going to stay here with Vulcan."

"No child," Vulcan protested. "You must go to Titus with Emily. You will be safer there."

"I'm not leaving," Stella insisted. She looked at Paelen. "You may need to fight. But you can't do that while holding on to me. Let me stay with Vulcan. It is safer for you."

Paelen hesitated. "You are concerned for me?"

Stella nodded and kissed him on the cheek. "Of course I am. We're friends, remember?"

"She's right," Joel said softly. "There's no telling what's going to happen when we reach Titus. At least she'll be safe in this cave."

Vulcan accepted Stella back. "Maxine and I will take good care of her."

"Maxine is here?" Stella cried.

Vulcan smiled gently. "She has missed you almost as much as I have."

"Go," Jupiter said. "And may the power of the stars be with you."

Emily nodded and looked at the Olympians. "Don't give up," she said as she climbed back up onto Pegasus's back. "We'll return, and when we do, we'll have Saturn and the Titans with us."

WITH AGENT B SEATED BEHIND HER ON Pegasus, they took off and flew away from the war room on Mount Helicon. As they headed back toward Tom and Alexis's cave, Paelen cried out, "Over there! Look how big they've grown!"

In the distance they could see two glowing blobs that were the mutant Titans. The colors flashing inside their gelatinous bodies were sparking like lightning. Each stood higher than the tallest giants and was grossly enlarged by feeding off of Olympus and the Olympians.

"Emily!" the female Titan shouted. Her voice echoed across the distance like a roaring avalanche. *"You cannot escape us. Soon we will feed on you and Riza. No one will dare stand against us!"*

The two Titans started to ooze toward them. That sight alone would give Emily nightmares for the rest of her life. They didn't walk. They didn't fly. They slid, like thick pudding pouring out of a bowl and onto the floor.

"We need more than the Titans to stop them," Joel called from the back of Chrysaor. "We need Riza. Only a Xan can defeat them!"

Hearing Joel's words cut through Emily like a knife. Yird's message rushed back to her head. *In a time of great need, you must call out your mother's full name and the last door to power will open and the final metamorphosis will begin. You will become Xan.*

The choice was hers, but did she have the strength to make it? Remain as she was, or commit her life to being a Xan. "I can't do it," Emily said aloud. "Not yet."

"What?" Agent B said. "What can't you do?"

She looked back into his intense blue eyes. "I can't do something I know I should. I'm not that strong."

His arms were around her waist and he gave her a light squeeze. "You'll do the right thing when the time comes," he said. "I have faith in you. We all do."

Emily frowned, searching his face for something that told her he knew the decision she was facing. "What if I don't find the strength?"

"You will," he finally said. "You just have to believe in yourself."

But did she? Emily doubted it. If she did, she would have already told Pegasus to turn around and go back to the mutant Titans. It would be so simple: Face the blobs, call her mother's name, and it would all be over. Why couldn't she do it?

Racked by guilt and insecurities, Emily kept flying toward Alexis and Tom's cave. When they touched down in front, she saw evidence that the mutants had already been here. Not one tree or plant was left. Panic gripped her as she slid down from the stallion.

"Tom, Alexis!" She ran into the cave, but no one was here. Had they been absorbed by the blobs? "Cupid, are you here?"

Joel was already pulling the first gemstone from the sack. "Emily, I'm sure they all got away. They can fly. That makes them faster than those things out there."

"I hope so, I really do," Emily said. "But Cupid said he'd meet us here."

"Not with those monsters in the area," Paelen said. He was standing at the entrance of the cave, keeping watch.

Agent B was working with Joel to set up the gemstone against the back wall of the deep cave the way Arious had told them to. They felt the ground rumbling as the Titans headed their way.

"Hurry," Paelen called. "I can see them. They are getting closer!"

As Joel and Agent B struggled to set up the stone, Chrysaor squealed and pushed Agent B aside. "Hey, back off, pig!" the ex-CRU agent said.

Emily suddenly remembered the first time she'd met Chrysaor. Back then, she and Pegasus had been his prisoner. He has used a gemstone mounted to a cave wall, just like this, to access the Solar Stream to the Nirad world.

"No wait! Joel, Agent B, let him work. Chrysaor has done this before."

They stood back and watched the winged boar expertly use his snout to mount the gemstone to the wall.

"Hurry!" Paelen cried. "They are almost here!"

Chrysaor stepped back and squealed loudly.

Instantly the cave wall fell away and they were facing the blazing light of the Solar Stream. Chrysaor looked back at everyone, squealed, and then ran into the light.

"He said to follow him!" Paelen said as he charged into the blazing light. Pegasus nickered and gently nudged Emily forward. She looked at Joel and then Agent B. "Let's go."

They ran together into the Solar Stream.

The journey to Titus was short. No sooner had they entered the Solar Stream than they were coming out into daylight.

"It looks just like Olympus," Paelen said.

"This is amazing," Agent B said softly. "It's so beautiful here."

Emily sighed sadly. "This is what Olympus looked like just a short time ago."

There were cobbled roads lined with statues—though the statues were of people Emily didn't recognize. Stunning marble buildings filled the area. Fountains and art were everywhere. Most of all, Emily was thrilled to see all the plants, flowers, and animal life.

The last time she had been here, Titus has been destroyed by Saturn's weapon. Nothing lived, and it was a barren dust bowl. But Jupiter had said that it was becoming livable again. Then Riza's father had done the rest when he'd sent the Titans home from Hawaii and Olympus.

What she had seen in Urania's pool was correct. The Titans had abandoned war and were concentrating on rebuilding their world.

Paelen put his arm around her. "We can rebuild Olympus. It will look like this again."

"If we survive the mutants," Emily said darkly.

The Solar Stream had deposited them in the middle of a public square, and their arrival hadn't gone unnoticed. Some of the Titans around them looked frightened and moved away quickly. But others wore expressions that were openly hostile as they realized that Olympians were standing among them.

Several large Titans rushed at them. One of them had wings and looked a lot like an older Cupid, with sculpted features and blazing dark eyes. Another resembled Mars, and was all muscle. All of them looked as beautiful and powerful as the Olympians.

Emily held up her hands. "Please, it is urgent we speak with Saturn. Titus is in terrible danger."

"It is you who is in danger, Olympian," the winged Titan said, pointing an accusatory finger at her. "You have defied the Xans' ban on interworld travel. That was foolish indeed."

Pegasus whinnied in threat and came forward.

"I will do as I please," the Titan said back to him. "Who are you to tell me what to do?"

Pegasus nickered and whinnied.

"Pegasus?" the winged Titan repeated. "I do not know that name."

"But you should," a stern voice called. "It is a name from the past, and a name known to many of us from Tartarus."

Emily watched a large, commanding Titan approach. There was something very familiar about him. He almost looked like a younger Jupiter, but it wasn't Saturn. He had the same piercing blue eyes and same shape face. His build was muscular. He was followed by several others, all bearing weapons.

She frowned, struggling to remember who he was and where she'd seen him.

"Hyperion," he said to her unasked question.

Emily gasped while Pegasus whinnied and Chrysaor squealed. He had been in Tartarus when she'd fired on Saturn and his most powerful followers.

Agent B stepped forward. "Hyperion—I know that name. If I remember correctly, you are Saturn's brother and Jupiter's uncle."

"Do not speak that criminal's name here, human," Hyperion spat. He started to look among them. "I see Pegasus. He was always with the one called Emily. Where is she?"

"She's not here," Joel said.

Emily shook her head. "No, Joel. No more games. This is far too important." She faced Hyperion. "I don't look the same as I did before, but I'm Emily Jacobs."

"Do not lie to me, girl," Hyperion said. "I fought her in the bowels of Tartarus and will never forget her face. You look nothing like her. In fact, you look very much like my grandniece, Diana."

Emily held up her hand and summoned the

Flame. "I told you, I've changed. But it's still me, and I remember you, too. You, Saturn, and several others burst through the door in the cell block where you were holding Joel and Prometheus."

Hyperion was eyeing the flames in her hands. "Continue . . ."

"There's not much more to tell. Saturn attacked me and I fought back. I destroyed three of you and hurt the rest. I am sorry if I injured you, Hyperion. I swear I never wanted to. But Saturn wouldn't listen to reason."

Hyperion's eyes widened. "It is you!" He looked back at the others around him. "Seize them! Seize them this instant. They have returned to start another war!"

20

AFTER BEING CAPTURED BY HYPERION, they were escorted to a new prison building. The cells were clean and bright and mostly empty except for one directly across from Emily. It contained a young satyr who sat glumly on the floor. There were shackles on his goat legs and another chain around his waist, which was attached to a ring on the wall. His hands were bound by another chain.

"Not the best start to our new friendship with the Titans," Joel said from the cell beside the satyr. He was locked up with Paelen, Chrysaor, and Agent B. "Not here five minutes and already we've been captured and locked away."

Emily and Pegasus were standing at the bars of

their cell. "It could have been worse. They might have started a fight."

"Doubtful," Paelen said. "Once Hyperion realized who you were, he knew better than to try to use force or violence."

"We're wasting precious time," Agent B said. "Why won't they listen to us?"

"Hyperion never listens," said the soft voice of the satyr. "He prefers to lock people away before learning if they are innocent or guilty."

Emily looked at the young satyr. He couldn't have been much older than ten. "What did they accuse you of?"

The satyr stood up. "They say I stole some jewels from Saturn's wife, Rhea."

"Did you?" Emily asked.

"Not exactly. I just borrowed them. I would have put them back—eventually."

"So you are a thief," Paelen said, suddenly interested.

"That is one of the things they call me," the boy said. "But I am more than that. I am going to be a hero."

"What's your name?" Emily asked.

"I am Jai-me the Magnificent!"

"Jai-me the Magnificent?" Joel repeated. He punched Paelen lightly. "What is it with you thieves and your magnificent names?"

"I am not a thief!" Paelen cried. "How many more times must I say it to convince you?"

"Once a thief, always a thief," Joel teased.

"Why have they put you in chains as well as the locked cell?" Emily asked.

Jai-me grinned. "Because I can escape anywhere they lock me."

Joel looked at Paelen again. "You two could be twins. You're always saying the same thing."

Emily looked from Paelen to the satyr. "I wouldn't exactly call them twins," she said, knowing the thick wall separated them and they couldn't see each other.

The sound of a heavy door opening caught everyone's attention. Emily peered down the long marble corridor and saw Hyperion and several of his men marching toward them.

"It is about time," Paelen said. "We have told you of the danger; you must let us out of here!"

"Silence!" Hyperion commanded.

He and his people stopped before Emily's cell and

the door was opened. "You and Pegasus will come with me."

"What about us?" Joel asked.

"You will stay here until we figure out what to do with you."

Agent B came to the front of the cell. "Look, I know you have bad blood with the Olympians, but that doesn't mean we're not telling you the truth. Titus is in terrible danger."

"I would take the word of a filthy Olympian before I believed a single thing out of a human's mouth."

"Then you're a fool," Agent B spat. "And you all deserve what's coming."

Hyperion moved closer to their cell. Emily could see the tension in the Titan's shoulders. Agent B was making him angry, and that was a very dangerous thing to do to Saturn's brother.

"Hyperion," she quickly called. "Agent B is right. We keep telling you that Titus is in danger. Why won't you believe us?"

"Believe you?" Hyperion said as he turned back to her. His blue eyes blazed. "Believe the one who nearly destroyed us?"

"I didn't do that."

He nodded. "Yes, you did. Because of you, we were all imprisoned in Tartarus."

"Yes, after you and Saturn attacked Olympus and Earth."

"You had no place getting involved in that squabble."

"Squabble?" Emily cried. "*Squabble?* Saturn locked his kids away in prison because he was paranoid they'd overthrow him. Because he did lock them away, they *did* overthrow him. But all of that won't matter once those mutant Titans get here and start eating everyone."

"What do you mean mutant Titans?"

"That's what we're trying to tell you. There are two really huge bloblike creatures that used to be Titans. Right now, they're devouring Olympus and absorbing all the Olympians' powers. When they finish there, they are coming here."

"That is a lie."

"No, it's not! They told me their plan!" Emily cried. "They intend to come here and kill you all. Why else do you think we'd risk coming back here if not to warn you?"

"She's telling you the truth!" Agent B spat. "Put away your ego for once and listen to her. We've seen them up close and know what they can do!"

"That is not possible. The Big Three . . ."

"The Big Three are useless against them!" Agent B cried. "They have tried combining their powers, but nothing works. If those blobs devour Jupiter and his brothers, their powers will be absorbed by them and they will truly be unstoppable."

"Please, Hyperion," Emily begged. "Take me to Saturn. Let me tell him what's happening."

Beside her, Pegasus started to whinny and snort. He pounded the marble floor with his golden hoof.

Hyperion tilted his head to the side and nodded. "Agreed."

Emily had no idea what Pegasus had said, but the frightened expression on Paelen's face told her it wasn't good.

Emily and Pegasus were led away by Hyperion and his guards. They spoke little as they walked through the main city of Titus. Everywhere Emily looked, she could see the beauty of the restored world. There were

Titan children playing in the street with large, strange insects, and the sweet fragrance of flowers filled the air.

"This looks so much like Olympus used to," Emily said to Pegasus. "It's beautiful."

Hyperion looked back at her. "We have all worked very hard to restore our world."

"It shows," Emily said. "Olympus used to look like this until the mutant Titans came." She didn't bother to mention the damage the Titans themselves had done to Olympus as well during their invasion. She needed them to understand that the blobs were a danger to them all.

Up ahead she spied a wondrous palace that was almost twice the size of Jupiter's. Fountains sprayed rainbow water in the air, and enormous flowers were growing around it in the gardens.

Emily saw several centaurs working with satyrs, digging in the gardens and planting flowering trees. Not far away, several giants were lifting marble stones into place as they built another home. Everywhere she looked she saw evidence of how the Olympians had come from the Titans. They truly were one people.

"This way," Hyperion said as they arrived at the base of the palace steps. He looked back at his guards. "Stay here and wait for us."

The men nodded and took their positions.

"Aren't you afraid I might try something?" Emily asked as they climbed the steps.

He shook his head. "Pegasus has vouched for you. He said he would not fight us or try to escape if you did anything. He had offered his life in exchange for your good behavior."

Emily looked sharply at Pegasus. The stallion nodded to her. She could see the trust shining in his bright eyes. His absolute faith in her warmed her heart. She reached over and stroked his neck. "Don't worry. I won't do anything. I promise."

Hyperion studied her and Pegasus closely. He looked back at Pegasus. "Neptune is truly your father?"

Pegasus snorted and nodded.

"That makes you my great-nephew. But do not misinterpret our family connection. My loyalty is to Saturn and Titus. I will do as I must."

"And we will do anything we can to stop those monsters from destroying both worlds," Emily said.

Hyperion raised an eyebrow to her but said nothing more.

They passed through the front doors of the palace, and Emily saw riches she'd never dreamed possible. While Jupiter's palace was adorned with art, flowers, and beauty, this palace was filled with golden treasures and jewels. Even the furniture was gold.

Servants fluttered around, cleaning and arranging everything. They looked at Pegasus with dismay, as if they expected him to make an especially bad mess. Were the situation any less critical, Emily would have said something. Instead she looked away and followed Hyperion.

When they approached the throne room, Emily saw the same area she had seen in Urania's pool. Nothing had changed. She hesitated and felt a flutter of fear as she neared the entrance.

"This way," Hyperion said. His voice wasn't harsh, but it was commanding and left no room for debate or argument.

Emily took a deep breath and followed him into the room.

Saturn was there, seated on a throne at the front.

Emily realized it hadn't been that long since their last encounter in the skies over Honolulu. Saturn and his Titan warriors had arrived in their flying chariots to fight the Olympians. If it hadn't been for the intervention of the Xan, the outcome would have been much worse.

"Come closer . . . ," Saturn's deep voice commanded. "Come to me, Flame of Olympus."

Emily did as she was told and walked up to Saturn. She had expected to find him alone, as he had been in the vision. But instead the room was filled with senior Titans.

Several women stood at the front of the gathering, and Emily immediately recognized one of them—though she looked very different with her golden blond hair piled high on her head and wearing a stunning silken gown. The first time Emily had seen her was in Lorin's mind. Her name was Phoebe and she'd been in Tartarus with the rest.

Phoebe frowned at Emily and then looked beyond her, as though she expected to see someone else enter. Her disappointment when no one else came was obvious.

Another thing Emily noticed about the gathering was the expressions on the faces of Saturn's council. They were not hostile, but curious, with perhaps a trace of fear.

"Closer," Saturn commanded.

Emily walked up to the leader of the Titans. Seated on his raised throne, he was an imposing sight. He was similar in looks to Jupiter, though his eyes were much harder and his expression unreadable. With Jupiter, Emily could always tell what he was thinking—but not with Saturn.

There was only one thing Emily could think of to do. She knelt down on one knee and lowered her head. "Great Saturn, I come to you begging for your help."

There was a collective gasp from everyone in the room.

"Silence!" Saturn boomed. He leaned forward on his throne. "Rise, Flame."

Emily stood and gazed up into Saturn's unreadable eyes.

"You have changed, Emily," he said. "You are the image of Diana."

Emily nodded. "I know, sir. The Xan gave me a new body, and Diana offered part of herself for them to do it."

"You are Olympian now?"

Emily shook her head. "To be honest, I'm not sure what I am anymore. There is Olympian in me, but also Xan and some of my human father."

"Not a lot," Saturn said. "I sense no trace of human in you at all."

"I guess not," Emily said sadly.

From behind her, Emily heard a soft woman's voice. "Saturn, please. Ask her. Where is Lorin?"

Emily turned back to Phoebe and saw the begging in her eyes. "How is my girl?"

Emily lowered her head. "I am so sorry, Phoebe, but Lorin has died."

"What?" Phoebe gasped. "No. You lie. I still feel her."

"I'm not lying. You still feel her because her powers have been absorbed by two monsters, and they are using it. She gave her life saving others."

Phoebe was shaking her head and started to weep, while Saturn eyed Emily suspiciously. "No one other than you or a full Xan had the power to defeat Lorin."

"I swear it wasn't me or the Xan," Emily said. "That is why we came here."

"Ah, yes, monsters are devouring Olympus," Saturn said. "Hyperion has told me what you said."

"It's true. They are destroying Olympus even as we speak."

"What care have I should Olympus fall?"

"You don't understand," Emily said. "Those creatures are gaining power and size with each Olympian they consume. Their plan is to come here and devour you next. I'm certain by the time they've finished with Olympus, no one here will be strong enough to stand against them."

"You called them 'mutant Titans,'" Hyperion said. "Explain yourself."

Emily looked at both Hyperion and Saturn. "Do you remember when we fought in Tartarus? I wounded some of you, but there were three who vanished."

"Yes," Saturn said slowly. "You killed them, though you could not defeat me. I hold too much power, even for you, Flame of Olympus."

"It doesn't matter who won!" Emily cried. "Don't

you get it? I didn't kill those Titans. I wounded them. After that, they fled to Earth and hid deep under the ground. They've been feeding off anything they could catch for thousands of years, absorbing their prey's energy and power. They are the ones who created the Olympian clones, so that they could consume their power."

"This is impossible!" a voice from the gathering said. "Stories designed to frighten us." Three large Titans came forward. Emily recognized them from the fight in Tartarus. They were Saturn's other brothers, Iapetus, Crius, and Coeus. The family resemblance was astounding. They looked just like their nephews, Pluto and Neptune.

"She is spinning lies to confuse us," Crius exclaimed. "A distraction so that Jupiter can start his invasion of Titus."

"Yes," Coeus agreed. "The Flame of Olympus seeks only to destroy us now that Lorin is gone."

"No!" Emily insisted. "I came here to beg for your help. They are killing the Olympians. If we don't stop them now, they will come here and destroy all of you."

Saturn looked at Emily. "That is impossible. Olympus has its Big Three. They will stop them."

"They've tried!" Emily said. "But it didn't work. The mutants are stronger. With each minute we delay, their power grows. Please, believe me. I came here with a message from Jupiter. He and his brothers will surrender to you if you save Olympus."

"Lies!" Saturn cried.

Beside her, Pegasus started to whinny. Never before had it been so critically important that she understand what he was saying. But for all their time together, and despite her Olympian body, his language was still a mystery to her. But the Titans understood.

"Who were the three Titans?" Saturn asked, in answer to Pegasus. "They were Dictate and the siblings Pern and Pearth."

"Are those the three Titans who vanished?" Emily asked.

Saturn nodded. "Dictate was a weak-willed Titan but very powerful. He could read minds and control wills."

"And the other two?" Emily asked. "Were they brother and sister?"

"Yes," Hyperion answered. "They were not particularly loyal to us. But they possessed great power and could be convinced to serve."

It suddenly all made sense. Dictate had used his mind powers to control humans into serving them and creating the CRU. The others used their powers to build the pit beneath Charing Cross. Now that she knew who they were, it was even more critical that the Titans joined the fight.

"Saturn, Hyperion." She looked back to everyone else in the room. "If you've ever believed anything in your life, I beg you to believe me now. Dictate is the Titan who killed and absorbed Lorin. When he did, Pern and Pearth attacked and devoured him so they could steal his power as well as hers. I swear on the lives of everyone I love, those two are now destroying Olympus. They will come here next, and when they do, you won't be able to stop them."

There were murmurs from the gathering. Emily could feel fear rising among the Titans. Whether they believed everything or not, they'd started to believe some of what she'd said.

Pegasus whinnied again and pawed the ground. He

faced every member of Saturn's family and nodded.

"But would Emily allow it?" Hyperion demanded.

"Allow what?"

Pegasus turned to Emily and invited her to peer into his eyes. When she did, she saw the vision of Saturn and his brothers touching her head and reading her mind as Jupiter had done thousands of years ago, when they'd first faced him in the past.

She knew what he was proposing. But letting the Titan leadership into her mind to see the mutants also meant letting them see other parts of her life—private parts that were meant only for her.

"Well," Saturn demanded. "If you truly wish for us to believe you, you should not hesitate in showing us the creatures you claim are destroying Olympus."

Emily looked at Pegasus again. "Should I?"

He nodded and nickered softly.

Emily looked at Saturn and then his four brothers. "I'll do anything to save Olympus and you. Please, come and read my mind—read both our minds and see what those monsters are doing."

Saturn appeared stunned by her quick agreement. "If this is some kind of trap for us . . ."

"It's not!" Emily said. "But each moment you delay means more Olympians die. Please, hurry."

Saturn rose and walked toward her. With each step, Emily felt the danger she was putting herself in. But she had no choice. They had to see it for themselves. Hyperion was the first to reach her side, followed by the others. The last to arrive was Saturn.

"You know that you cannot alter what is in your mind. Once we enter, we will see only the truth."

"And the truth will terrify you," Emily said.

Soon she was completely encircled by the most powerful Titans. She tried to look brave as Saturn and his brothers each reached forward and laid their hands on her head.

Unlike the first time Jupiter had done this in the ancient past, the Titan approach was brutal as they tore through her mind like lightning. There wasn't a single piece of thought or memory that didn't have a Titan prying through it.

Emily fought to hold back the one bit of information that was precious to her—the message from Yird telling her about the final metamorphosis she faced. But as she tried to keep them away from that small piece of her mind, she felt Saturn's incalculable power forcing its way through her barriers.

Saturn and his brothers accessed the final piece of information that was in Emily. When they finished, they broke contact and staggered back. Saturn shook his head and looked at her in stunned recognition.

"So, tell me, Emily," he demanded. "What will you be? Olympian or Xan?"

PAELEN STOOD AT THE BARS OF THE CELL, shaking his head. "They have been gone too long. I do not like this."

"Em will convince them," Joel said. "She has to. Without them, Olympus is lost. We just have to give her more time."

"How much more?" Agent B said. "Paelen is right. Each moment we waste here, more of Olympus will fall. We've got to get out of here and back there."

Paelen started to push against the bars, but they didn't even move. Joel joined him, but even with Agent B and Chrysaor shoving the door, nothing happened.

"It will not work," the satyr in the next cell said.

"Titan steel is far too strong for you. You need magic to open the doors."

"Magic?" Joel repeated. "Oh great, we're toast."

"I could do it," Jai-me said.

"If you could, why are you still imprisoned?"

"Because they have me in chains. Were it not for them, I could easily open the door. I would release you as well."

"If you can open the doors, why can you not open the chains on you?" Paelen asked.

"It is different metal. These chains are silver. I cannot command silver because it burns me."

"Who is this kid?" Joel said.

Paelen shrugged. "I think he may be a satyr. They burn if touched by silver. Wait here. I will see." He lowered himself to the floor. "Keep an eye open for the guards and warn me if anyone comes in."

"What are you going to do?" Agent B asked.

Paelen grinned up at him. "Hurt myself."

He fed his arms through the bars, and they all heard the cracking and popping of bones as his body extended. Longer and longer, thinner and thinner he became, until he was like a snake.

Paelen slid out of the cell and into the one next door. When his full body was through the bars, he winced as he pulled himself back into his normal size.

The young satyr stared in amazement. "I wish I could do that."

"I would not, if I were you," Paelen said as he stiffly climbed to his feet. "It really pinches. Now, let me take a look at you."

The satyr was young, not overly tall, and, at best, came up to Paelen's chest. He had pointed ears and an elfin face with wild brown hair and golden eyes. There was a chain that went around his waist and was fastened to a ring on the wall. Without a shirt between him and the chain, the silver was burning his skin raw. The other chain around his wrists was doing the same, and where the manacles closed on his hooves, the silver was burning the coarse brown hair off.

"They really did not want you to get away, did they?"

Jai-me shook his head. "I think Saturn wants to execute me slowly with the silver."

"For what?" Joel said. "Just because you stole some jewels?"

"They belonged to his wife. He cares deeply for her."

Paelen leaned in closer and whispered in his ear, "From one thief to another, you must never steal from the leaders. It will only bring you disaster. I know. I have tried it myself."

Jai-me nodded and held up his hands to show the burn welts on his wrists. "I have learned my lesson."

"I hope so," Paelen said. There was so much about this young thief that reminded him of himself when he was younger. "Now, let us see about getting these chains off of you."

The silver of the chains was strong, but Paelen was stronger. With a bit of effort, he broke the chains around the satyr's waist and from his wrists and hooves.

In gratitude, Jai-me threw his arms around Paelen and hugged him tightly. "Thank you!"

Uncomfortable at first, Paelen finally sighed and patted the satyr's back. "You are very welcome. But in exchange for freeing you, you said you could open the cell doors."

"I can!" Jai-me said excitedly. He clopped forward

and stopped before the cell door. He smiled brightly at Paelen. "It is simple. I put my hand on the lock and say 'open.'"

They all heard a click, and then the door swung open.

"That is very clever," Paelen said. "I wish I could do that."

Jai-me grinned as though Paelen had given him a gold coin. "I still wish I could stretch my body like you can. Then no one could ever catch hold of me."

Paelen grinned. "It does help. So, will you free my friends?"

Jai-me nodded and quickly opened the other door. He looked at Agent B and Joel. "Are you truly humans?"

Joel nodded.

"I have never seen humans before," the satyr said. "You really stink."

"Hey," Joel said. "I don't go around insulting you for having the legs of a goat!"

Jai-me looked down at his legs. "That is because they are beautiful. I keep my hooves very well polished."

"Ignore him," Agent B said. He gazed around the large cell block. "Now, we've got to find out where Hyperion hid our gemstone for the Solar Stream. Then we can locate Emily and Pegasus and get out of here."

"I know where he put your things," Jai-me said.

"How?" Joel challenged. "You were here when he brought us in. You couldn't have seen."

"I know because I have seen him take other prisoners' possessions and lock them away." He held up his hand to show a large ring on the middle finger. "See this? It belonged to a centaur that Hyperion locked away. I freed it for him."

"Did you free the centaur?" Joel asked.

The boy shook his head.

"And will you give him the ring back?"

"Maybe."

Joel looked at Paelen. "I can't believe it. You're worlds apart, but you two are exactly the same."

Chrysaor squealed and approached the satyr.

"There is no need to yell at me," Jai-me said. "Of course I will show you where Hyperion keeps the items. It is this way."

The young satyr led them down the long corridor and paused before the door at the end. He pressed his ear to it and nodded. "There is no one out there." He carefully pushed the door open and poked his head out. "Hurry. Follow me."

They ran across an open corridor and then through another door. This led to more holding cells. As they made their way along the corridor, they saw some of the cells contained prisoners.

Jai-me touched each door he passed and commanded the lock to open. "We might need a distraction," he said as the Titans were freed from their cells.

Most of the prisoners ran in the opposite direction. But a group of around ten started to follow Paelen and the others.

"What crimes have they committed?" Agent B asked.

Jai-me shrugged. "I do not know. But sometimes Saturn gets angry and locks away people who displease him—and who have never committed a crime."

"Like me," a lovely woman with black and white wings said. She was around fifty, and her solid black eyes never stopped darting around. Instead of hair, her head was covered in fine black feathers. With her large dark eyes, she looked more bird than a woman with wings. Her voice was high-pitched and sang like a mourning dove. "All I did was design a cloak that Saturn did not like. So he locked me away until I come up with a better design."

"How long have you been in here?" Paelen asked.

The woman shrugged. "I do not know anymore. I lost count after one hundred and fifty-two days. I think he has forgotten about me."

"What?" Joel cried. "Just because you made something he didn't like?"

When the woman nodded, Agent B said, "So Saturn is still bad-tempered."

"He is getting better," she said. "In the past, he would have had someone who displeased him executed. Now he just locks us away."

Paelen looked back at the other prisoners who were following them. "Did you all displease him?"

Everyone nodded.

"That's it," Joel said, looking around. "We're definitely in trouble. There's no way Emily could convince Saturn to help Olympus. He's too busy being a dictator."

"Have you come from Olympus?" a strong-looking young man asked as he stepped forward. He was fiercely muscled with light blond hair and shocking green eyes. He was wearing a tunic styled much like they wore on Olympus, but his left shoulder had a gold emblem emblazoned on it.

"Yes," Joel said. "But we're not here to attack you. We need Saturn's help."

"I do not fear attack from you, human," the young man said. "I want to ask if you know a woman called Fiora. She is my mother."

"Your mother is Olympian?"

He nodded. "I am Argon, warrior of first rank in Saturn's forces. My mother and I were separated just after the war, a long time ago. I have not seen her since I was very young. I joined the force, hoping to find her."

"I am sorry," Paelen said. "I do not know such a woman. But I am sure she is safe."

"If you are from Olympus, why have you come here?" the bird woman asked.

"Because Olympus is being destroyed, and we need Saturn's help to save it."

"Destroyed!" Argon cried. "You must take me there immediately. I have to find my mother."

"You help us get out of here, and you can come back with us," Joel said. "But you won't like what you find. Olympus is in ruins."

"I care only that my mother is safe."

"We must hurry!" Jai-me said. "They may soon discover we have escaped."

Paelen looked back at the large group that was following them. "Please, you must not all come with us. We will draw too much attention. Go the other way. Find your own way to freedom."

But no matter what he said, the group of escaping prisoners continued to follow them. Paelen realized it was true. These were not hardened criminals. They were innocent people looking for help and a way out of their imprisonment.

They passed through another bright, clean, empty cell block until they reached a new corridor. "Down at the end is where they lock the prisoners' items," Jai-me said. He clopped forward and reached the door. It too was locked, but it soon surrendered to his magic.

Joel and Paelen ran inside and searched for the sack containing the second Solar Stream gemstone. But despite the many items inside the storage room, it was not among them. "It's not here!" Joel said angrily.

"Perhaps they gave it to Saturn," Paelen offered. "It may be at his palace with Emily."

"That's just great," Joel said. "Fist he takes Emily, and now he's got our only way off this rock. How the heck are we supposed to get into Saturn's palace?"

"Joel, calm down," Agent B said. "The fastest way to get captured is to panic. Now, what do we know about the palace?"

"It's big and made of marble?" Paelen offered.

"Be serious," Agent B snapped.

"I am. How do you expect us to know anything about Saturn's palace? Let alone how to get into it?"

"I know a way in," Jai-me offered. "That was how I got into trouble in the first place. I have found a secret entrance." He looked at Paelen. "But you told me not to do that anymore."

"That is true," Paelen said. "And I meant it. But

we do not wish to go there to thieve. We must find our friend and the gemstone that will take us home."

"So it is different?"

"Yes," Paelen said. "Will you show us the way?"

When the boy nodded, Agent B said, "Perfect." He looked down at his clothes and then to Joel and Paelen in their jeans and shirts. "But we're not going anywhere dressed like we've just come from Earth. We need to blend in."

Joel nodded and went back into the storage locker. He came back holding up items of clothing. "There's plenty of stuff in here."

"Clothing is my specialty," the bird woman said, stepping forward. "If you really want to look like a Titan, you must trust me."

Within minutes, Saturn's designer had them looking like they had lived on Titus all their lives. When they were ready, the large group of prisoners followed Jaime through the maze of the building.

Joel kept looking around. "If this is a prison, why are there no guards?"

"Because the cells are impossible to open," Jai-me

said. "So far, I am the only one who has ever suc-ceeded."

"So there are no guards?" Agent B asked.

Jai-me shook his head. "Not that I have ever seen. They are only here when there is a new prisoner to lock inside or release."

"Which isn't very often," Argon added.

After a few more turns, they were led up to the doors in the back of the building. Jai-me used his powers to open them, and everyone slipped outside into the bright sunshine.

"All right," Agent B said, taking over. "Everyone wanted out of the prison. You are out. But you can't stay with us. We need to move quickly and not worry about stragglers. Trust me. You are much safer away from us than with us."

Most of the prisoners agreed. They offered their thanks and drifted away. But Argon remained. "I am a trained warrior in Saturn's forces and can help you. In exchange, you will take me with you to Olympus so I may find my mother."

Joel looked at the others. "Not until you tell us why you were in prison."

Argon shrugged. "I had a disagreement with my commander, and he took exception to my comments."

"And they locked you away for that?" Paelen said.

"Yes," Argon said. "My commander was Hyperion."

Agent B frowned. "There seems to be a pattern here. All roads lead to Saturn or his family."

"And to prison," Paelen said. "We must get Emily away from him as soon as possible." He looked down at Jai-me. "Take us to the palace as quickly as you can."

Thanks to the workings of the bird woman, they were able to walk around in daylight without causing too much interest. A few people paused to stare at Joel with his exposed silver arm, and Agent B. But they did not approach.

"They sense you are human," Argon explained. "And cannot understand how you are here. But because I am with you, they should not challenge us."

Paelen was grateful to have one of Saturn's warriors with them. Each time someone looked at them strangely, Argon gave them a warning look that kept them walking.

"I must learn that look," Paelen said, screwing up his face and trying to look threatening.

Joel shook his head. "It'll never work for you."

"Why?"

"Because you look like a constipated raccoon doing that."

"Oh . . ."

"Boys, that's enough," Agent B warned.

As they walked, they told Argon and Jai-me about the mutant Titans attacking Olympus and their plans to bring their ferocious appetites to Titus.

"Will they really come here?" Jai-me asked fearfully.

"If we don't stop them, they will," Joel said. "That's why we're here. We were hoping that Saturn and his strongest fighters might join the fight to stop them."

"I cannot see that happening," Argon said. "Ever since the Xan brought us all back here from Earth, Saturn has changed. I do not know that he cares about anything anymore. He spends all his days at the palace. We rarely see him."

"Wait," Joel said, stopping. "Are you saying you were in Hawaii?"

Argon nodded. "After we escaped Tartarus, we

were ordered to Earth. I did as I was commanded to do. But before I could engage the Olympians there, the Xan stopped us. We were all delivered back here and warned from fighting with the Olympians. We are never to use the Solar Stream again."

"Olympus was given the same warning," Paelen said. "Though we have been given permission to use the Solar Stream to visit a few worlds. Coming here was not one of those, but we had no choice. Not if we hope to save Olympus."

"Then we must fight for both our worlds," Argon said.

"There it is," Jai-me called. He pointed to a massive marble palace standing tall and proud. It was easily double the size of every building around it. "That is Saturn's palace. My secret entrance is at the side."

"Wow!" Joel cried. "I thought Jupiter's palace was big, but that place is gargantuan!"

Argon nodded. "It may appear peaceful, but do not be fooled. Saturn has a lot of protection here. Getting in to find your friend will not be easy. I just wish I had my weapon with me."

"I know where the armory is," Jai-me offered. "We will walk past it when we enter. They have lots of weapons down there."

"Perfect," Agent B said to the satyr. "Lead on."

They continued walking toward the palace, but as they drew near to the large steps leading up to the front entrance, they stopped. A number of guards were waiting outside.

"Those are Hyperion's guards," Argon said. "Your friend must still be inside."

"Why post them out here?" Agent B said. "Saturn knows who Emily is and what she's capable of. Why wasn't she escorted by all of them?"

"Because there are stronger guards hidden inside," Argon said. "You will not see them, but they are there. I was once offered a position in the palace, but I turned it down. I do not relish the thoughts of spending all day or night hidden inside a hollow pillar or behind a wall waiting to be called upon."

"So it's a fortress," Joel said.

"Yes, I am afraid so."

Jai-me shook his head. "Perhaps it is. But if you know where to go, you can avoid being seen." He turned away from the guards and walked along the front of the palace until they reached the end.

"It is down here," the satyr said as he led them along the side of the immense palace. He looked around to make sure no one was watching and pointed toward the back. "Follow me. We have to run into that flower bush."

He darted off first, followed by Joel, Paelen, and Chrysaor. Finally Agent B and Argon brought up the rear. They forced themselves into the flowering bush, grunting and complaining.

"You never said it had thorns!" Joel cried as the thorns cut into his bare legs.

"I am sure I did," Jai-me said.

"No, you did not," Paelen muttered as he winced when a sharp thorn caught his cheek.

"We're being ripped to shreds," Joel complained as he struggled to follow the small satyr.

"It is not my fault if you are giants." Jai-me made it to the back of the bush, where it butted against the white marble wall of the palace. "Down here there is a loose stone that can be removed."

He slipped his thin fingers into the small seals

around the stone and started to pull. The marble block was almost bigger than him, but despite his size, he was strong enough to pull it out of the wall.

Paelen and Joel looked at each other and their eyebrows rose. "That little guy is stronger than he looks!" Joel said.

"I am," Jai-me agreed. "Now, it might be a bit tight for you, but try to squeeze through. We will arrive in the storage room."

Jai-me was first to slip into the palace, followed by Paelen and then Joel. It was soon apparent that Chrysaor could not fit through the hole. Instead he agreed to keep watch from the bush and call instructions.

Agent B forced himself through, followed by Argon. They landed on the floor of the storage room, and Paelen's eyes went wide at the sight of all the valuable items strewn around.

"I would be a wealthy man if I owned half of these things."

Jai-me grinned. "I am a wealthy man because of the things I have taken from in here."

"No," Joel corrected. "You're a wealthy boy who still likes to get into trouble."

Jai-me shrugged his shoulders. "But at least I know where I am going."

Argon shook his head and sighed. "Enough chatter. We do not have time to play. Just show us the armory."

Both Paelen and Jai-me said, "Who is playing?" at the exact same time.

Joel shook his head. "See what I mean? Twins."

"Boys." Agent B sighed.

Jai-me crept forward through the piles of discarded golden furniture and pieces of art. He finally stopped before a set of double doors. Pressing his ear to the door, he nodded. "We are alone. Come. The armory is this way."

They slipped into a long, dark corridor that held many doors. The satyr moved with the confidence of one who had been in here many times. He stopped before an unmarked door. "This is it."

Everyone was stunned when they entered and saw what had to be thousands of weapons mounted to the walls, on tables, and heaped into piles on the floor.

"There are enough here to defeat Olympus twice!" Paelen cried.

Jai-me nodded. "Perhaps, but Saturn had all the weapons gathered up and locked in here. Only a few of the guards carry swords now."

"I wonder if Riza's dad had something to do with this," Joel said. "Only a Xan could get the Titans to surrender their weapons."

"We did not surrender them," Argon said. "We chose to put them down. War is wasteful, and none of us have a taste for it anymore."

"But you attacked us a short time ago," Joel said. "You even came to Hawaii to get us."

"And we paid for that mistake," Argon said. "When we were returned to Titus by the Xan, everyone agreed that the time for warring was over."

"But you're still in Saturn's forces," Joel said. "You said so yourself."

"Yes, I am. I joined to defend Titus against the Olympians, not to attack them. What happened recently was a reaction to being locked away in Tartarus for so long. Now that we have our own world back, there is no need to fight."

Agent B nodded. "Well, I hope you all have one fight left in you. Those mutant Titans destroying

Olympus will soon set their sights on here if they're not stopped."

"We will," Argon said. He reached forward and lifted up a sword. "I do not wish to fight my brothers here in the palace, but to free your friend and get to Olympus, I will."

"Hopefully, it won't come to that," Agent B said. He picked up his own sword and nodded at it appreciatively. He turned to the satyr. "Does this palace have dungeons? Where would Saturn keep Emily?"

"Why would Saturn need a dungeon when he has the prison?"

"I don't know, but he's got to keep important prisoners somewhere," Agent B said.

"There is one place he may keep her," Jai-me said. "There is a small chamber off of the throne room."

Paelen nodded. "Take us there."

Once everyone was armed, the small satyr led them back into the corridor. "We will take the back stairs," he said softly. "They are always quiet."

They followed Jai-me through the bowels of the palace, keeping to the lesser used passageways and stairs. On two occasions they saw servants in the corridor. But Argon once again used his rank and position to get them out of trouble.

"Maybe we should wait until night," Jai-me suggested. "It is always quieter at night."

Paelen shook his head. "We do not have time to waste. If Saturn is not going to help us, we must get back to Olympus to do whatever we can to help them."

"But we will be seen and captured."

Argon stopped. "He is right. But that also gives me an idea." He approached Joel and Paelen. "Give me your weapons."

"We can't fight without them," Joel complained.

"That is the point. Most of the guards in here will not yet have heard of my imprisonment. We might get farther through the palace if it looks as though I captured you. Then, if we are challenged, I will give you back your weapons and we will fight our way though."

Agent B inhaled deeply and looked at Joel and Paelen. "He's right. We're in Saturn's stronghold. It's too busy during the day to sneak in. We'll have to face them head-on."

"We are so dead," Joel said.

"Not necessarily," Agent B said. "They won't be expecting us. We're already inside the building. Most of the guards are posted outside. We'll just have to bluff our way through the rest of it to get to Emily."

Joel reluctantly handed over his weapon to Argon.

"If you are certain there is no other way," Paelen said as he too surrendered his weapon.

"I can think of none," Argon said.

Agent B nodded. "There isn't. Not here, not now. Just be ready to take your sword back at a moment's notice."

Argon received the swords into his arms. "All right, I will stay at the rear. Jai-me, you lead us in to where you believe they are holding the girl. If we encounter any resistance, come to me for your weapons."

As they started to walk up the stairs, Joel looked at Paelen. "If this doesn't work, we won't have to worry about Olympus. These guys will kill us first."

"Do you have another suggestion?" Agent B asked.

Joel looked back at him and shook his head. "No. That's the trouble."

They made their way to the main level of the

palace, passing several servants and even a couple of guards. When they saw Argon holding his weapon up and the other weapons in his arms, they nodded to him and kept walking.

Paelen watched everyone responding to Argon and leaned closer to Joel. "Who is this Argon?"

Joel shrugged. "I thought he might be one of the Argonauts."

Argon heard the comment and said, "No, Joel, I did not serve on the ship *Argo*. It was Olympian. But my mother told me about it and said she named me after it."

Paelen looked back at Joel. "What is the *Argo*?"

"A guy called Jason used it to find the Golden Fleece," Joel said. "I'll tell you about it later—if there is a later."

They continued through the main floor of the palace unchallenged. But when they neared the throne room, everything changed.

"Argon?" a voice called from behind them. "Why are you not in prison?"

Everyone turned and saw one of the guards that had escorted them to their prison cell. When his eyes lit on Paelen and the others, he started to shout, "Guards, guards, set off the alarms. The Olympians are attacking the palace!"

"So much for our clever plan!" Joel shouted as he dashed up to Argon and pulled his sword from his arms. "We're going to have to fight!"

In an instant, what appeared to be solid marble walls suddenly burst open and guards rushed out. Two other guards opened a secret door in the pillars down the corridor and came running toward them, shouting and brandishing their weapons.

"This is it, boys!" Agent B said, retrieving his sword and holding it up. "Fight for your lives!"

EMILY STOOD IN THE THRONE ROOM WITH
Pegasus, facing Saturn and his four brothers. They
had read every inch of her mind and then Pegasus's. They knew everything that was happening on
Olympus.

"Do you understand now why we are here?"

Saturn nodded and rubbed his chin. He looked at
his brothers. "If she is part Xan, is there any way she
could have manipulated her thoughts?"

"Perhaps," Iapetus said. "Though I do not believe
she could have altered Pegasus's."

"What?" Emily cried. "After all of that, you still
don't believe us?"

Hyperion came closer, the hardness gone from his

eyes. "As leader of the Titans, Saturn must be extra cautious. The lives of everyone depend on him. But I, on the other hand, am not constrained by such responsibilities."

He looked at all his brothers. "I believe if we do not assist Olympus now, in its greatest time of need, those creatures will come here and devour us all."

Emily turned back to the large gathering of Titans. "Please, I'm begging you. You must help us defeat them before it's too late."

The mood in the room changed from distrust and fear to nods of acceptance and agreement in their part of the struggle for Olympus. But all of that vanished the moment alarms started blaring and guards in the corridor started shouting that the palace was being attacked.

Hyperion lunged forward and caught hold of Emily. "This was a trick?"

"No!" Emily cried. "I swear everything we've told you is true!"

"Then who is attacking us?" he harshly demanded.

"I don't know! Maybe it's the mutants!"

Hyperion shoved Emily back toward Saturn and

pointed a shaking finger at her. "You will stay here."
He summoned some of his men and ran for the door.
As he exited, he shouted back to his brothers, "If she
makes one move against us, kill Pegasus—he is her
weakness!"

Pegasus whinnied in protest as more Titans
swarmed around him.

"Leave him alone!" Emily shouted.

She tried to run to Pegasus, but Saturn's hands
slamming down on her shoulders stopped her. "Do
not move, Emily," he warned darkly. "And do not
dare call your mother's name and change. You will
not complete your metamorphosis before we kill your
beloved Pegasus."

"Please, Saturn," Emily begged. She turned to face
him. "I don't know what's going on out there, but it's
not me! You must believe us. Olympus needs you."

"Perhaps it does, or does not. But until we discover
the source of the alarm, you will not do a thing. Is
that understood?"

Emily looked back at Pegasus and nodded.

Time seemed to stand still as everyone in the
throne room stood, staring at the door. The shouts

outside grew louder for a time and then stilled. Tension climbed as they watched and waited for word.

Finally, Hyperion returned. His face was unreadable.

"Well?" Saturn demanded. "What has happened?"

Hyperion walked over to Emily. "Your little deception did not work."

"What?" Emily demanded. "I don't understand."

Moments later, Joel and Paelen were shoved brutally into the throne room. Joel had a large cut on his forehead, and his silver arm was badly dented. Paelen also bore the wounds of a recent fight.

"Joel!" Emily cried.

"Em, are you all right?" Joel tried to break free of the guards who held him, but the Titans were too strong.

"I'm fine. What are you doing here?"

"We came to rescue you."

Agent B was dragged into the throne room by two large Titans. He was unconscious and his head was bleeding from a deep wound. Emily broke away from Saturn and ran to him. "What did you do to him?" she demanded of the guards. She reached out to Agent B. At her touch, his wounds started to heal.

"They attacked us," one of the guards reported.

"That's a lie!" Joel challenged. "You guys attacked us first!"

"Silence!" Hyperion commanded. He looked back at Saturn. "Brother, Emily's people were captured in the palace, not far from this throne room."

"How did they get in?" Saturn demanded.

"They had help." Hyperion ordered. "Bring them in!"

Two more prisoners were dragged into the throne room. Emily recognized the satyr from the cell beside Joel and Paelen. He was being restrained by two Titans but was kicking at them with his sharp goat hooves. The other young man she didn't know. He struggled in the arms of the guards, who held him firm.

Saturn gasped and Crius ran forward and faced the muscular youth. "Argon!" he harshly demanded. "What are you doing here?"

"Hello, Father," Argon said coldly.

"Father?" Paelen cried. "You did not tell us your father was Crius!"

"What difference would it have made?" Argon said.

"A big difference!" Joel cried. "Just whose side are you on?"

"I am on the side of peace," Argon said. "Father, uncles, you must listen to us. Olympus is being destroyed."

Saturn's expression was black as thunder. "So in response you helped these people break into my palace to attack us?"

"No, we came for the girl and the gemstone that will lead us back to Olympus. I must go there to find Mother."

"Your mother?" Crius exclaimed. "Have you lost your mind?"

"Maybe I have, Father. But I need to find her. We have been apart for too long. Now that Olympus is in danger, I must go to protect her."

"Your mother chose to side with the Olympians against us!" Crius cried furiously. "Her crime is unforgivable."

"You gave her no choice!" Argon shouted back.

Emily listened to the argument between Argon and his father. In this, their greatest time of danger, they were arguing over old allegiances? When Saturn joined in, Emily felt her own temper start to flare.

"Shut up!" Emily fired two blasts of flame into the ceiling high over their heads, bringing burning chunks of marble crashing down to the floor.

"Em, calm down," Joel warned. "Don't lose your temper!"

It was already too late. Emily felt the Flame rumbling in her core, demanding to be released. It wouldn't take much to set it free. "I can't believe you people!" she cried. "Olympus is being destroyed, Titus is next, and all you care about is who sided with whom a thousand years ago? Have you heard yourselves?"

She turned on Saturn and pointed an accusing finger at him. "And you, old man. All these years, hating and warring against your sons just because someone once told you they would overthrow you? Get over yourself, Saturn! Family is all that matters, and right now, your children are fighting for their lives. What are you going to do about it?"

"How dare you!" Saturn boomed.

"How dare I?" Emily exploded. "How dare you, Saturn, and all you Titans! All the Olympians wanted was peace. They were going to release you from

Tartarus right before you broke free and attacked them. They have never done anything against you. You have always been the aggressors, and that's just too stupid for words because you're the same people! You are family!"

"Emily, please stop," Paelen warned, "before it is too late."

"It's already too late!" she raged. "The Olympians—your family—need you, but what are you going to do about it? Nothing! Well, that's just fine! But we are leaving here, Saturn. . . ."

Emily's temper finally blew, and she burst into a full flame that covered her entire body. The fire crackled and roared and gave off searing heat that drove everyone back. "You are not going to stop us. We are going to Olympus to try to save them. So you will bring that gemstone to me right now, or I'll really get mad and show you what the Flame of Olympus can do!"

Everyone around her took another step back as Emily's Flame grew in intensity. Each second that passed, the flame climbed higher and grew hotter.

"Em, please, you gotta calm down!" Joel said. "You're about to go nuke!"

Emily's heart was racing as her anger stoked the flames higher. "Not until Saturn brings us that gemstone!"

"All right, all right!" Saturn shouted. "I will return your gemstone. But you will turn off your Flame right now!"

Emily was panting hard and tried to pull the Flame back inside, but she couldn't. She hadn't been this angry in a very, very long time and somehow couldn't calm down in the face of these Titans who would do nothing to save the Olympians.

Pegasus came as close to her as the heat would allow. He nickered softly and lightly pawed the floor. His head bobbed up and down and he snorted. He alone cut through her rage. He alone had the power to calm her fiery temper. Little by little, with Pegasus standing before her, the flames started to diminish. Emily took several deep breaths until they vanished completely.

Since receiving her new body, Emily hadn't released the Flame. Now that she had, she felt physically exhausted. She stumbled to Pegasus and put her arms around his neck.

Joel came up to her. "It's over, Em. Just relax. We'll go back to Olympus and do what we can. Maybe we can evacuate some of the Olympians to Xanadu."

Emily reached out to Joel. "Why won't they believe us?"

"They can't," Agent B said as he joined her. "They've hated the Olympians too long. They don't know how to change."

Emily was grateful to see him conscious. "Are you all right?"

He nodded. "All the better for seeing that light show of yours. That was really something."

"It was indeed," Saturn agreed. He approached her and looked at Joel, Paelen, and the others. "You all care so much for Olympus?"

They nodded.

The leader of the Titans turned to Agent B. "You are wrong. We are still capable of change." Saturn looked to his brothers and to the large gathering in the throne room. "Love them or hate them, they are still our children. Titans, arm yourselves for battle. We journey to Olympus!"

23

EMILY COULD HARDLY BELIEVE HER EYES AS she watched Saturn and his four brothers climbing into their chariots, the same ones they'd used against the Olympians just a short while ago. This time they were going back to Olympus to save it.

All around them, other powerful Titans used whatever means they could to travel. Each carried several weapons and was gearing up for war.

She was seated on the back of Pegasus with Agent B directly behind her. His arms were around her waist, partially holding her up after she'd expended all her energy in the Flame. Joel was beside her on Chrysaor. He looked up at her and smiled.

I love you, he mouthed quietly.

I love you too, she replied silently.

"Ah, young love," Agent B teased as he squeezed her waist. "It just warms my heart. . . ."

Emily looked back at him. "Really? After what you just saw, you really want to tease me like that?"

He grinned and nodded. "Bring it on. . . ."

Finally Emily smiled too. But it was a haunted smile filled with fear and anxiety that even with the Titans' help there would be no stopping the blobs from devouring Olympus.

The gemstone had been set up against the strongest wall of Saturn's palace, and as they prepared to open the Solar Stream, Saturn called to Emily, "Flame of Olympus, lead us in."

Emily nodded to him and reached forward to pat Pegasus's neck. "Here we go, Pegs. Are you ready?"

Pegasus twisted his neck to look back at her. He nickered softly and nodded. To her left, Paelen also waited and nodded. "I am ready."

Joel grinned up at her. "I was born ready!"

Emily smiled at him and then sat up higher on Pegasus to gaze around at the warriors surrounding them. Hyperion was beside Saturn and acknowledged Emily with a nod, as did his three other brothers.

Argon was behind her with the rest of his forces and called to Emily, "We are ready to go on your command."

Emily looked down at Joel a final time. "This is it. Let's go."

Pegasus whinnied loudly, opening up the Solar Stream. Charging forward, he ran into the swirling brightness.

Just as coming to Titus was a fast journey, the trip back to Olympus seemed even quicker. They soon burst free of the blazing lights.

Emily gasped. They hadn't been gone long, but in that time the damage to Olympus was unimaginable. Where they arrived near the remains of Jupiter's palace, not one tree or bit of growth could be seen. The brown earth beneath their feet was covered in a toxic slime.

Joel, Chrysaor, and Paelen were next to appear. Their shocked reactions were exactly the same.

"They're actually devouring the planet!" Joel cried.

Saturn and his forces followed. Emily watched their shocked faces as they viewed the dying world. "Surely this cannot be Olympus," Saturn cried.

Emily nodded. "We told you, those monsters are eating everything."

"Where are my sons?" Saturn asked. "Take us to their war room."

Emily looked back to Paelen. "Ask your sandals to take us there."

Paelen leaned closer. "This is our last chance, Emily. Should we really trust Saturn? What if it is a trick?"

"Then we are all going to lose," Emily said. "Please do it."

Paelen looked down at his sandals. "Take me to Jupiter."

The sandals flapped in acknowledgment and lifted him off the ground. Pegasus flapped his wings and took off behind Paelen. Joel and Chrysaor launched into the air, followed by the legion of Titan warriors.

"I hope they're still alive," Joel called.

"If they weren't, Paelen's sandals wouldn't have moved," Emily explained.

They flew away from Olympus's main city and toward Helicon. Emily gazed down on the remains of the world she loved. Somehow, it all seemed wrong. The sky above them was the usual bright blue with the sugar-sweet, fluffy white clouds. The sun was shining brightly, and a warm, gentle wind blew. But everything beneath the sky was gone.

There was no birdsong, no buzzing insects. Not even a blade of grass grew in the rich, fertile soil. They flew over what used to be the nectar orchards, but they too had been devoured by the mutant Titans.

Emily turned back to Saturn and his people. The shock on their faces was absolute. Around them was the proof that if they didn't stop the mutants here, no world stood a chance against them. How long before the blobs turned their monstrous appetites on Titus, Earth, or Xanadu?

In the distance, Emily heard the roaring sounds of thunder and saw lightning flashes in the clear sky.

"There!" She pointed. "There they are!"

The closer Pegasus flew to the battle, the larger the rock in Emily's stomach grew. She was still too far away to see the Olympians fighting, but from a great distance she could see the two mutant blobs. They had grown to impossible sizes, standing taller than her whole apartment building and spreading out just as wide.

Emily heard the roar of Saturn's voice. "Titans, attack!"

Before she could look back at them, Emily felt the air around her whoosh as the Titans flew past. Saturn and his people attacked the mutants. Blasts of power exploded in the air, and the sounds of the creatures screeching echoed across the land.

"Saturn!" a high, booming female voice roared. *"Have you come to feed us?"*

In response, Saturn and his brothers fired more blasts at the monsters. Hyperion commanded his fighters to attack from the rear. Soon the two rampaging mutants were surrounded by the fighting Olympians and Titans working together.

The effort the Titans were making was more than Emily could have dreamed. But her hopes were quickly dashed when she saw it was in vain. The Titans were as ineffectual against the mutants as the Olympians were.

"It isn't working," Agent B said. "Nothing can stop them!"

Emily heard a voice calling her name. She looked down to the ground and saw her father and Diana waving at her.

"Pegs, look. Dad is there. Please take us down!"

When Pegasus landed, Emily slid off the stallion's back and ran into her father's arms. She held him tightly, grateful that he was still alive.

"Where have you been? We've been so frightened!"

"We went to Titus to ask for Saturn's help."

"What?" Diana cried. "That is madness!"

"No, it's not. Look!" Emily pointed up at the sky, where Saturn and his brothers were beside the Big Three, uniting their powers against the mutant Titans.

Diana's mouth hung open. "How did you do this?"

"We told them the truth. If they didn't help us now, the mutants would move on to Titus." She looked all around. "Dad, have you seen Riza? Is she here?"

Her father shook his head. "No, I haven't seen her, and we really need her now."

"She must still be sick," Joel said as he arrived and hugged Emily's father. "We're on our own here."

Emily felt herself tearing up with relief that her father was still alive. She hugged him again. "There's so much I have to tell you, but we just don't have time. Have you seen Tom and Alexis? What about Cupid? Are they all right?"

Diana nodded. "I saw Cupid carrying Venus earlier today. He was gaining speed in the sky to open the Solar Stream. The Sphinxes left for Xanadu a while ago. We expected them to stay and fight with us."

"Alexis is going to have a baby," Emily said. "Tom won't let her."

Diana nodded. "That explains it. I am glad they will live."

Agent B approached, and Emily introduced him.

"You're Agent B?" her father cried.

The ex-CRU agent nodded. "It's nice to see you again, Steve. But, unfortunately, I think our meeting will be brief." He looked back at the raging battle. "Has anything stopped them?"

Emily's father shook his head. "No, everything we shoot at them just goes right through them. Neptune and Triton brought a massive tidal wave and crashed it down on them. All it did was flood the land."

"The Titans are our last hope," Diana said. "But I fear they are too late."

Emily's father caught hold of her. "Em, listen to me. I want you and the boys to take Agent B and follow the Sphinxes. Get to Xanadu. Olympus has fallen; it's just a matter of time now."

"No!" Emily cried. "The Titans are here. We have to give them a chance."

Diana shook her head. "I am grateful for Saturn's help, but it will not save us. Nothing can stop them."

Her father put his arms around her. "Emily, you are everything to me. I have loved you from the moment you were born, and will love you forever. But you can't stay here. I can do many things, but I can't watch you die."

Emily looked back to the battle, feeling more guilt than she could imagine. She had created the mutants. She was the cause of this disaster.

As she watched, the blobs cast out tendrils and plucked Titans out of the sky. They were quickly consumed in the grotesque mouths. Her father and

Diana were right. Her hopes for a Titan rescue had failed.

Pegasus approached her and nickered softly. He pressed his head to her, and Emily knew exactly what he was saying. The time for the final decision was upon her. She nodded at him and turned to her father. "No, Dad, we haven't tried everything," she said sadly. "There is one more thing I can do."

"I don't like the sound of that," he said.

"Neither do I," Agent B agreed.

"Em, what are you talking about?" Joel demanded.

Emily looked around at those she cared most about. To save them, she would have to accept the final metamorphosis. "Dad, I think I can stop them. But to do it, I must change again, and it will be permanent. I won't be the same person you knew. There will be no coming back for me, and my destiny will be set." She looked at the stallion. "But somehow I have the feeling this was always meant to happen."

Pegasus whinnied and nodded.

Emily didn't know what he was saying, but she had a pretty good idea. "You're right. This was always going to be my destiny." She reached up and brushed the white hair from his eyes. "It's just like long ago when I had to walk into the flames at the temple to save you. I did it back then, and I'll gladly do it now if it means keeping you safe."

"Em, you're scaring me," her father said. "What are you going to do?"

Emily embraced her father tightly. "The only thing I can. I'll be all right, Dad, I promise. And no matter what happens, whatever I turn into, I will always be your little girl."

"Emily, do not do this," Diana said. "We will find a way."

"There is no other way," Emily insisted. "And we all know it."

"No!" her father cried. "Em, I'm not going to let you give yourself to those monsters in exchange for our lives."

"I'm not. I promise," she said. "That wouldn't stop them anyway. They must be destroyed, and I can't do it the way I am."

"I don't understand," he cried. "Emily, tell me. What are you going to do?"

"Yeah, what are you planning?" Joel demanded.

"Let us come with you—Paelen and me—we've always been a team."

Emily took a deep breath and let it out slowly. She went up on her toes and kissed him softly. "You can't come with me, Joel. Neither of you can. Not this time."

"Why not? What are you going to do?"

She looked at all of them. "The thing I was born to do. I am going to accept my final metamorphosis and become a full Xan. Then I'm going to stop them."

Their shocked voices followed Emily as she climbed back up on Pegasus and he trotted away. Right before the stallion opened his wings to fly, Joel came running up to her. "Em, wait!"

Emily looked down at him. "Don't try to stop me, Joel. I have to do this."

"But what do you mean you're becoming a Xan? You've already got some of their powers. What more can you do?"

"A lot," Emily said. "Not long ago Riza's father came to me and gave me a choice. I could stay as I am and live as an Olympian, or I could become what was always meant for me, a Xan. But when I accept,

I will be expected to work with Riza on Xanadu. The power is already in me, Joel. I just have to embrace it. But it will mean another change."

"Will you be alive?" he asked.

Emily nodded. "If this works, yes."

He reached up and caught hold of her hand. Bringing it to his lips, he kissed it tenderly. "Then whatever you become won't matter. You could look just like Riza and it won't change how I feel. I love you, all of you, no matter what."

In this, the worst of times, those were the best words she could ever hope to hear. "No matter what happens to me, Joel, I will always love you too."

Joel took a step back. "You be careful, Emily Jacobs, and come back to me!"

"I will!" she promised.

Pegasus opened his wings and started to fly.

Emily felt a strange calmness descend on her as she and Pegasus climbed higher in the sky. They circled over her family and friends, waving and calling to them, before heading toward the mutants—and her destiny.

◦ ◦ ◦

Emily looked at the devastation around her. Was it already too late to save Olympus? Was the damage too great?

Up ahead she spied Jupiter, now on the ground. He was standing with his two brothers. They were holding hands and summoning the power of the Big Three, working in tandem with Saturn and his brothers. But it was useless. No amount of power could slow the blobs.

When Jupiter saw Pegasus and Emily in the sky, he tried to warn them away. Emily waved back but shook her head.

"Take us closer, Pegs," she said. "I need to face them when I change."

Pegasus whinnied and climbed higher in the sky. Moments before they rose above the monsters, they heard them calling her name. *"Emily!"* they cried as one. *"Give us your power! Feed us!"*

"Emily, get away from here!" Hyperion called as his chariot passed close beside them. The winged horses whinnied at Pegasus but followed Hyperion's command and kept flying.

"You know what's coming. I have to do this!"

Hyperion bowed to her and moved his chariot away.

Pegasus flew closer to the blobs, as they pulsed and grew excited in anticipation. "Yird, I pray you were right," Emily muttered.

Just as Emily prepared to call her mother's name, she felt invisible arms catch hold of her and Pegasus. The strength in the grasp was so much stronger than it had been under Charing Cross Station. In that instant, Emily feared that they were now too powerful even for the Xan.

"Feed us, feed us, feed us," chanted the two monsters.

Pegasus screamed as he tried to break the invisible grasp, but the power of the creatures was too strong. Emily suddenly realized this had been a terrible mistake. She was too close to them and shouldn't have tried it without Riza.

"Feed us, feed us, feed us . . . ," they chanted.

Saturn saw her distress and shouted for his fighters to expand their efforts. He was trying to buy her time to change. But the Titan effort was in vain. The invisible hands of the creatures contracted further. Emily couldn't breathe, and Pegasus stopped screaming and could only struggle weakly in the deathly grip.

Emily had only seconds. But as the blood raced in her body and her mind was starved of oxygen, she feared that she needed to actually say the name aloud and not just in her head.

"*Mom!*" she called with her mind as panic set in. "*Mom, open the door!*"

But nothing happened. Her full name, Emily suddenly remembered. She had to say the full name.

"*Sarah Jane Brady-Jacobs, please open the door. Let me become a Xan!*"

EXPLOSIONS WENT OFF IN EMILY'S MIND AS the final door to power burst open. Her brain flashed with memories older than time itself. Yird's whole existence was there for her to see—then his parents and their parents before them and every generation back through the depths of time. The lives they had lived, the good things they had done for millions of endangered species across the universe and beyond.

Colors flashed as worlds flew by. The Xan traveled at the speed of thought. Cared more deeply for one another than she'd imagined possible, and their love for all life forms was limitless. For all their exterior calmness, the Xan were filled with deep emotions.

Time stood still as Emily's body changed. Each cell, each tiny piece of DNA, was rewritten and altered or, perhaps, restored to what it should have been. As she changed, somehow she understood that this was always meant to be. Perhaps a caterpillar didn't know that they would ultimately turn into a beautiful butterfly—but they knew by their nature alone that a monumental change was coming.

Emily, too, knew this change was always coming. She had felt it all her life—a haunting siren song of destiny calling to her. That same song was what had drawn her up to the roof so many years ago, that night when Pegasus had first crashed there.

It had called again and led her to Olympus. It had invited her to accept the first part of her metamorphosis to become the Flame of Olympus. And little by little, that same voice beckoned her to this moment, when she would finally burst free of the cocoon that had been Emily and emerge a full Xan.

The metamorphosis finished and her mind burst free. Emily could feel everything, hear stars singing in the eternal cosmos as suns were born and died and reborn again. She could hear the beating heart of every Olympian and Titan as they struggled to fight the monsters.

When Emily came back into herself, she realized she couldn't feel the life force of the mutants. They weren't alive. They weren't dead. They just were. All she received from them was a deep insatiable hunger that could never be satisfied.

Shaking her head, Emily felt Pegasus fading away beneath her as the life was crushed out of him.

"No!" she howled, and her voice, the voice of the Xan, echoed across all of Olympus. At the speed of thought, she put a bubble of protection around herself and Pegasus, breaking free of the mutants' grip.

"Pegs!" Emily cried. She touched his neck and offered him all the healing power she possessed. When the life within him returned, she transported her beloved Pegasus to Xanadu and away from danger.

Across the vast distance, Emily could feel the strong beating of his heart and blazing life force. She rejoiced, knowing he was safe. Now alone, she hovered above the mutant Titans and summoned her powers to destroy them. But it was as she feared. Not even the Xan had the power to destroy them.

Emily held out her arms and used every ounce of focus she possessed to lock the mutants in a bubble. If she couldn't destroy them, maybe she could contain them long enough for everyone to evacuate Olympus.

The two blobs screamed and shrieked in rage as they realized they could no longer consume the world around them. But as the moments ticked by, Emily realized this was only a temporary solution. She couldn't hold them long enough to save the Olympians. It was only a matter of minutes before they broke free of her grasp.

"Riza, if you can hear me, please help me," Emily called out to the universe.

"I am here." Riza appeared in the sky beside her.

Emily stole a glance over at Riza and could feel her "sister" was recovered. "I can't hold them for long. Please help me destroy them."

Riza gazed down at the mutant Titans and shook her beautiful head. "We can't destroy them. They are too powerful now. Soon they will break free and devour everyone."

"No, they won't!" Emily insisted. "I have an idea how to stop them, but I really need your help."

"What do you want me to do?"

"Are you strong enough to transport everyone off of Olympus and get them to Titus? It's not far."

"Send them to Titus?"

"Yes," Emily cried. "Can you do it?"

"I think so, but that will only give us a bit of time. They will follow us. You know they will."

"We won't give them that chance."

Emily glanced down and saw Saturn and his fighters landing on the ground near Jupiter and his brothers. For as much as Emily's powers contained the mutants, it also kept the Titans and Olympians from attacking them. Directly beneath her, the two gelatinous blobs screeched and tried to break free of the bubble that bound them. The more they fought, the harder it was for Emily to hold them.

"Riza, please, get everyone to Titus. Then I need you to tell the Big Three to turn the Solar Stream, just like they were going to do to Earth because of the clones."

"Yes, I remember. But they can't turn the stream now. My father changed it."

Emily cursed—it seemed everything was against them. "What if the Titans joined them? If Saturn and his brothers united their power with the Big Three, would that be enough?"

"If I also joined them, yes. What are you planning?"

"You know what I'm planning," Emily cried. The strain of containing the mutants was starting to show, and she could feel herself weakening. "I need them to turn the Solar Stream on Olympus. Destroy it. Destroy it all and the mutants with it!"

"Emily, no!" Riza cried. "You'll be destroyed with them. I can't let you do it!"

"Please, trust me; I won't be destroyed. I'll transport out the moment it gets here. But we don't have long. I am getting weaker. Do it now. Please get everyone to Titus and turn the Solar Stream!"

Riza looked down. Beneath them the blobs tried to lift off the ground and push out of the walls that contained them.

"Please, Riza," Emily begged. "Save the Olympians."

The beautiful Xan floated in the sky, looking serene as always, but Emily could feel her raging emotions.

Riza shook her head. "Emily, have I ever told you that you're crazy?"

"No."

"Well, you are!"

"Yeah, I know. That's why you love me so much. Now, go, and get everyone away from here!"

Riza vanished, and Emily focused fully on containing the blobs. Their tendrils shot out in all directions and their screaming increased.

"You can't stop us, Emily. We will absorb you and everyone you ever loved!"

She knew they were baiting her. Hoping she might lose her temper and release her hold on them. She wasn't going to be drawn in. But the longer she had to wait, the more she could feel her grip slipping. Soon they would escape.

"Riza, hurry," Emily called.

A moment later all sounds, apart from the blobs, stopped. Emily dared not look down for fear of breaking her focus. But she could feel it. Riza had not only transported the Olympians and Titans off the planet, but she had also taken every other life form with them. She hadn't left so much as an ant, worm, weed, or even bacteria behind. The land, oceans, and skies were completely devoid of life. Olympus was now a dead, empty world. Empty, except for her and the two screaming mutant Titans.

"It won't work, Emily!" they screeched. "We will devour you and follow them. There is nowhere they can go to escape us."

Floating in the sky and using every ounce of power she had, Emily was shocked to hear the mutants start to laugh. It was a high cackling sound, filled with menace. *"We will devour you all!"*

Soon the hair on Emily's arms started to stand up. She gazed up into the sky and gasped. A blazing ribbon of fiery light was flashing in the atmosphere high above Olympus. She had only ever traveled within the Solar Stream. This was the first time she'd seen it from the outside. It was wondrous and terrifying in equal measures—a living, moving stream of pure energy cutting across the sky.

"You did it, Riza," Emily said softly as she watched

the Solar Stream drawing near. "The Olympians and Titans are finally united."

"What is that?" the female cried.

"You want to devour it all," Emily shouted back. "Go ahead. Let's see how well you digest the Solar Stream!"

The air around them crackled as the roaring Solar Stream approached. Closer and closer it came, burning up everything in its path.

"No," the mutants cried. *"It will not destroy us. We will consume you all! The Solar Stream will feed us. Feed us, feed us . . ."*

Emily felt the approach of the Solar Stream like sunburn on her skin. At first it only tingled, and then it started to sting. But like staying out in the sun too long, the burning increased. Soon the blue of the sky and the white fluffy clouds were replaced by the flaming oranges and white of the living Solar Stream.

Emily had promised Riza that she would leave the moment the Solar Stream arrived. She felt guilty for lying to her. But she had to. There was no way she could hope to hold the mutants long enough for the Solar Stream to obliterate Olympus.

"Forgive me, Dad, Pegasus, everyone. I will love you always. . . ."

Emily closed her eyes and felt a searing blast of pain as the Solar Stream flashed across the sky and touched down on the ground, destroying Olympus and taking her and the screaming mutants with it.

EMILY WOKE IN HER BEDROOM, KNOWING it was time to get up for school. Somehow, she always knew when it was time to get up. She looked over to her clock radio and saw that it wasn't working. The power was still out.

She sat up and felt as though she'd slept a thousand years. Her police officer father had said he'd be working late and that she shouldn't wait for him. The storms over New York were getting worse, and the police force was stretched to the limit. He didn't know when he'd be home.

Emily yawned, stretched, and gazed around her room. Suddenly it all came back to her, crushing her like a lead weight—like it did each morning.

Her mother had died of cancer just a short time ago, and she and her father were alone. Tears that were always so close to the surface came to her eyes.

How could they go on without her? Her mother's death had left a huge hole in Emily's heart that she didn't think could ever be filled.

Climbing from her bed, Emily winced as she stepped on something. She looked down and saw that she'd broken the wing off her glass Pegasus. It was always on her nightstand and she had no idea how it had fallen to the floor. But seeing it broken made the tears she'd been holding inside start to fall.

Her mother had given it to her with a book of Greek myths. It had always been one of her favorites, and she could remember many nights when they would read it together, enjoying the stories of Zeus, Hera, or Heracles. But her favorite had always been the story about the winged stallion, Pegasus, with Bellerophon and the golden bridle.

Emily dressed and walked into the kitchen. Because of the blackout the refrigerator wasn't on and the orange juice was warm. But the milk was still good, so she poured herself a bowl of cereal.

She carried her breakfast into the living room. Her mother always told her not to go near the windows during a storm, but she couldn't help it. The window seat was her favorite spot, and she always felt closer to her mother there. Emily sat before the glass, eating her cereal and gazing up Broadway.

New York was strangely silent, though there was still traffic on the road and people walking on the sidewalks hidden beneath their umbrellas. The sky overhead was dark and rainy, but even in the worst weather, the city was always bustling.

"Emily?"

Emily jumped, and her cereal bowl went flying as she screamed at finding a tall alien standing in the middle of her living room. His head nearly touched the ceiling, and his hands hung long at his sides. His skin and eyes were like pearls, and despite her fright, he was the most beautiful thing she'd ever seen.

"Emily, do not fear. I am not here to harm you."

There was something very calming in his voice. It was so familiar.

"Who are you?" she asked softly.

"You know who I am."

"You're Yird," Emily heard herself saying. How could she know that? Why wasn't she frightened anymore? An alien was standing in her living room and she wasn't panicking. Why?

"Emily, my child, the time has come for you to make your choice."

"I don't understand."

"It is simple. Do you want to stay here, living the life you always expected to live—safe with your father and growing up in New York City? You will marry and have children and grandchildren, and then you will die, a content old woman."

"Or?"

"Or you can have another life. A life far from here, filled with wonders you can never imagine. You will travel the universe at the speed of thought. Live on a world teeming with life and creatures that love you. I can give you either life, Emily. You have earned the right to choose."

The previous night, Emily had dreamed. She'd dreamed of a winged stallion that meant more to her than life itself—her very best friend and the one that made her complete. Many others filled this strange life and gave her great joy. But there was the *one*, above all others, that she yearned to return to.

"Pegasus," she whispered without understanding what she was choosing. "I need to find Pegasus."

The strange, tall alien nodded. "If that is your choice, you shall have him. But know this, once you do, there is no returning here or to the life you would have had in this city, on this world."

"There is no life without Pegasus," Emily answered.

Yird came forward and placed his hand on her head. Her mind burst with memories of everything she'd gone through from the moment Pegasus arrived in New York to the destruction of Olympus.

"It was real," Emily gasped. "It wasn't a dream."

Yird nodded. "Yes, my child. It was real, and everyone there is waiting for you to return. But *you* had to make the choice." He waved his hands, and the walls of the artificial New York City landscape fell away. They were in the Arious control room. The supercomputer hummed softly. "Welcome home, Emily."

Emily was suffering a profound sense of disorientation. "I—I don't understand. That wasn't real?"

"It was real enough for you," Yird said.

"But what if I'd chosen to stay?"

"Then you would have stayed. Your body would have been kept here, safely protected in Arious, and your mind would have lived a normal human lifespan on Earth, never to remember the Olympians or Xan. And when you grew old within your mind, you would have died and Arious would have destroyed your body."

"So my life in New York would have been a dream," Emily said softly. She looked around. "And this, Xanadu, Olympus, and all of it would have been the reality I missed."

Yird nodded. "I told you, Emily, the choice for your final metamorphosis had to be yours and yours alone. But there is no Olympus anymore. That is reality. It was destroyed by the Solar Stream. The survivors are now living on Titus. It was you who united them. There will be no more wars. In fact, Saturn has stepped down. Jupiter now rules Titus. But his father is to be his closest adviser. I believe this arrangement will work."

"That was real." Emily gasped as the final memories returned to her. "Did it work? Did the Solar Stream destroy the mutants?"

"Yes."

"How did I survive?"

Yird smiled and it lit his whole face. "You are Xan. Anything is possible."

The image of Yird vanished, and Emily was left alone with Arious. "What happens now?"

"Well," Arious said. "First you go back to Titus to see your family and let everyone know that you are safe. There is much work still to be done to settle everyone. Then, when you are ready, you and Riza will return here to take up your duties as Xan. Rhean still needs help if everyone there is to survive."

"But I can go back to Titus for visits, right?"

"Of course," Arious said. "And there is nothing stopping them from coming here. Xanadu is sanctuary to all. I know some will choose to live here, and they will be welcomed."

Emily could hardly wait to get back to Titus. She needed to know who had survived, but mostly, she needed to see Pegasus.

"Did we lose many?" she asked. "What about my father and Diana? Vulcan and Stella and everyone I know?"

"Many Olympians perished, but you were lucky. Those you care for most survived. Many are wounded, but Riza is healing them."

"Is Pegasus all right? Did he arrive here safely?"

"See for yourself."

The doors to the control room swished open, and Pegasus charged in. "Emily, my pet, are you all right?"

Emily staggered back, hardly able to believe what she'd just heard. It was a voice, deep, strong, and comforting, coming from Pegasus. "Pegs? Is that you?"

"Of course it is me," he nickered. His eyes twinkled with laughter. "Who else would it be? Please do not say that pretender, Tornado Warning!"

Emily's hand flew up to her mouth and her heart started to race. Was this just another dream within a dream?

"Emily?" Pegasus said. "What is wrong? The color has drained from your face."

"I—I, Pegs, I can understand you!"

"What?" Pegasus cried. "That is impossible!"

Emily nodded. "Say something. Anything. Please, let me hear you again."

"Can you really understand me?" he said. "For real?"

"Yes, yes, I can!" Emily looked back at Arious. "How is this possible?"

"You are Xan now, Emily. There isn't a language spoken in the universe that you can't understand."

"Chrysaor, too? I can understand him?"

"All of them. Riza will explain how it works. But for now, go back to Titus and take a break. You've earned it."

Emily threw her arms around Pegasus's neck. "It's true. It's really true, Pegs. I can finally hear you, and we can always be together!"

He lowered his head against her, holding her tightly. "Yes, we will, pet, always. Come," he said warmly. "Let us go back to Titus and show them that you are all right. I know Joel will be very happy to see you again."

Pegasus lowered his wing and invited Emily up onto his back. "So, do you wish to take us there with your power? Or shall we take the long way and use the Solar Stream?"

Emily leaned forward on his neck, feeling joy at the powerful stallion beneath her. "Let's take the long way. I want to savor this moment with you."

Pegasus chuckled. "All right, just as long as you do not get all soppy on me."

Emily gasped and then started to laugh. She looked back at the computer. "Maybe it was better when I couldn't understand him!"

Pegasus bucked lightly and laughed along with her. They made their way through the temple and reached the outside jungle. The air was clear and humid and filled with the sounds of life. This was to be Emily's new home once the Olympians were settled on Titus.

Emily expected to see Earl and Frankie and the Sphinxes here. "Where is everyone?"

"They have journeyed to Titus to help with the resettlement."

Looking around at the lush jungle, knowing that this would soon be her new home, Emily couldn't have been happier.

"Take us to Titus, Pegs!"

Pegasus whinnied and entered into a gallop. He leaped gracefully into the air. "Then Titus it shall be!"

Acknowledgments

I BELIEVE OF ALL THE PEOPLE WHO HAVE helped in the production of this book, the biggest thanks of all should go to the many nameless and faceless people who lived thousands of years ago—people who loved stories perhaps more than anyone because for them, they weren't myths. Who am I talking about? The ancient Greeks and Romans. Those amazing, imaginative people created some of the most endearing characters in existence.

Without them, there would be no Pegasus. No Chrysaor, no Zeus/Jupiter, and no Olympus. You, my dear reader, would be sitting here holding a different book.

So as we draw this series to a close, I want to thank

these cultures for their amazing imagination and continued contribution to modern literature.

For six years, Pegasus has been a huge part of my life. He's been my constant companion, and it's hard for me to set him free. But he must be free. His stories must go on without me. But boy oh boy, will I miss him . . . though he'll always be in my heart.

As always, though, there are others who I want to send a big thank-you to. Veronique Baxter and Laura West, my amazing agents, have always got my back and I appreciate it. Thank you. I also want to send a special "Tom H" shout-out to Fiona Simpson and everyone at Simon & Schuster for taking such great care of me and Pegs. An even bigger thank-you coming your way!

I would also like to thank John McAllen and the staff of Charing Cross Station, London, for giving me a wonderful private tour of the secret and hidden places under the station. As you can see, John, there was a little damage done to Charing Cross, but it did survive the book!

And as always, my dear readers and friends, I would like to thank you for taking Pegs and me into your hearts. I hope that when you close this book, you smile too, thinking of Pegs soaring free—and that you might look out for the many other stories I plan to be part of.

Finally, I always say it and I always will. Be kind to Earth. It's the only home we've got. Take care of it and all the animals that live here with us. They have no voice, so you must speak for them.

Now, as we must say good-bye to Pegs, I have actually written a poem for him, but I have never claimed to be a poet. So I hope you don't hate it.

PEGASUS AND ME

Many years ago, I heard a sound in the night
A voice softly calling, though it gave me a fright
But curiosity untold, made me be bold
I climbed the stairs to a dream and a wonder to behold

With mane soft as silk and wings white as snow
Eyes warmest brown that held a magical glow
He dipped his head low and beckoned to me
To climb on his back and set myself free

From astride sweet Pegasus, all could be seen
Olympus to Xanadu and worlds in between
Laughing by day, cheering by night
No limits for us, on this magical flight

But the time has now come for our journey to end
A tearful good-bye, all my love will I send
My Pegasus soars free, while I here, remain
To the stars he'll ascend, so wildly unrestrained

But maybe one day when many years have flown past
As thunder claps boom and my dreams run their last
To my roof he'll return, to collect me and fly
Until then, sweet Pegs, I'll wait, by and by